A HERO'S SURPRISE

BAYTOWN HEROES

MARYANN JORDAN

Cover: Graphics by Stacy

ISBN ebook: 978-1-956588-43-9

ISBN print: 978-1-956588-44-6

❦ Created with Vellum

Author's Note

Please remember that this is a work of fiction. I have lived in numerous states as well as overseas, but for the last thirty years have called Virginia my home. I often choose to use fictional city names with some geographical accuracies.

These fictionally named cities allow me to use my creativity and not feel constricted by attempting to accurately portray the areas.

It is my hope that my readers will allow me this creative license and understand my fictional world.

I also do quite a bit of research on my books and try to write on subjects with accuracy. There will always be points where creative license will be used in order to create scenes or plots.

BAYTOWN, VIRGINIA

The game playing on the widescreen over the bar only marginally held his attention. Jose Martinez had gone to the Sunset Restaurant in Baytown for a blind date but now sat alone. He'd received a text apology from the woman pleading a headache and canceling at the last minute. Reading between the lines, he discerned she had as little interest in the blind date as he did. A wave of relief washed over him now that he didn't have to feign interest.

He sipped his water, relaxing for the first time all day. He hated blind dates and rarely accepted them, but his mom had twisted his arm.

"Jose! You need to find a good girl. Settle down and make babies. And this girl... I just met her mother at church, and I'm sure she'll be perfect for you!"

A chuckle escaped as he shook his head in amusement. His mom was good at twisting the arms of her children even though they were all adults now.

Glancing at the time on his cell phone, he debated

what to do. Most of his friends would be at the pub watching the game or at home with their families. Still hungry for dinner, he decided to order at the bar. It might not be the evening he envisioned or preferred, but he never minded his own company. As the oldest growing up in a small house with a large family, he'd learned at an early age to spend time alone whenever he got the opportunity.

By the time he'd enjoyed the meal, the game was over and replaced by another one he had no interest in. Sighing, he leaned back on his stool and sipped his beer. Looking into the mirror behind the bar, he viewed the restaurant behind him. It was a quiet night with several couples and families enjoying themselves. It wouldn't be long before the vacationers descended upon Baytown for the warmer season, and the restaurant would be packed most evenings.

Raucous female laughter from upstairs met his ears, and he wondered if a bachelorette party was in full swing. The Sunset Restaurant often hosted wedding events. The nearby rental houses made it easy for people to cut loose and drink too much while still making it to bed without getting behind the wheel.

Tossing back the last of his drink, he reached for his wallet, ready to signal the server to bring him his bill. Instead, his attention was snagged when a pretty dark-haired woman slid into the bar seat two down from him. Her blue dress was fitted but modest with a skirt that flared out, hitting her almost at her knees. Black heels completed her outfit, giving her legs length even though she was petite.

2

Her eyes were not on him, but as he watched her in the mirror behind the bar, she sighed and pushed her hair away from her face. At the sound of more laughter from upstairs, he caught a grimace crossing her expression.

Just then, she glanced over at him and offered a pinched smile as she shook her head. "If you've been down here listening to that noise, I should apologize."

"I just assumed some people were having a good time," he said. "Bachelorette party?"

She nodded and sighed. "I really wanted to get away from it. I don't even know the bride very well. She's a coworker who asked me to be in her wedding, but we're not close. I think she needed someone else to even up the number of bridesmaids and groomsmen. I agreed, which was more to being raised to be polite than a desire to be in the wedding party."

An image of his mom drilling manners into him and his siblings raced through his mind, and he chuckled. "Believe me, I understand."

She turned slightly on the stool to face him fully, and he did the same. "Isn't it weird how we were raised as children can be so ingrained that even as adults, we respond to situations that go against what we want just because we think it's what we're supposed to do?"

He nodded slowly, thinking about why he was in the restaurant tonight. "You're exactly right. Do you want to hear something funny?"

She tucked a strand of hair behind her ear, cocked her head, and smiled. "Absolutely."

"I was here tonight for a blind date that my mom

3

insisted on. Now, mind you, my mom had never met this woman. She simply ran into the woman's mother at church one time, and they decided to set this up."

The woman's eyes widened, and her mouth dropped open. "So you accepted a blind date even though your mom didn't know the woman?"

His brows lowered, and he shifted uncomfortably on the stool. "Yeah, that's right, but now that I hear it stated from someone else, it's not very flattering for me, is it? Especially since I had no desire to have the date in the first place."

She threw her head back and laughed. "Please, don't feel bad! I swear that sounds like something I would do!"

He inclined his head toward the bar. "Can I buy you a drink?"

She held his gaze momentarily, and he wondered if she would deny his offer. Finally, her lips curved upward, and she nodded. "Sure. Thank you." She glanced toward the empty stool between them. "May I?"

"Please, allow me." He moved to the seat closer as the bartender brought their drinks and placed them on the polished wooden bar.

She stuck out her hand once he was settled. "I'm Karen. Karen Anderson."

He took her hand in his. "Jose Martinez. It's nice to meet you, Karen."

"It's nice to meet you, too, Jose." She picked up her drink and lifted it for a toast. "Here's to lone drinkers celebrating how our parents raised us to be extra polite. If it wasn't for me saying yes to a bachelorette party that

I had no interest in and you agreeing to a blind date you weren't thrilled about, we wouldn't be sitting here right now."

He threw his head back and laughed. "You've got that right!"

They clinked glasses, then each took a sip.

"Are you just visiting Baytown for the wedding?"

"Yes. I was born and raised in the Northern Virginia area and have never been to the Eastern Shore before. The bride read about Baytown in a magazine and decided it was perfect for her bachelorette weekend."

As they continued to chat, he discovered she worked as an office manager in a real estate office. After admitting she'd lived with her parents for years to save money, she expressed excitement over moving into her first apartment.

As soon as he said he worked for the Virginia Marine Police, her brows lifted in surprise. "I'm embarrassed to say I've never even heard of the marine police."

"We provide law enforcement on the water, specifically around here, for the Chesapeake Bay. Everything from search and rescue, boating safety, enforcing recreational and commercial fishery laws to responding to accidents and emergencies."

"So if I'm ever on the water out here and have trouble with my boat, you might be the one who rescues me."

"I promise if I ever saw you needing assistance, I'd be there."

She threw her head back and laughed, her hand

resting over her heart. With great drama, she exclaimed, "My hero!"

They continued to chat for the next hour, and while he couldn't say he felt a spark, there was definite flirtatious interest. And if he read her signals right, she was interested, too.

"I'm going to go out on a limb here," Karen said. She sucked in a deep breath and let it out slowly while tucking her hair behind her ear. Her fingers fiddled with the cocktail napkin, now wet from the condensation on her glass. "Um… I'm not staying with the other bachelorettes since I'm not acquainted with any of them. But I do have a room in the small downtown hotel." Her gaze darted up to his, and she swallowed audibly. "Any chance you'd like to come back with me?"

His teeth dug into his bottom lip as he tried to keep his smile from widening. She appeared nervous, but it added to her appeal. "I'd consider it an honor and a pleasure, Karen."

A giggle slipped out as she ducked her head and blushed. "Well, I don't know about the honor, but I have a feeling it will be pleasurable."

He signaled for the server and paid for his dinner and their drinks. He waved away her protestations that she should pay her bill. "Remember, Karen. My parents raised me to pay a lady's tab."

She laughed again as they slid from their stools. He didn't mention that his mother would be mortified to think he was going to sleep with a woman he'd just met. *Thank God she never knew what my Navy days were like.* Glancing to the side, he had a feeling that Karen's parents would have had the same objections based on what she'd indicated.

They walked out of the restaurant together, and it only took a couple of minutes to follow her and park downtown. Walking into the lobby of the Baytown Hotel, they headed to the elevator. Once on the third floor, he escorted her down the hall, where she stopped outside one of the rooms and dug into her purse for the key card.

It had been a long time since he had been in the hotel because he didn't make it a habit to pick up vacationing women. Some of his good friends and coworkers had enjoyed the single life to its fullest, and he wondered how many of the rooms here they'd been in. Stepping into Karen's room, he shook that thought out of his head. The last thing he wanted was to take his attention off her by thinking of his friends doing exactly what he was getting ready to do.

She tossed her purse onto the dresser next to the widescreen TV, then turned and smiled as she moved closer. "This will sound so cliché, but I almost never do this. Picking up a guy in a bar and taking him to a hotel is a new experience for me."

She smoothed her hands down the front of her dress as he stood close without touching her. "There's no pressure here, Karen. We won't do anything you don't want to. If you've changed your mind, I can walk out the door right now, no worries."

She held his gaze and smiled. "That's a really nice offer, Jose. But honestly? I don't want you to walk out

7

MARYANN JORDAN

that door. I guess I just told you what I did because I'm a little nervous about expectations."

"Then why don't we throw out expectations and just have a good time for tonight? And if at any time you want to stop, just say the word."

She tilted her head to the side, considering his words carefully. Finally, she nodded, stepping closer and gliding her arms around his neck. Lifting on her toes, she angled her head and kissed him lightly. She settled back on her heels and grinned. "I like the sound of having a good time... just for tonight only."

Wrapping his arms around her, he pulled her closer. "I do, too." He didn't care about her experience level but was glad she'd verbalized that she understood a hookup. One time. No hard feelings when he walked out. No sharing phone numbers with hopes of a repeat performance.

Her smile widened as she nodded, and he lowered his head to seal his lips over hers.

A couple of hours later, he dressed while she slipped into the bathroom for a shower. She was wrapped in a robe when she emerged, smiling almost shyly. An evening with a pretty woman who'd had no expectations other than sex had been good, but he was anxious to get home.

She walked him to the door and smiled up at him. "This was really nice, Jose. Thank you."

"I told you that it was my honor and pleasure. It was absolutely both," he admitted, smiling.

With a final goodbye, he walked out the door. He didn't often hook up, but when he did, she fit the bill

8

perfectly. Pretty, funny, a good conversationalist, and no expectations or hurt feelings when it was over. There also hadn't been sparks, fireworks, tingles, or jolts—none of the things he thought he might feel when he met someone he wanted to spend more than a few hours with.

Once at home, he showered before falling into bed. When they returned from early church service, his parents expected his presence at their house for brunch. No way would he be able to get out of a family meal. He knew his mom would have questions about his blind date, and she was part bloodhound sniffing out details and part guard dog when it came to her children. Telling her that his blind date stood him up would not go well.

An hour later, he sat at his parents' table, surrounded by familiar chaos. His dad, Carlos, sat at the end, the place of honor he'd held for as long as Jose could remember. His dad's black hair was now liberally sprinkled with gray around the temples, but his five-foot-eleven-inch frame was just as trim as when he was a much younger man.

He and his brothers had their father's olive complexion and lean build and the height of the men on his mother's Italian side of the family. Her two brothers were over six feet tall.

His sister Rosemarie sat across from him, continually jumping up and down as she bounced her toddler on her lap while her husband, Stanley, kept an eye on their two other rambunctious children.

His brother Jimmy sat next to their father, talking

business since they were both in the fishing industry. Jimmy's wife, Katy, sat next to him, also helping keep an eye on Rosemarie's kids.

His sister Bethany held her phone down in her lap to keep their mom from realizing what she was doing. He shook his head and chuckled, not surprised when their mom called out, "Bethany! No phones at the table!"

She sighed and rolled her dark eyes. "I know, Mom, but I'm trying to study."

"You can do that when it's not time to eat. Anyway, how can you study on an empty stomach? Eat, and you'll learn more."

At their parents' house, Mom's rules prevailed, and Bethany dutifully turned off her phone and slid it into her pocket.

There was an empty chair at the table for his other brother Jonas, who was currently on tour in Germany, serving in the Army. It didn't matter how many extra chairs they might have to put around the table to accommodate everyone. Their mom insisted that Jonas's chair always be there for family meals, even if he couldn't be there.

"I can't believe Paula's daughter stood you up!" his mom grumbled as she sat down.

He opened his mouth, but she shook her head. "You know we have the blessing first! Carlos, pray."

His father looked around at his family, a slight grin curving his lips. Jose knew his father smiled because he was proud to have his family together but also amused with his mom. They were a perfect team. She managed to rule the roost while still giving deference to her husband. And while Carlos was confident in his role as the patriarch, he usually allowed his wife to have her say. And considering they'd been married for thirty-five years, raised five children, and all still got together on Sundays for lunch, Jose figured his parents must have done something right.

As soon as the prayer was over, everyone dug in, plates piled high with food. And it only took his mom a moment to jump back in.

"I can't believe the rudeness of some people today. In my day, if you agreed to meet with someone, you met with them, no matter what!"

"She said she wasn't feeling well, Mom. If she was ill, then I'm glad she stayed home."

"Pfft! If she was in such a bad way, she could've let you know early, and then you wouldn't have wasted your time going to the restaurant to meet her."

"Now, Mary," his dad said. "If she wasn't feeling well, then we certainly wouldn't have wanted her to be around Jose. What if she passed something to him? And then he brought it to lunch today, and we all got sick?"

Jose hid his grin, noticing his siblings did too. His mother's eyes widened, and she crossed herself. "Of course, you're right, Carlos!" Looking up at Jose, she bounced her head up and down. "I'm glad you didn't meet with her. Goodness knows what illness she may have."

His mother's diatribe hit a snag when Justin, one of Rosemary and Stanley's children, started crying when he didn't get the biggest roll.

"Hers is bigger than mine!" he sobbed, pointing at his sister's plate.

"Stop fussing, or you won't get any bread at all!" Rosemarie said, lifting her brow and giving the *mama look*. Mary jumped up to get more rolls from the oven, making sure that a large one ended up on the plate of her tearful grandson.

Jose was grateful for the direction change in their focus so that it was no longer on him. The conversation flowed, and he, Jimmy, and their dad spent several minutes chatting about their jobs on the Chesapeake Bay. They worked for a major fishing company, and as part of the VMP, he patrolled the waters. Their jobs were different, but their livelihoods all came from their love of the bay.

By the time lunch was over and everyone helped with cleanup, he hugged his sisters and brother goodbye before moving to his mom. Pulling her shorter, slightly plump body close to him, he kissed the top of her head. "Thanks for lunch, Mom."

Her arms wrapped around his waist, and she hugged him in return. Mary Martinez did many things well, and her deep hugs were among the best.

She leaned back, clutched his cheeks with her hands, and pulled him down so she could kiss each cheek. "I don't want you to worry about anything, Jose."

He didn't have a chance to ask what she was referring to when she bulldozed ahead.

"Forget Paula's daughter! I'll find you someone better to go out with. It's not good for you to be alone."

"Mom, I've got my friends, I've got my job, I've got

the American Legion, and I've got my family. I'm hardly alone."

"Pfft!" She grumbled in her usual way. "Those are all good, but they won't give me more grandbabies!"

"Grandbabies! Jimmy and Katy will soon be thinking about children, and there's always Bethany and Jonas!"

"I want grandchildren from all my children! And you're the oldest, Jose. You should be setting the example!"

Arguing with his mom would've been a waste of time, and it didn't really matter. Her concerns came from a deep place of love for her family. Kissing her again, he moved to the door to shake his dad's hand, accepting the clap on the back.

His dad leaned in and said, "She means well."

He nodded. "And I love her for it."

Heading back home, the smile was still on his face. He'd had a fun evening with a lovely woman, even if he'd never see her again. He had a lunch with his family. And now, he was looking forward to going home and enjoying his afternoon alone, relishing the peace and quiet.

2

ONE MONTH LATER - ALEXANDRIA, VIRGINIA

Melanie Landers walked through her small living room and down the short hall by the kitchen to get to the front door of her older Northern Virginia townhouse. She peeked through the security hole first, then threw open the door with a wide smile on her face. "Karen! I didn't think you were coming until later, but I'm so glad you're here! You can help me decide between the cheap Walmart curtains or the cheap Amazon curtains! Plus, I've got paint chips for the kitchen. Touch of Lemon or Buttercream." Furrowing her brow, she pondered aloud, "Why are paint colors so often named after food?"

Her best friend, Karen, remained standing on the front stoop. Her usual smile was not in place as her lips were pinched together.

Startling as it dawned on Melanie that something was wrong, she reached out and grabbed Karen's hand, drawing her inside the house. "Honey, what's going on?"

Their gazes held for a moment before Karen exclaimed, "Oh, Melanie, I'm in big trouble."

Leading her to the worn but comfortable sofa, she sat and pulled her friend down next to her. Karen's fingers were cold, and Melanie tried to warm them with her own as they stayed clasped together. Her bestie was usually smiling when they were together, but this tearful version of Karen scared her. "What kind of big trouble? Are you talking about going to jail and needing bail money? Or your parents are pissed off again kind of trouble? Or a situation where you need me to get a shovel to bury a body? Or you just need a pint of ice cream and some wine?"

Her heart began to pound as her attempts to add levity were met with a tear falling down Karen's cheek. "Oh no. What's wrong? You're scaring me."

Karen took a deep breath. "Do you remember me telling you about my trip to the Eastern Shore last month when I went for that stupid bachelorette party for the lady in my office?"

"Of course, I do. You said the party sucked. A week later, the wedding sucked just as much when one of the bridesmaids slept with the groom, and the rest of you had to decide whether to tell her. Then that decision was taken out of your hands when the bridesmaid decided to announce it just before they all walked down the aisle."

When Karen's expression did not break into a smile at that memory, Melanie shook her head. "God, I'm so sorry. I'm rambling. You have me so nervous I'm just blabbing. Please, I'll shut up, and you tell me what you need to."

At that, Karen snorted while a little smile escaped. She continued to clutch Melanie's hands.

"Remember the man I met at the bar that night?"

"The policeman, right? The one you said was really nice, and you slept with him." When Karen had told her, she'd been both surprised and impressed. Neither of them had ever been so bold before. Melanie wasn't opposed to casual sex but had always waited until she had gone out with someone at least long enough to determine that there was some affection. Karen had only slept with someone she'd been in a relationship with. So, for her to have a one-night stand had been out of character, yet she'd seemed fine with her impulsive decision, saying it was liberating to break out of her mold.

"Yeah, that's the one. Well, it seems I walked away with something more than a good time."

Gasping, Melanie clutched Karen's hands even tighter. "Oh my God! Don't tell me he gave you an STD? I swear, we can go to a doctor and take care of it! In fact, we can call my doctor right now—"

"No, no!" Karen said, shaking her head. "I didn't walk away with an STD. He used a condom. But I guess nothing is one-hundred percent perfect."

Melanie's brain slowly caught up to what Karen was trying to tell her. Finally, as clarity settled, her mouth hung open, and her head moved back and forth. She whispered, "You're... You are...?"

"Yep," Karen said, popping the "p" on the end. "I'm pregnant."

For a moment, time stood still as Melanie tried to

process not only what Karen said but the life-changing implications. "Oh, honey... I don't even know what to say."

Karen pulled her hands away from Melanie's and wiped her tears before leaning over and snagging a tissue from the box on the coffee table. Blowing her nose, she nodded. "Everything has changed, Melanie. My life, career, plans, relationship with my parents, where I'm going to live—"

"Wait...what about your relationship with your parents and where you're going to live?"

Melanie and Karen had been friends since middle school. Karen's parents were ultra-conservative, never letting her wear pants or makeup while in high school. They'd decreed that her long hair should always be worn in a braid down her back instead of in the latest style. When they'd met, Karen was bullied by some mean twelve-year-olds in their class, and Melanie wasn't about to let it happen. She'd stood up for Karen, going so far as to punch one of the mean girls in the arm after school one day. She'd immediately gone home and told her parents what she'd done. Her mother's response? "Well, while I don't condone violence... it serves her right!"

That was how they first became friends. From that moment on, Melanie declared Karen to be her bestie. Melanie's parents had given Karen a fun place to hang out that was so different than her home, and Karen had often declared that she liked Melanie's mom and dad more than her own.

Even though Karen was now in her midtwenties and

had her own life, Melanie knew she'd struggled to deal with her parents still passing judgment on most of her life choices. But surely, they would accept the situation once they became used to the idea of a grandchild. And since Karen now had her own apartment, Melanie couldn't understand why she'd need to change housing.

Karen sucked in a deep breath and wiped her eyes again. "I just found out a few days ago, and knowing that I'm going to have the baby, I told my parents yesterday." Her shoulders slumped. "I knew they wouldn't be happy, but I didn't expect them to disown me."

Gut punched, Melanie found it hard to catch her breath. "No fucking way!"

Nodding slowly, Karen said, "In their words, I was a complete disappointment. I was a fallen woman. I was a woman who needed to repent and couldn't do so with a child out of wedlock. Then they told me not to come back because, as far as they were concerned, they didn't have a daughter."

Furious beyond all belief, Melanie jumped to her feet and stomped around the room, fuming. "Your parents have made me crazy for the past fifteen years! I can't believe they've done this. Those words surpass even the cruelest things they've ever said!" Turning, she hastened to the sofa again and plopped down, pulling Karen's hands back into her grasp. "But don't worry. As soon as they cool off, they'll come around."

Karen lifted a brow, her expression showing her incredulity. "Really? Come on, Melanie. Do you really think that?"

Melanie opened her mouth, then snapped it closed. Her shoulders rounded as they drooped, and she shook her head.

"And to add insult to injury, I know I'll have to find a new place to live. My tiny one-bedroom apartment won't be big enough for a baby. Plus, with an upstairs and a downstairs neighbor, they'll complain about the noise."

"Then move in here with me!"

Karen startled, her nose crinkling. "Melanie, you didn't even take a moment to think about that offer!"

"What's there to think about? We've been best friends since we were twelve years old. My townhouse has two bedrooms, and even though it's not very big, there's no one above us or below us. And I can help out with the baby when it comes."

Karen burst into tears, flinging her arms around Melanie. The two women hugged, not speaking for several minutes, each lost in their own thoughts. As Melanie slowly continued to digest the information and changes in Karen's life, she leaned back and held her friend's gaze. "What about the father? Have you had a chance to tell him?"

"No. And I'm not going to."

Now it was her turn to blink, her incredulity showing. "What? Karen, you have to tell him! It's his child, too!"

"I know, I know. But think about it, Melanie. We were just a one-night stand. And let me emphasize that...ONE. NIGHT. Neither of us wanted more."

"I understand, but things have changed. Your life is

now going to alter completely. And even if he originally only wanted one night, he needs to be informed about the baby."

"Not now, Melanie. Right now, I'm only a month along. I'm not about to tell him until I'm farther along and am sure that I'm able to carry the baby full-term. Plus, I don't want to be one of *those* girls."

"What are you talking about? What kind of girl?"

"I wasn't trying to trap him, but you know there are women out there who might do that."

"It has nothing to do with whether he thinks you're trying to trap him. The bottom line is you're pregnant with his child, and he deserves to know. And you deserve to have the help. Financially at the very least."

"I just don't want to deal with him right now. Later? Maybe, I'll see. As far as money goes, I make enough that I can share rent here with you and have plenty left over to take care of the baby's needs. I have health insurance through my job. And I've already checked, and there is maternity leave. But beyond that, I don't know, Melanie. I've only known about the baby for a couple of days, so I'm still wrapping my mind around everything. But I hope that no matter what, you'll hang with me."

Throwing her arms around Karen again, Melanie pulled her in tight. "Oh, honey, I'm going to hang with you. We've got this. You and me. Screw your parents. Screw the people in your apartment building who would complain about a precious baby's noise. And screw anyone who doesn't understand your decisions. I'll stick with you, and we'll do this together."

"Well, we've got some time to figure everything out."

"When are you due?"

"I haven't been to the doctor yet, but I should have the baby in early spring. I can do three months of maternity leave and then will find a daycare starting at the beginning of next summer."

"That's perfect! My summer break from teaching starts at about that time. So I have over two months to take care of the baby when you go back to work! Then you won't have to have daycare until it's almost five or six months old."

A small light was now visible in Karen's eyes, and Melanie smiled. With tears still sliding down her best friend's face, Melanie pulled her closer into her embrace, hoping to give her strength. God knows they would need it. Then thinking about the little baby Karen would have, Melanie smiled. *Yeah, we've got this.*

But she was still going to talk Karen into telling the baby's father. Regardless of what happened, it wasn't fair for his life to continue in blissful ignorance while Karen's changed completely.

3

8 MONTHS LATER

Jose stood in the wheelhouse of the thirty-three special-purpose craft, guiding it out of the Baytown Harbor. Fellow VMP officers Joseph Newman and Callan Ward joined him on morning patrols. Jared Dobson, Andy Bergstrom, and Bryce Townsend were in a similar vessel just ahead. All good men. All good law officers. And all good friends. It dawned on him usually at least once a day that he was damn lucky to have the career and life he did.

Each day was a little different with the ever-changing weather on the bay. Today, the water reflected spring in the cloudless blue sky. It was still chilly enough for jackets to be worn, but he'd been able to forgo the heavy coat needed when on winter patrol.

As the other vessel headed toward the south, he steered toward the north. Besides routine patrols of the shoreline, bay, and the many inlets, they would randomly check and board some of the fishing vessels today. Many of them were local, and they knew and recognized the fishermen. They'd stop anyway just to have the connection with those who made their livelihood harvesting the oysters and clams, or fish for crabs, rockfish, and drum fish.

They also would stop and check recreational fishermen's catches and licenses. Vacationers were often intrigued with the idea of fishing from their boats, giving no thought to following the regulations or obtaining the required licenses.

"Is Jimmy out today?" Callan asked as they approached some of the oyster beds.

"As far as I know, he is." Looking ahead, he laughed when he spied his brother's bright red cap. Their mom had knitted it, saying that she wanted him to be easily seen in an emergency. It didn't matter that he had followed in their dad's footsteps and had been fishing since he was little. Their mom had never gotten used to him choosing to be an oyster fisherman rather than working on one of the larger boats like their dad.

Carlos had worked the crab boats, pulling up the pots. But Jimmy liked the low, flat bottom boats, and then standing in waist-deep water with his waders on, digging through the oyster beds with the rake to pull them up. No matter how many times Jimmy had explained to their mom, she always assumed that only his head would be sticking out of the water. Hence, she knitted the red cap to make him more visible in case a boat came too close.

"Never mind!" Callan called out. "I see his hat!"

They slowed as they neared, not wanting the waves from their boat to interfere with what the oystermen were doing. Gently maneuvering closer, Jose waved in return as his brother grinned up at him.

"What are you going to wear when it gets too hot for that hat?" Joseph called out.

"Hell, I figure my mom will have me wear this every day of the year!" Jimmy yelled back. "And if she doesn't, then Katy will!"

They all chuckled, then Jimmy sobered and called out, "Did you hear about Richard Grissom's boat being stolen?"

Shaking his head, Jose glanced at Callan and Joseph to see if they knew what Jimmy was talking about. From the expressions on their faces, they didn't either. "Did he report it? Because we haven't gotten anything on that."

"I don't know. We passed his dock coming out here, and he was still cussing and fuming!" Jimmy said.

One of the other fishermen standing next to Jimmy added, "He said something about going out in his other boat to see if he could find who took it."

Rolling his eyes, Jose sighed. Richard was a hothead under the best of circumstances, and the last thing they wanted was him out on the water, accosting anyone in a boat that looked like his.

"Okay, thanks. We'll keep our eye out for him. But he'd better report it because the sooner he does, the sooner we can start looking."

By the way, brother," Jimmy said. "Katy told me that Mom's already talking to one of the women at church with a granddaughter who recently graduated from the community college. You'd better stay away unless you want Mom trying to hook you up with a twenty-year-old."

"Well, shit," he grumbled, trying to ignore the smiles from the others.

They said their goodbyes and pulled away. He continued to steer the boat up the shoreline while Callan got on the radio to see if Richard had called in a stolen boat report.

Their dispatcher, BobbieJean, radioed, "You got me just before I was going to call it out. It seems he called into the sheriff's department first, and they relayed it to us. And from what we can tell, he's already been out on the water trying to find who might have taken it."

"Yeah, we heard. Send over the boat specs, and we'll keep our eye out."

"When you finish patrols, come on in. Chief Coates will meet with Sheriff Hudson during lunch, and then he'll bring the rest of you up to speed at your staff meeting."

The rest of the morning's patrols went smoothly, with only a few citations given out. It was one of their calmer patrols on the bay. And despite their efforts, they didn't see Richard or anyone in a vessel that matched his boat's description.

By lunchtime, they headed back to the harbor, and once their vessel was secure, they walked to the Seafood Shack where the other officers were already at a large table. Once they gave their orders to the servers, they settled in for their break.

As the conversation flowed, Jose looked around the table, once again considering himself lucky with his choice of profession and friends. And whereas many of them had been single when he first started working for the VMP, now it seemed that most of them had found what still eluded him.

Callan married his high school sweetheart, Sophie, after years apart and a long road to get back together. Joseph, a player-bachelor before he met his wife, Shiloh, was now utterly devoted to his new family, including helping to raise Shiloh's niece, Rachel. Jared had met his wife, Billie, who also worked on the Bay for the Chesapeake Bay Foundation as a water analyzer. Andy had also fallen for a woman he rescued before realizing she was someone he'd known in high school. And, of course, their captain, Ryan, had fallen for the new doctor in town, Judith.

It hit him that he and Bryce were the only single officers at the table. Others worked at the station, but with this group, he was now in the minority.

"So," Andy began, grinning at him. "Is your mom seriously still trying to play matchmaker?"

"And with a twenty-year-old?" Callan laughed, shaking his head. "I can't even imagine trying to have a conversation with someone that young right now."

He couldn't help but wince at his mom's latest attempt to find a potential wife for him. "Somehow, because I'm the oldest, I think I've become her poster child for who she needs to get grandbabies from. But hell, you're right. A twenty-year-old? Jesus, eleven years might not seem that much of a difference to some people, but I can't fathom going on a date with someone that young."

"You'd feel like an old man, for sure!" Joseph agreed. "Rachel is seventeen now and super mature. But hell, that's a whole different age bracket!"

"I keep thinking that if I ignore my mom's machinations, she'll stop. But this is my mom we're talking about."

The server brought their food, and he was glad for the interruption. But as the others talked, he ate his burger in silence as his mind rolled to his mostly nonexistent dating life. The occasional, mutually agreed upon one-night stand was fine, but those were becoming rarer and rarer. He wasn't opposed to finding someone to fall in love with, but he knew it couldn't be forced. Until then, he was willing to wait for the sparks.

"Come on, push, Karen," Melanie encouraged, her heart pounding with adrenaline as she allowed her best friend, Karen, to squeeze the feeling out of her hand. *Oh God, I hope I remember everything from the birthing coach lessons!* Melanie was such a planner and had studied birthing techniques with Karen, memorizing all the coaching information she could get her hands on. But now, it seemed as though all her lessons were thrown out the window with each of Karen's grunts. *I know how to teach science to teenagers... not how to birth a baby!*

As soon as Karen fell back against the pillows on the hospital bed, Melanie grabbed a washcloth and dabbed her friend's sweat-dripping forehead. "You've got this, honey. You're doing great."

The last months had seen a multitude of changes in their lives, but they'd weathered it all with their friendship intact.

Within a few weeks of Karen telling her that she was pregnant, Melanie helped gather a few friends, and they moved Karen into Melanie's townhouse. While she originally had not wanted a roommate, sharing it with her best friend in need was different. It only had two bedrooms, but she gave Karen the larger of the two, knowing that a crib would also have to go in there eventually. Karen tried to protest, but once Melanie made up her mind, there was no changing it.

Karen's job working for a major real estate company had proven to be perfect. Her work hours were regular, and the health insurance was excellent. Plus, the office was located just down the street from a hospital, making doctor's appointments easy to schedule.

Melanie's parents had always considered Karen to be like a daughter and supported Karen's decision to be a single mom. They'd even bought the nursery furniture. Melanie knew it was bittersweet for Karen, thrilled to be around people who were excited about the baby's coming while her own parents did nothing.

"Augh!"

Her attention jerked back to Karen, who bent forward with a grimace on her face and her body straining in childbirth. Melanie had gone to the birthing classes with Karen, but fear was starting to creep in with her friend in the full throes of labor. As she helped support Karen's back, her eyes were riveted onto the doctor tucked away on a stool between Karen's knees. A flash moved through her mind of how undignified childbirth was, but she kept that thought to herself.

"You're amazing, Karen. You've got this."

When the doctor called for another push, Karen screamed out, following the doctor's every direction. Suddenly the activity down below seemed different, and Melanie looked into the mirror that had been set up and watched as the baby's head crowned. *Oh God... it didn't look like this on the video I'd watched!* Melanie had wanted what her parents had—a good marriage and one day children. But now, staring at the mirror, she wasn't so sure about the children.

Soon, the doctor assisted the baby out of Karen's laboring body. Karen had decided she didn't want to know the sex, and Melanie supported anything Karen wanted.

As the baby slipped out, the doctor called, "It's a girl!"

Melanie gasped in awe, and Karen burst into tears. "Is she okay? Is she okay?" Karen begged, her eyes wide as the nurses were checking her out.

The little one let out a wail, and the doctor looked up, grinning. "She looks perfect."

Melanie looked down at Karen's exhausted expression and grinned widely. "Do you hear that? She's perfect! Just like her mama, she's perfect!"

A few minutes later, the baby was placed on Karen's chest, skin to skin. The moment was beautiful, but Melanie stepped back slightly. As much as she was a part of their lives, she wanted this moment of bonding to be between Karen and her daughter. And she no longer wondered about having children of her own. *If I can have that expression on my face, the birth process is worth it.*

After several minutes, Karen seemed to realize that Melanie wasn't right with her. Across the room, she called out, "Come see your niece!"

While Melanie wasn't related by blood, Karen had already declared that she would be her baby's aunt, and Melanie wasn't about to argue with that decision. Stepping closer, she leaned forward to kiss Karen's forehead, resting her hand on the baby's back.

"I'm going to name her Suzette. What do you think of that?"

Tears welled in Melanie's eyes and slid down her cheeks, overwhelmed by the moment. "I think it's perfect."

Melanie had agreed with Karen on just about all her decisions. Well, almost everything. Karen made it to full-term, but she'd never tried to contact the father from Baytown to tell him she was pregnant. It was the only thing she and Karen had argued about. But as time went on and the pregnancy progressed, Karen wouldn't relent.

Now, looking down at the beautiful baby, with the perfect scrunched-up nose and tiny little fingers, she wondered about the man who didn't even know his daughter existed. And hated that he didn't have the choice to be here or, if he chose, to miss the moment.

4

TWO MONTHS LATER

Melanie stood outside the hospital room, staring through the door. An ache like none she'd ever felt before in her life made it almost impossible for her to remain standing. Karen lay in the bed, her head shaved, and tubes and wires coming out of her body connected to machines that beeped and clicked and whizzed and whirred. Karen was so pale, and her eyes closed, seeming to sink into her face.

Melanie's parents walked up behind her. She looked down at Suzette swaddled in her arms. Nuzzling the sweet baby and inhaling her scent, she gently handed her over to her mom.

How are you holding up, sweetheart?" her dad asked. She turned and faced him, terrified to speak. Then her gaze dropped to Suzette, and her heart squeezed once again.

After Karen gave birth to Suzette, they'd settled into their new routine. Karen was the quintessential new mom, both nervous and perfect all at the same time.

And Melanie relished the role of favored aunt. They've been amazed at how much poop could fill a diaper, how much spit-up a tiny baby could project, and how Suzette managed to pee just as soon as they'd changed her. They laughed at her adorable face and loved the clothes they dressed her in. And Melanie cataloged it all by taking a thousand pictures. For a month, everything was perfect. And then everything changed.

Melanie had been at school in the middle of teaching a high school class when she received a call to hurry home. As soon as she got there, she found Karen lying on the floor, still cuddling Suzette as she protected her with a mother's instinct. Rushing over, Karen managed to gasp that her head hurt so bad, she thought she might need to go to the hospital. When Melanie tried to get her to stand, Karen's legs gave out from under her. Fear threatened to choke her, but rallying, she dialed 911. Her voice remained steady when on the call with the EMTs but shook with adrenaline when she called her mom to come help with Suzette while she went to the hospital with Karen.

Tests, images, surgery, biopsy, and diagnoses all led to despair. A malignant brain tumor that was growing so fast, the doctors only gave Karen a few weeks to live.

Melanie railed against the news, but with a baby to care for, she was thrown into a situation she couldn't have ever imagined. No matter what Karen was going through, Suzette still needed to be fed, changed, held, rocked, played with, and loved.

Her school had given her permission to take leave, and her parents had put off a trip that they had planned for her father's work. And for weeks, she sat by Karen, both at home and in the hospital, thinking surely the doctors were wrong. But they weren't.

Earlier that day, the doctor had called her from Karen's room. His kind face was full of empathy, and she was grateful. She wasn't sure she could have talked to him if he'd been businesslike.

But his words sliced through her even though she knew they were true. He told her that she was nearing the end, and it would be best for the baby to be brought by today. He also told her that Karen had had visitors earlier. Her heart leaped at the idea of Karen's parents coming by, but that wasn't who made the trip. It was an attorney with his legal assistant. Karen had asked two nurses to be witnesses as she had letters dictated and then gave them to the attorney to be handed out upon her death.

Karen had already talked to Melanie, pleading for her to become the legal guardian of Suzette. In truth, Karen didn't need to plead, listing all the reasons she could think of. While Melanie's heart was breaking, she couldn't imagine a day without Suzette in it, so she'd readily agreed.

But now, staring into the tearful faces of her parents, Melanie dragged in a shuddering breath that hitched painfully as anguish ripped into her world. "I don't know how to do this, Mom. I can't bear to say goodbye to my best friend or let her go. And I look at Suzette, and my heart aches so badly that Karen will never see her grow up, and Suzette will never remember her mother."

The tears fell as her father pulled her into a deep embrace. She reveled in the feel of his strong arms around her.

After a moment, Suzette woke and began to squirm and cry. Leaning forward, she kissed the baby's sweet head. "Why don't you go ahead and take her home, Mom? Karen had a chance to hold her earlier, and the doctor said it might've been the last visit."

As her parents walked down the hall, she pulled in another deep breath and wiped her tears. Turning, she moved into the room and sat on the edge of the bed, taking Karen's frail hand in her own. Karen's eyes fluttered open, and her lips managed to curve upward in the tiniest of smiles. Speaking was difficult, but Karen managed. "Thank you. From the time we were twelve until this moment and beyond, you have been the greatest friend I could've ever had."

Once again, Melanie's tears fell unheeded, dropping onto the pile of blankets keeping Karen warm. "I feel the same way. You're in my heart always."

"I talked to a lawyer…"

"Yeah, the doctor mentioned that. You don't have to talk about it now, Karen."

Karen nodded slowly. "Yes, I do. I've had my wishes written out. Suzette will become your daughter. I don't think my parents will care, but I wanted it done legally, just in case."

Melanie simply nodded, unable to form words.

Karen's eyes flooded before they spilled down her cheeks. She finally managed to say, "I left letters. They'll tell you what to do."

Melanie listened as the beeping monitor slowed and was barely aware of several nurses and the doctor coming in to stand nearby. She wanted to scream for them to leave and beg for Karen to stay. Swallowing past the lump in her throat that threatened to choke her, she leaned forward and whispered, "I'll always love you, Bestie. I promise I'll take care of Suzette as though she was my own."

Karen's eyes fluttered once again, and with her weakened voice, she managed to whisper in return. "Best friends forever."

One month later

"Are you sure?" Melanie's mother asked, folding some of Suzette's clothes that had just come out of the dryer.

Snorting, Melanie shook her head. "Honestly, Mom? I'm not sure about anything anymore."

A month ago, she had buried her best friend. The funeral had been beautiful, filled with Karen's friends and coworkers. Her parents had been informed but chose not to attend, giving the excuse that it was God's will for their daughter to die for having lived a sinful life. Melanie had finally lost her cool, screaming at them every insult she could hurl, not caring that it made her look like she was possessed. She didn't normally handle unpleasant situations like that, but her own grief spilled out into anger.

And somehow, it had been cathartic. She managed to

get through the funeral with the help of her own family and friends. Suzette had barely left her arms, and even though many had offered to hold her on that horrible day, Melanie couldn't let her go. It was the piece of Karen that lived on, and if she ever needed it, that was the day.

It was later that evening after everyone had gone, and she and her mother had put Suzette down to sleep. She had already read the legal documents with the attorney. The guardianship paperwork was standard, and she'd sign everything necessary before the funeral with the attorney. But he had given her two letters. One had her name on the outside. And the other one was addressed to Jose Martinez. *Suzette's father.*

She wanted to rip his open and read it, but she forced her fingers to lay it to the side while she threw herself into the role of *mom* for Suzette.

And now, the high school year was over, and she'd had the time to think and plan what was next.

She looked around at her townhouse that only two years earlier she'd been so excited to move into. Her parents often traveled, but Melanie relished her home. When Karen had moved in, she'd been happy to share her space. But now, it was filled with memories that threatened to drown her. *Life changes when we least expect it.*

"This is the perfect time to deliver the letter to Suzette's sperm donor."

"Melanie!" her mother chided.

"I know! I know! That's a rotten thing to say! It's not his fault that he didn't have a choice to be here. It's just that it's hard for me to be rational when…" The words faded as she swallowed deeply and stared unseeing out the window. "When nothing in all this mess is fair."

They were silent for a long moment, hearts aching. "I miss her, Mom." She turned to face her mother as a tear dropped onto her shirt. "You know how people say that when someone they love dies, they often start to call them and then realize that person isn't there. But that doesn't happen for me. Because every second of every day, I have Suzette and am one-hundred percent aware that Karen is gone."

She squeezed her eyes shut and breathed deeply, trying to keep the tears at bay. Her mother's arms surrounded her, and they clung to each other until she could finally catch a breath that didn't hitch in her throat.

"I'm amazed at how well you're hanging on."

She scoffed. "Being a mom to Suzette and vowing to keep Karen's memory alive for her is the only thing that keeps me going every day."

"No judgment here, Melanie. Sometimes the best we can do in life is find something that lets us get from one day to the next. I promise you, though, it will get easier." She tilted her head to the side. "But Baytown? Are you sure?"

"You and Dad are getting ready to take a month-long trip to Paris that you've put off long enough. I don't want him to lose the contract because you cancel again." Her father taught Art History at George Mason University and had planned a tour of museums in Paris for a paper he was writing. They'd easily postponed their trip, but she hated for them not to go at the earliest opportunity.

"Anyway, I don't know how this will go. With budget cuts, my teaching job here is on the line, so I applied to the North Heron school system when I saw they had openings for a science teacher. Plus, I'm ready to leave this townhouse, although it's bittersweet. Moving away from the last place Karen lived is hard, but staying here is hard, too." She shrugged and added, "I feel like I need a change of scenery. I've got to go to Baytown with Suzette anyway to talk to Mr. Martinez. It's what Karen asked of me in her letter. To inform him about Suzette and take her to meet him. Then whatever he decides to do about wanting to be in her life will be up to him."

"And what if he wants more?"

"Well, we'll have to figure out co-parenting. People do it all the time in divorces. Or even just when they never get married to begin with." She sighed again. "But I have to honor Karen's last wishes."

A week later, after the movers loaded her belongings, she hugged her parents goodbye, buckled Suzette in her infant car seat, and climbed behind the wheel. Sucking in a deep breath, she let it out slowly. With the baby monitor mirrors she'd set up in the car, she could see Suzette's bright-eyed face from the back-facing carrier in the back seat.

"Okay, baby girl. Are you ready for an adventure?"

The response was a gummy grin, and as she drove down the street, she whispered, "And are you ready to meet your daddy?"

The same gummy grin was the only response.

5

BAYTOWN

Jose looked around the table in the VMP conference room. Their staff meeting was more crowded than usual. Not only were most of the officers sitting around the table, but Colt Hudson, Sheriff of North Heron County, was present, as well. He brought along several of his detectives, Hunter Simmons and Sam Shackley. Jose was friends with all of them from having worked with them before and from the active American Legion they belonged to.

Having other law enforcement personnel at some of their meetings wasn't unusual. While the Virginia Marine Police had jurisdiction on the water, with the crimes that traversed both water and land, the sheriff's department shared their resources as well as jurisdiction.

Today's topic was one that had been building over the past few months. Boat thefts. It wasn't unusual for an occasional boat to be reported stolen, but often upon investigation, some of those were when the owner had not secured the vessel, and it had drifted away with the tide only to be found later. Occasionally, when a boat was stolen, usually a single miscreant acted alone and impulsively.

But recently, it appeared the area was plagued with a possible boat theft ring.

"What makes this difficult," VMP Chief Ryan Coates said, "is that we're not looking at any one type of boat being reported missing. There have been speedboats, fishing boats, single engine... nothing that would tie in the perpetrators as searching for a particular type of boat."

"It also doesn't help that we're not finding the boats reported stolen," Callan added. "So other than checking at the last place it was docked, we don't have a lot of evidence to investigate."

"The reported thefts have come in from a variety of places," Sam said, looking down at his tablet. "Personal docks outside of homes. A garage in Easton. An empty lot next to the owner in Seaside."

"But so far, none from a dock or harbor that has security cameras," Colt stated, his gaze moving around the table.

Joseph nodded. "And that would indicate they know where the cameras are, or at least, see them. More owners are installing security cameras around their docks, but the last one reported stolen had no such security."

"We may be dealing with a professional boat theft ring," Sam surmised.

"And that just means they'll be a lot harder to catch," Andy grumbled.

Jose usually remained quiet at the larger integrated staff meeting unless asked a question. Not that he didn't have opinions, thoughts, or ideas, but he preferred to use the time to mentally correlate the information coming in.

Ryan looked his way. "Jose? Thoughts?"

He rubbed his chin as he stared down at his tablet, studying the images of stolen boats before lifting his gaze to the others. "With the randomness of the types of vessels being stolen, we have to consider the possibility of copycat thefts. We could have a professional thief who has targeted certain boats, and since the local newspapers have reported what's happening, someone else could be capitalizing on the situation."

The others nodded, but he took a little pleasure in the possibility of being correct. It was one thing to go after an organized, professional theft ring, but it was a lot more difficult if local copycat assholes were also using the opportunity to steal a boat.

The meeting continued, and more ideas were bounced around, but Jose's mind had already moved to how they could encourage the locals to better monitor and secure their vessels. Having grown up around boats, he knew the importance of watercraft to the livelihood of many who use them daily. And he wasn't discounting those who had spent a great deal of money on pleasure craft only to have them stolen from the docks at the back of their houses.

Standing quickly as the meeting concluded, he

shook the hands of Colt, Hunter, and Sam before heading out to the dock. Once aboard the vessel, he readied it to go out on patrol. Today, Andy was steering, and he stood on the bow with Jared, letting the breeze hit his face as they moved out into the water. The water was choppy, but with the clear skies above, the waves only added to the beauty of the bay.

"Is Billie out today?" he asked.

Jared nodded. "She said she was going to be testing the water at Winslow Inlet."

Jared's fiancée Billie worked for the Chesapeake Bay Foundation, and a part of her duties was to analyze the water quality around the bay.

"I don't suppose she'd—"

Jared threw up his hand and shook his head. "I know what you're going to say, and believe me, with the news about the boat thefts hitting the news, she's already been looking."

Jose chuckled, knowing Billie's tenacity as well as Jared's protectiveness. "And how are you handling that?"

"Hell, you know Billie. She's going to do what she wants to do and what she thinks is right regardless of what I say."

"That's true, but you found a smart, protective woman who will be cautious."

The crinkles at the sides of Jared's eyes deepened as he smiled. "You're right about that. I got lucky as fuck that I met her, and even luckier than fuck that I didn't screw things up too badly."

Now laughing aloud, Jose shook his head. When Jared met Billie, fireworks exploded, and they weren't the fun kind. They'd fussed and fumed and fought until they fell in love. While it wasn't exactly the way Jose wanted a relationship to start, he couldn't deny that it worked for Jared and Billie.

Just then, the dispatcher radioed the location of a stalled boat in the bay.

Andy steered the vessel toward the west, farther out into the deeper water. They soon came upon the stalled twenty-two-foot pleasure craft. He looked over his shoulder and said, "Radio for Bryce if he's available." Bryce had been a mechanic in the Navy and, of all of them, was the best at diagnosing and possibly offering a quick fix for a boat to make it back to the harbor without having to be towed. And since Bryce was on the larger VMP vessel this morning, it would make sense for them to come in case towing was necessary.

Once they'd approached, he tossed the lines to tether the stalled vessel to theirs. "Wait until we board after securing your boat," he called out to the man standing nearby. Another man was near the wheel, and a woman was seated but clinging white-knuckled to the seat. "Are there just the three of you?"

"Yes. I'm Judd Malrooney. This is my brother-in-law, Tim, and my sister, Julie."

"I'm Officer Martinez, and we've got someone coming to see if we can get you started or if we'll need to tow you to the Baytown Harbor."

"That's not very convenient, Officer. If we have to be towed, it would be best if you could take us back to our rental house."

"I'm afraid that if you need to be towed, then it's back to the harbor, not to a private residence."

Judd grumbled, but Jose ignored him while catching Jared's narrow-eyed scowl. He was always amazed at people... most overflowed with gratitude for being saved, but a few groused when they didn't get their way.

A few minutes later, Andy reported that the other police vessel was approaching. Jared had already examined Judd's engine but had been unable to get it started. Callan steered the other VMP vessel and maneuvered to the other side of Judd's boat so they could tether to it, too. Bryce deftly leaped to the smaller vessel. Jose noted that Judd stayed right with Bryce every minute as though he expected the officer not to be able to do his job. Jared followed to provide backup if Bryce needed it.

The woman suddenly leaped from the seat and raced to the edge of the boat. Leaning over while clutching the edge, she threw up. Jose hustled over to her as Tim patted his wife's back.

"She started getting sick when the engine stalled, and we were rocking back and forth in the waves."

"Oh God, Tim," she cried. "Don't even talk about the movement!" She began to dry heave again.

"Ma'am, let's get you to our boat. We'll take you in so you can be seen by the EMTs."

Tim nodded his acquiescence. Jose held his hand out to assist the woman onto his vessel, but she was almost too ill to walk. With his hands on her upper arms, he guided her forward until Jared could lean over and pull her the rest of the way to their boat. Once she was secure, he called the station to let Ryan know that one of the passengers they were bringing in was ill. Disconnecting, he slipped his phone into his front jacket pocket just in time to see the woman lurching toward the side. She grabbed the edge and leaned too far over as she began to throw up again.

Hustling toward her, Jose held her shoulders to keep her from toppling over the side of the boat while she retched. Leaning forward to get a better hold on her, he watched as his phone slipped from his pocket and fell into the bay.

Biting back the curses that threatened to erupt, he focused on the woman since his phone was beyond rescue. He was furious for not having secured his phone in his back pocket. Getting her settled once again with her husband, he stalked into the wheelhouse.

Bryce reappeared on deck with Judd hustling after him.

"Try it now," Bryce said.

Judd pressed the start, and the engine sputtered, then roared to life. Judd thanked him, beaming. Bryce wiped his hands and approached, reporting, "It's working for now, but it's only temporary. You need to take it in—"

"Yeah, yeah, I'll get right on that," Judd said, dismissing Bryce. Turning, he yelled, "Tim. Julie, get back on board."

"I'm having them take us to the harbor so she can be seen by the EMTs," Tim replied.

"Why? She's just seasick. It'll pass!"

"I'm not willing to take that chance, Judd."

"You're ruining the trip," Judd exclaimed, his face red.

No longer willing to let the boat owner call the shots, Jose stepped up. "We're taking them to the harbor. You can follow—"

"I'm not giving up my fishing trip!"

Turning, Jose untied the ropes that attached the boats, and Callan did the same on the other side. Waving toward Andy, Jose indicated for them to start back to the harbor, leaving a fuming Judd alone with his boat.

Once underway, he walked into the wheelhouse. "I am so fucking sorry about your phone," Andy said. "I looked over and saw it falling into the water."

"I can't believe it. It was an old phone that needed replacing, but it still worked." He sighed heavily. "I'll go to the store in Easton this weekend and get it replaced."

"Why wait for days?" Jared asked.

"Because I'm working for the next four days. I'll let my family know I'm out of touch. Surely, someone can get along without a cell phone for four days!"

"Well, as long as people know how to get ahold of you if they need to," Andy said, tossing a wave to Callan and Bryce as their boat moved back into the bay.

"My family are the only people who call me anyway. I highly doubt I'll miss any important news."

6

Melanie stood with Suzette in her arms and looked around the small apartment. *Small? More like minuscule.*

The trip from Alexandria to Baytown should have only taken four hours. She had avoided the major highways and traveled along smaller roads to enjoy the trip more. One pit stop was necessary for a blow-out diaper change. That delay meant that she arrived after the movers, and with eye rolls and huffs, they made it obvious that they were in a hurry and she was holding them up. Then they'd proceeded to unload her belongings so fast that it was amazing they'd managed to get the few pieces of furniture and the numerous boxes into the right rooms.

Her parents lived frugally, a trait passed on to Melanie. So the small size didn't matter to her as long as there was room for the most important things.

Eyeing the small space, she was glad she'd taken the time to look at her furniture measurements. She had already donated Karen's bedroom furniture to a local women's shelter in Alexandria, and her extra few pieces that didn't fit had been stored in the storage unit behind the apartment building. That caused more eye rolls and huffs from the movers.

The apartment's living room was only big enough for a loveseat, her rocking chair, and an end table. She didn't want a coffee table to take up floor space. The bedroom held a twin bed she had purchased after getting rid of her double bed. She also managed to squeeze the crib and a dresser against the wall.

While there would've been room for a small table and chairs in the dining area, she opted not to fill that space, keeping it open for a toy chest, a highchair, and Suzette's swing. Melanie had decided she could eat her meals sitting on a single stool at the counter.

Now that the movers had left, and she was alone with a slumbering baby, she doubted her sanity for the umpteenth time just that day. *I've uprooted my life just to drop a bombshell on someone I don't know, on the off chance that he might want to find out he has a daughter and spend time with her.*

She dropped her chin to her chest and fought back the tears. Concentrating on breathing deeply, she finally blew out a cleansing breath and walked into the tiny kitchen. *A cup of tea will surely help. Or at least it can't hurt!*

A knock on the door caused her to jump in surprise, and she hurried over to keep whoever was outside from waking Suzette. Opening the door quickly, she stared at two teenage boys, each with a box in their hands. Recognizing her red-marker print on the outside, she cocked her head slightly in confusion.

"You left these by your vehicle. Figured you wanted them," the smaller of the two said. He was wiry and bounced up and down, energy pouring from him. His eyes were bright, and his smile immediately had her smile in return.

"Oh, good grief! I can't believe I left those two outside. Thank you so much!" She glanced over her shoulder and said, "Can you set them just inside? I've got a sleeping baby, so you'll need to be quiet."

"No problem," the taller one agreed, carrying the larger box. He was much larger than his friend and had a quiet, solemn air about him.

She stepped back, and they placed the boxes gently on the floor. She pulled out a couple of ten-dollar bills from her wallet. "I really appreciate this. I had forgotten them and would have hated for them to be stolen or get wet." She handed the money to them. "What're your names?"

The smaller one grinned as he pocketed the ten. "I'm Trey. This here is Ricky. I live with my mom on the first floor. Ricky lives a couple of apartments from you on this floor."

"Well, thank you, Trey and Ricky."

"That one was heavy," Ricky said, inclining his head toward the box now on the floor. "It says books. Who's got that many books?"

She chuckled softly. "A lot of them are science books."

The two boys stared at her as though she just admitted she'd dropped down from another planet.

"Science? Why the hell– um… sorry, but why would you have science books?" Trey asked, his gaze now peering inside the apartment, his obvious curiosity flowing.

"I'm a teacher. I usually teach biology."

"I hate biology," Ricky muttered. "Failed the state test. Probably will fail it again."

"Yeah, but you passed the class," Trey said, his gaze bouncing from Ricky and then back to Melanie before firing off more questions. "Are you going to teach at Baytown High School? Is that why you're moving here?"

She hesitated but finally gave the only answer she could. "I'm not sure. I have a teaching job with the county but haven't been told what school. Things are kind of up in the air for me." Shrugging, she smiled. "We'll see."

"If you stay, you could help me and Ricky with biology," Trey suggested. "We gotta pass the state test for graduation, but both of us failed it."

"Well, I'm sure I could tutor you some over the summer if your parents say it's okay."

Ricky's scowl indicated that being tutored during the summer was the last thing he wanted, but Trey turned to him and said, "I know what you're thinking. But we gotta pass it."

"Since this was my move-in day, we won't make any plans now. Let's see how things go," she suggested, surprised she'd made the offer with all she had going on.

She loved working with teenagers, but now wondered if she would have the time. Seeing the interest on Trey's face, she smiled. Teens could be challenging, but she loved getting to know the individuals underneath some of the bravado they showed their peers.

As the two boys walked out, Trey grinned. "My mom will be thrilled if I get some help, and Ricky's uncle doesn't give a shit—um... sorry. He doesn't care what Ricky does."

Waving goodbye, she glanced around the apartment building, hating how run-down it appeared. The apartments faced a concrete breezeway with a metal railing alongside the outer edge, overlooking the parking lot. The inside was clean, but the outside gave evidence that the landlord cared little about the aesthetics of the building. *Housing is so hard to get. I suppose he doesn't have to care.*

Glancing over the rail, she spied Trey and Ricky ambling down the stairs and grinned. She missed working with teenagers.

Suzette woke soon, and Melanie spent the afternoon caring for her while putting a few things away. After microwaving a frozen meal and eating it between feeding and bathing Suzette, she finally sat in the rocking chair, ready for her first day on the Eastern Shore to end. She was exhausted as she gently settled Suzette against her shoulder and patted her back. She rocked back and forth, the motion as soothing to her as it gently soothed Suzette to sleep.

Her mind rolled to the possibilities that unfolded

before her, knowing she didn't want to waste time acting on the reason she'd come.

Suzette's father could outright rebuff her. *Fine! If he doesn't want to have anything to do with her, I'll take her away so she'll never know a day of rejection.*

He could decide to raise her himself and cut me out. *No way! First of all, that's highly unlikely. And second of all, he'll find me only willing to compromise, but I'll never give her up.*

She closed her eyes and whispered, "Oh, sweet Suzette, what have I done? This could be the biggest mistake of my life."

"No, it's not," Karen whispered back. *"You're brave when I never was. You're doing what I had been afraid to do. And you are honoring my last wishes when I should have done it myself. You're doing it for me. You're doing it for her."*

Melanie continued to rock a sleeping Suzette. She hadn't told anyone, not even her parents, that sometimes in the quiet, Karen talked to her. She refused to think that she might be crazy or delusional. Instead, she found comfort in still having the occasional conversation with her best friend.

"Okay, I'm going to do this," she whispered.

She had already programmed Mr. Martinez's phone number into her phone. With Suzette tucked against her heartbeat, she reveled in the baby's steady breathing and sweet scent. Then she pulled her phone from her pocket. Locating the number, she pressed dial. It rang several times before going to voicemail.

Hello. You've reached Jose. Leave a number at the tone, and I'll call you back.

"Hello, Mr. Martinez? My name is Melanie Landers. I'm in Baytown right now and need to speak to you as soon as possible about a personal matter. Please call me back at this number."

Disconnecting, she let out a long breath, noting her shaking fingers. She hoped he would get the message soon and return her call. The faster she completed the initial meeting with him, the sooner she hoped she could get rid of the butterflies in her stomach that had turned into a brawling catfight in her gut.

Three days. Three days of leaving messages only to be met each time with the same voicemail message.

Hello. You've reached Jose. Leave a number at the tone, and I'll call you back.

"No, you won't, you worthless prick!" she grumbled as she tossed her phone into her purse. Moving into the living room, she smiled at Suzette in her playpen and calmed her ire. It hadn't taken long to discover the location of the Virginia Marine Police station. *At least, I hope it's the station he works at.*

And tired of constant messages left with no return, she wasn't waiting any longer. Karen used to tease her about being so impatient. *I think I've shown great restraint.*

She certainly had things to fill her time while waiting for the call that never came. She and Suzette had gone to the grocery store twice since Suzette decided to scream in the middle of the vegetables during their first visit. She had gone to the small dollar store to grab a cheap shower curtain. Her apartment building was north of Baytown, so she drove into town so she could stroll with Suzette around the park.

But to her mind, three days was more than enough time to allow Mr. Martinez to return her call. She realized he might not make it a habit to return the calls of strangers or maybe he thought she was a robocall. But whatever the reason, she was no longer willing to wait.

Melanie's parents encouraged her to be independent, and some of her coworkers had often called her the take-charge teacher who would jump in and get things done. She'd volunteered to tutor after school, sponsor clubs, and take kids out for road cleanups and other community service projects. So sitting around waiting for Mr. Martinez wasn't going to happen.

Scooping Suzette up from her playpen, she snuggled her, blowing raspberries against her tummy. "Okay, little darling. I hope you're ready for this." She placed her into the carrier and added, "God, I hope *I'm* ready for this!"

Grabbing the crammed-full diaper bag and her purse, she walked out of the apartment and over to her small SUV. She carefully clicked the carrier into her car seat and climbed behind the wheel. It only took fifteen minutes to arrive at the Baytown Harbor, where she easily found the sign indicating the Virginia Marine Police station. Parking near the front, she sat for a moment, her fingers still wrapped around the steering wheel. Finally, she sucked in a deep cleansing breath and let it out slowly. "Okay, this is it. I can do this. I can do this."

Suzette's car seat was also a carrier that could snap into the stroller. Once fastened in, Melanie slung the diaper bag over her shoulder and grabbed her purse. Feeling like an alpine hiker heading to the summit with full gear, she walked to the station's door and entered, pushing the stroller in front of her.

She blinked as she came out of the bright sunshine and fumbled to push her sunglasses up onto her head. A counter was near the front with a pleasant-faced woman sitting behind the glass partition. Her graying hair was pulled back into a bun, and her blue polo had VMP embroidered over the left breast pocket.

"Oh, what a lovely baby," the woman said, her warm gaze upon Suzette.

"Thank you," Melanie acknowledged.

"What can I do for you today?"

Placing the diaper bag onto the floor, she pushed the stroller closer. "I need to see Mr. Jose Martinez. Um... I believe he works here?"

"Yes, Officer Martinez is assigned to this station. Do you have an appointment?"

The single second of elation that hit her when finding out she had the right place of employment was quickly dashed at the idea that she couldn't see him without an appointment. Her smile drooped. "Oh no. I'm sorry. I didn't know that I would need one."

"Well, he's often out on the water when on duty. Is there something that another officer can help you with?"

"No, I'm afraid not. It's…" She hated to tell the receptionist that it was a personal matter, fearing that she'd be told to go away and contact him privately. Considering she'd been trying to do that for three days, she wasn't in the mood to hear someone suggest she do what she'd already done. Finally, she gave in to the truth. "It's actually a personal matter. And I'm sorry, but before you suggest that I try to contact him, I've tried."

The woman's owl-like expression gave no indication of what she thought of Melanie's comments. Just then, Suzette began to squirm a little, and Melanie knew she was on borrowed time before a full-blown meltdown might occur. *Please, baby girl, just hang on a little bit longer.*

The woman smiled again and said, "I'm BettsAnn. I can see your little one is about to get fussy. If you want to take a seat, I'll call to the back to see if Officer Martinez is out on patrol or is in the station."

She felt sure that her gratitude must have shown forth on her face like a beacon. "Oh, thank you." Turning, she rolled Suzette next to the few chairs that were pushed to the side of the small reception area. Since no one else was around, she placed a diaper bag in one seat, laid her purse on top, and then bent forward to coo and entertain Suzette, praying they didn't have to wait long.

After only a moment, BettsAnn walked back into the room, moving to sit at the counter again. She smiled softly but remained quiet. Before Melanie had a chance to ask again if Officer Martinez was available, a tall, dark-haired man walked from the back. He wore a navy-blue uniform with various patches sewn on the sleeves and over the front pocket. He was at least six feet tall. Muscular, but lean. His face and arms were tanned, and his eyes were so dark that she felt the intensity of his gaze from the distance.

She sucked in a hasty breath. *Black hair. Olive complexion. Dark eyes.* Glancing down, she stared at Suzette, seeing the same.

He approached, and she jumped to her feet. Looking behind him, she observed several other uniformed men standing just inside the hall where he'd come from. She wanted a more private place to talk but was now filled with uncertainty. All the speeches she'd practiced over the past month flew out the window. As she stared up at his dark eyes peering at her in polite curiosity, no words came forth.

"I'm Officer Martinez. May I help you?" His voice was smooth. Soft, but strong.

Suzette fussed louder, and Melanie bent to wiggle her fingers in front of the baby, hoping she could distract her for another few minutes. Looking up, she drew courage from his gentle expression. "I need to make sure I have the right person. You are Jose Martinez?"

"Yes."

Glancing behind him to the men who had now moved forward in abject curiosity, she swallowed deeply. "I'm sorry to bother you at work, but I couldn't get you to call me back. I've left numerous messages over the last few days, asking you to meet with me."

He grimaced and shook his head. "My phone has

been unavailable." Still holding her gaze, he added, "I'm sorry, but I didn't catch your name."

A wince crinkled her nose. She was so focused on distracting Suzette's impending meltdown that she'd forgotten to introduce herself. Before she could speak, Suzette's face scrunched, and she cried out mournfully. Bending, Melanie unbuckled her and lifted her up, cuddling her against her shoulder. Bouncing her slightly, she rocked back and forth, returning her gaze to Jose.

"I'm sorry. I'm Melanie Landers. I need to speak to you about a personal matter." Her gaze shifted to the small crowd surreptitiously nearby without being too close. "Is there somewhere private we could speak?"

"I'm afraid, Ms. Landers, that I'm on duty right now. If you could tell me what this is in reference to, I'm sure we could set up a mutually agreeable time to meet."

By now, Suzette had reached the limit of her three-month-old patience and was letting everyone in the vicinity know that she wasn't happy.

Melanie continued to bounce her slightly while leaning down to shove her hand into the diaper bag, grabbing the pacifier. Inwardly kicking herself that she hadn't gotten it earlier, she tried without success to get Suzette to take it. She wasn't surprised. Once Suzette was in a full-blown, screaming meltdown, a pacifier no longer held magical properties. Dropping the pacifier back into the diaper bag, she then pulled out a bottle.

Suzette was marginally interested, but at least she quieted.

"Ms. Landers, I can see that this is not a good time

for you, any more than it is for me. I think your daughter needs your attention right now. Feel free to leave your contact information with our receptionist, and I will—"

Melanie's eyes grew wide, a red haze forming as she stared up at him, hearing the slight condescension his voice held. Forcing her voice to stay soft while her heartbeat galloped in her chest, she glared. "How dare you assume to know anything about me or this baby? That's the whole reason I've been trying to get you to answer your phone and contact me."

His dark brows snapped together, and he placed his hands on his hips, huffing slightly.

Just as he was getting ready to speak, Suzette's face scrunched again, and a loud, horrific sound emitted from her tiny body as she filled her diaper.

Melanie wanted to cry in frustration. She was at her wit's end, but Suzette needed her. No longer caring whether Jose was embarrassed in front of some of his coworkers who had eased forward behind the receptionist, she plastered a fake smile. She gently placed a still-screaming Suzette back into her stroller carrier with the horrific odor of a dirty diaper filling the room.

"I came by today to talk to you privately because I thought that would be easier on you. But let me just say, Jose Martinez, that you leave me no choice. This beautiful child is your daughter, Suzette. And when you're ready to have a conversation with me about her, just give me a call."

Wiping a bead of sweat from her brow, she then

turned to smile at Suzette. "Let's get you out to the car and get you changed, sweetheart."

"Wait!" he called out, stepping forward. "I don't know what you're trying to do, Ms. Landers, or what game you're playing, but I assure you this is not my child."

"Well, I have it on good authority that you are. Look, I realize this is a surprise—"

"You think?" he bit back.

Pressing her lips together, she kept her voice steady. "And I know you need answers—"

"I have never met you before. And I've certainly never…" He glanced down at Suzette as if afraid she might understand his words.

Melanie shook her head. "Slept with me? Is that what you were going to say?"

"Yes, it was," he argued, his voice harsh but soft as his gaze kept darting between her and Suzette.

"You would be right. But I hope you remember the young woman you did sleep with. Karen Anderson from Alexandria. About a year ago."

It only took a couple of seconds, but his expression changed from anger to wide-eyed surprise.

"Wha… but…" He stepped back, his brows lowered. "If this is Karen's child, why do you have her?"

"Karen was my best friend—"

"That may be, but it doesn't answer my question," he growled, still keeping his voice soft even though Suzette screamed loud enough to make it difficult to hear.

Glancing to the side again, she spied the expressions on the other officers' faces, ranging from shock to incredulity, and even scowls. No longer caring what anyone thought, she reached back into her purse and pulled out the letter. Walking straight up to Jose, she slapped it against his chest, causing him to reach up quickly to grab it before it fell to the floor.

"Her beautiful mother was my best friend. And she died last month, leaving her daughter to me. Legally. She left this letter for you."

"You can be assured that I'll check out your story. And there's no way I'd give you anything without a paternity test."

She narrowed her eyes, the red rage turning into an inferno, but managed to rein it in. Suzette was already screaming, and Melanie didn't want to make it worse. "And *I* assure *you* that I don't want *anything* from you. Nor will I let you near my daughter without a paternity test!" She let out a shaky breath, blinking as tears threatened to fall. "Karen told me who the father was and asked me to deliver that letter. What you do or don't do is up to you. I wrote my phone number and address on the back of the envelope. I'm here because I'm fulfilling the final request of my best friend." Leaning closer to be heard over Suzette's cries, she added, "I'm not here for you. I'm here for this little girl who is now my daughter."

Turning away with all the dignity she could muster, she slung the diaper bag over one shoulder, grabbed her purse, and began strolling a screaming, smelly little Suzette toward the door. The sound of footsteps rushing closer had her turn to see the receptionist rushing to hold the door open. Nodding her thanks but unable to speak with a tear rolling down her face, she pushed past.

"Ms. Landers!"

Melanie stopped but didn't turn around.

The receptionist hurried forward with a small card in her hand, and she dropped it into the diaper bag on Melanie's shoulder. "If you need anything, my number is on that card. I don't know what has happened, but I can tell you that Jose is a good man."

She held BettsAnn's gaze and then inclined her head toward Suzette. "I hope, for her sake, he is."

7

Jose stood in the lobby of the station, the envelope in his hand, and his mind whirling with the events of the past ten minutes. Barely aware that BettsAnn had run out after the woman, he looked up as she came back in. She walked over and sighed. "Go to the back and read the letter."

He nodded wordlessly and headed toward the hall crowded with the other officers.

Ryan inclined his head to the side. "Go into the conference room. It's empty."

He started to enter, then stopped at the sound of Andy's voice.

"You need company, man? We're here for you."

He turned, uncertainty filling him. On the one hand, he wanted to pretend the scene had never occurred. On the other hand, he was still in shock. He knew Ms. Landers was wrong... he didn't have a child. But as to what was happening, he was clueless to imagine.

Suddenly, the urge for counsel overrode the desire for privacy. Nodding, he said, "Yeah. Come on."

As he sat down, he wasn't surprised to see that everyone else had filed in. Ryan looked over at BettsAnn and said, "As far as anyone is concerned, we're in a staff meeting. And what happened here stays here. No one... and not even significant others, are to know. Jose will give his permission what information he wants to divulge and when."

"You got it, Chief," everyone agreed.

Jose laid the envelope with his name written on the front onto the table. He stared at it as though it was a snake ready to strike.

"Did you recognize the name she gave? Karen Anderson?" Callan asked.

Nodding slowly, he replied, "I've never been one to have a lot of random hookups. She was someone I met..." He closed his eyes and cast his mind back, trying to remember. Suddenly, he chuckled and shook his head. "It was the night I was supposed to have the blind date my mom set up. That woman backed out, and I was having a drink at the Sunset Restaurant bar. Karen came down from a bachelorette party that she didn't want to attend, and we started talking. We probably talked for an hour before deciding to go back to the downtown hotel."

A small smile curved his lips at the memory of her. "She was pretty. Dark hair with a sweet smile. She wasn't overly flirtatious. We just talked. And we both knew it would only be for one night. I left the next morning on good terms and never saw her again. In case you're wondering, I haven't really thought about her. There were no sparks, no real interest. Honestly? It was just sex with a very nice woman."

"I feel stupid asking this, but what about protection?" Joseph asked, wincing.

"Hell, after what Ms. Landers just came in dropped on me, I hardly think you should feel stupid asking anything. But yes, I used protection."

"There's a chance that that baby belongs to Ms. Landers, and she's just looking for a baby daddy scheme that helps her with money," Bryce said. "I mean, if not, why didn't Karen contact you to tell her she was pregnant?"

Shaking his head, he said, "I have no idea."

Ryan jerked his chin toward the table where the envelope sat. "Regardless of what's in that letter, you'll want to get a paternity test."

He swung his gaze at his boss, the word sinking in. Paternity test. Scrubbing his hand over his face, he groaned. "Shit. Yeah."

Ryan pulled out his phone and dialed. "Judith, how does someone get a paternity test around here?" He was quiet for a moment and then responded, "Thanks, babe. See you tonight."

Jose waited, grateful that his boss was married to one of the doctors in town.

"She's able to do the testing anytime. Once it's sent off, the results will be back in a couple of weeks. And she said that if you want to come in early, she'll be there at the clinic before anyone else comes in to protect privacy."

"Damn, thanks, Ryan." Grateful, he allowed his gaze to drop back down to the letter.

"I suggest we leave to give Jose a chance to read the letter by himself," Callan said. "But we'll be right here if you need us."

Once again nodding his appreciation, he cast his gaze around the table at some of the best men he knew. "Thank you. Really... thanks for the support."

The other officers walked past, their hands patting his shoulders as they moved out the door. Picking up the envelope, he flipped it over, observing the name Melanie Landers, along with a phone number and local address written neatly on the back. Sliding his finger under the seal, he pulled out the paper sheet, surprised to see the letterhead was from an attorney's office.

Dear Jose,

I'm dictating this letter to my attorney, whose assistant is writing it as I speak. I don't have much longer to live, but first, I need to right some past wrongs. I'm leaving this letter for my best friend, Melanie Landers, to deliver to you. Melanie had begged me to talk to you since I found out that I was pregnant. But I was afraid. And my fear kept me from doing what I should've done a year ago.

We both understood that the night we spent together was purely for pleasure, with no emotions involved. But I had not been with another man for over a year before you and no one after. It was a great surprise to discover I was pregnant. Melanie became my rock, allowing me to move in with her, and was my coach during my daughter's birth. I have given legal guardianship to Melanie, and it's only now, in the end, that I acknowledge I should've told you all along.

A paternity test is your right, and I hope you will agree. I want my daughter to know who her father is, but it's important for you to know that I never wanted you to feel an obligation. And I assure you that Melanie doesn't either.

I expected to raise Suzette by myself, along with the help of Melanie, her parents, and a few other friends. The idea that I'll never see my daughter take her first steps or any of the other life events that will occur breaks my heart. And while Melanie will be the best mother for Suzette in my absence, I know that it is unfair to take away the possibility that you could enjoy being Suzette's father if you choose to take on that role.

Whatever you decide, though, please do not attempt to take Suzette away from Melanie. I have given her guardianship because it is in Suzette's best interest.

I ask your forgiveness for not having told you at the time that I was pregnant. Please don't take my failure to act out on Suzette or Melanie. The responsibility was mine, and so was the failure. But as I leave this life, know that I loved my daughter with every fiber of my being. And therefore, I count our night together as fate because it brought this beautiful child into the world.

Karen Anderson

He laid the pieces of paper down on the table and clasped his hands together. Bowing his head and closing his eyes, he said a prayer for the woman who'd given birth and hoped that she'd found some peace before passing.

Lifting his head, he knew that was a peace he didn't

have. While the letter had given him some answers, there were a lot more questions out there. He looked over his shoulder and spied Andy standing near the door.

"Sorry, man. I didn't want to crowd you, but I wanted to be around in case you needed me."

He sucked in a deep breath and let it out slowly, his mind still filled with the events that had occurred.

"Did the letter give you any clarity?" Andy asked.

He stood and walked to the door, seeing most of the others still hanging around. Not wanting to read the words again right now, he handed the letter to Andy, allowing his friends to read what Karen had written at the end of her life.

"Damn, man, that's rough," Callan said, his voice quivering. "I can't imagine what it would be like to know that you're dying and have to take care of your infant child."

Callan and Sophie had a little boy, and Jose could only imagine how Callan was taking the words of the young, dying mother.

"Ryan is right," Jared added. "As heartbreaking as this letter is, you'll have to get a paternity test. And it'll take a couple of weeks to get the results."

"Yeah, so I better get right on that. Plus, I better go get my new cell phone, considering that Ms. Landers had been trying to get ahold of me the week that my phone had been sitting on the bottom of the bay."

"Christ, the timing sucked," Bryce said, shaking his head. "What are the odds?"

He nodded his agreement, then snorted. "Well, what are the odds of a rare one-night stand getting pregnant even though I used protection? Guess my odds aren't great right now."

Scrubbing his hand over his face, he reached out and took the letter from Andy, and folded it carefully before sliding it back into the envelope. Looking up at Ryan, he said, "I've got the next two days off. Tell Judith I'll be in for the paternity test first thing in the morning. Hopefully, Ms. Landers will bring the baby in, too, so we can get things moving along."

"I'll let her know to expect you," Ryan said.

"How are you doing?" Joseph asked. "This was a huge bombshell dropped on you."

"Honestly? I haven't got a clue," he admitted. "My brain can't catch up to all the craziness flying toward me. I can't seem to process it all."

"It's early. Give yourself a break," Andy said. "Ms. Landers just dumped this all on you."

"I agree," BettsAnn said, stepping closer. "But remember... Ms. Landers isn't the enemy here. It sounds like she gave a lot to her friend, including agreeing to become the baby's legal guardian. And to come here to handle all of this? Well, I'd say that's at least worthy of your appreciation."

The men stared at her, but she just smiled and turned to head back toward the reception desk.

Sighing heavily, Jose said, "I'm heading out to get a phone. Thanks for your support."

"Keep us in the loop," Andy said.

"Well, it sounds like I won't know anything for a few weeks." With that, he offered a chin lift in goodbye and headed out to his SUV. First stop? The phone store. After that? He had no idea.

8

Melanie sat in the rocking chair, singing softly as Suzette drank with gusto from her bottle. Fatigue pulled at every fiber of Melanie's being, and she was no longer sure that the move had been a smart plan. Even though her parents had left for Paris, if she'd stayed in Alexandria, she would have at least had a few friends she could have called on if she needed help. But here, other than the scribbled phone number from the nice VMP receptionist, she didn't know anyone. And she had never felt more alone in her life.

Of course, when she'd come into the apartment, Trey and Ricky were hanging outside. She almost didn't stop to talk but hated to ignore them. Trey, with his apparent enthusiasm, had told her that he'd asked his mom about the tutoring, and she was *tickled pink* according to him. When she'd looked at Ricky, he'd shrugged and said that his uncle didn't care, so if Trey was going to get some help, he would, too.

At least someone was happy to see me. The sucking

noises slowed, and she looked back down at the sweet-faced baby whose mouth was now slack with a little dribble of milk running down from the corner. She gently wiped her face, set the bottle to the side, and then lifted her ever so slowly to her shoulder. Patting her back while rocking, a few baby burps escaped, and Melanie smiled. She continued to sing and rock until she was sure Suzette was asleep. Standing carefully to avoid jiggling her, Melanie walked into the bedroom and bent with great care to place Suzette in her crib. Checking to make sure everything was perfect, she turned on the infant monitor and tiptoed out of the room, closing the door almost all the way.

Walking into the living room, she looked around at the disaster. A baby blanket was on the floor. The sink held several dishes and a pot still needing to be washed. A small pile of laundry sat on the sofa, needing to be folded. The diaper bin needed to be taken to the garbage, and the floor needed to be vacuumed. But right now, Melanie didn't have the physical or emotional bandwidth to tackle any of those jobs.

A knock on the door caught her attention, but it was so soft that she wondered if it was from her neighbor's door. The front door had no security hole, but she walked toward it when a knock sounded again. Making sure the chain was in place, she opened the door an inch and peeked out.

Her gaze immediately shot upward, seeing Jose standing just outside. Uncertain why he was there, she hesitated. "Um… I've just put Suzette down for the night." She thought he would turn and walk away, but he remained outside her door. She watched the crease along his forehead deepen at her words.

"Oh... well, I've... um... actually, I've come to see you, if that's possible."

She pressed her lips together and rubbed them together. "Mr. Martinez, I know we have a lot to discuss, but it took me a long time to get her to sleep, and I don't want to take a chance of her waking up—"

"Is she okay?"

Blinking at his hastily asked question, she jerked her chin back slightly. "Yeah. Um... it's still a new place and her schedule is all messed up. Um... so if you're here to argue, then we—"

"No." He shook his head with emphasis. "I don't want to argue with you, Ms. Landers. I read the letter, and I do have questions. I realize this is not the best time, but I can't think of anything else but to find out more. My mind is just stuck..." He sighed. "I'm sorry. I'm not making sense."

As tired as she was, she put herself in his place. A strange woman he'd never met showed up to his place of work with a baby and informed him that the baby was his. Considering the circumstances were unusual, to say the least, it was understandable that he would be reeling from the event. Nodding, she closed the door and slipped the chain off the latch. Opening, she whispered, "You can come in as long as we talk civilly and very softly. And ignore the mess—I'm still trying to get settled."

She moved back, and he walked past her, stopping just inside the door. Once she flipped the deadbolt, she waved him toward the sofa. He stepped past the laundry basket and had a seat. Such a large man sitting beside a pile of tiny baby clothes was almost comical.

Pressing her lips together, she pulled her thoughts back to the present. "I can offer you water or iced tea. I'm afraid that's all I have."

"No, nothing for me," he said. "Please, have something for yourself."

She nodded and walked to the kitchen, filling a glass with water from the tap before tossing in a couple of ice cubes. Taking a long sip, she walked back into the room and sat in the rocking chair.

"I apologize—"

"I'm sorry—"

They both stopped, and he offered a rueful chuckle while she shook her head and smiled.

"I'm not sure who should go first," she admitted.

"Please, you may," he offered.

She inhaled deeply before letting it out slowly. Closing her eyes for a few seconds, she felt the need to recenter her thoughts. Turning, she faced him and said, "I'm very sorry for approaching you at your workplace. It was never my intention to interrupt your life in that way. I just became desperate when I couldn't get you to return my phone call, but that's no excuse. I should've waited until the end of your workday."

"You offered to speak to me privately, and I was the one who refused," he said. "So if there is a fault about having witnesses, it's mine. But if you're worried about those people, they're not only my fellow officers, they're also my friends. I assure you that they will have the utmost discretion."

"I appreciate that." Her hands were clasped in her lap, and she looked down to see her short nails that hadn't seen a manicure since Karen had become sick. She could only imagine she looked like a mess with her hair pulled back in a sloppy ponytail and wearing an oversized T-shirt that still had remnants of spit-up on the shoulder. Glancing down, she hoped that spit-up was the least of the things that might have ended up on the shirt. Then giving her head a quick shake, she pushed those thoughts out of her mind.

"I also wanted to apologize for how I responded," he said.

She jerked her head upward, seeing him staring at her. Nodding slowly, she sighed. "I can only imagine your shock."

He nodded, but said nothing.

"For the record, I wasn't privy to what she wrote in your letter. When the doctor told us it was near the end, he said it would be best to bring Suzette to the hospital for what might be the last time. So I brought her, and they shared time together, and then I left. When I came back, the doctor informed me that she had called an attorney who came. She had drawn up a Will and dictated a letter to you and to me. She also had legal paperwork drawn up, giving me guardianship of Suzette."

She watched him with eagle-eyes as she spoke. He listened and nodded, and she breathed a little easier

77

when it appeared his expression stayed gentle. Pressing her lips together, she wasn't sure what else to say.

"Would you like to see her letter to me?"

A gasp slipped out as she nodded in haste. "Only if you want to share it, but if you do, then absolutely."

He reached into his pocket and handed it to her. It had been in her possession until a few hours ago, yet holding the envelope now, she felt her chest tighten at the knowledge that Karen's words were inside. "I find myself craving all the remembrances of her," she whispered. Then quickly, before he might change his mind, she pulled out the slips of paper, recognizing the attorney's stationery. Her gaze scanned the contents, not finding any surprises, but her heart warmed at Karen's words. When finished, she blinked back the moisture that had gathered in her eyes. She folded the letter, then slid it carefully back into the envelope and handed it to him. "Thank you."

He nodded, then dropped his chin as he stared at the letter in his hand. She studied him while his attention wasn't on her. Black hair shaved closer at the sides and a little longer on top. Physically fit. Athletic. He wore dark jeans with a black T-shirt showcasing his lean, muscular build. He was attractive, and it dawned on her that she'd never asked Karen what he'd looked like. But now, seeing Jose, she could see Karen being tempted... out of town, away from her parents, a handsome man at a bar. It held all the elements of a delightful chance for a night of fun.

"The one thing she didn't explain was why she never told me," he said, lifting his head.

She jumped slightly, pulled out of her musings, and cocked her head to the side. His tone captured her attention. A hesitation. A touch of fear. And maybe, a sliver of insecurity.

Suddenly, the desire to defend Karen's decision and make Jose understand, she rushed to explain. "I tried to get Karen to tell you as soon as she found out she was pregnant, but she was reticent. At first, she wanted to wait until she knew she could carry the child full-term. But I think the longer the pregnancy continued, the harder it was for her to tell you. Fear tended to rule Karen when it came to decisions. Fear that she wasn't going to do something right." She huffed slightly. "Me? I tend to just jump in with both feet."

"So it wasn't that she thought I was…" He seemed to struggle for the right description. Finally, he said, "That I was unsuitable."

"No, not at all! She once told me that she didn't want to be *that* girl. The kind to trap a man in marriage. She knew that what you two shared was one night only. She described you fondly but assured me there had been no emotional attachments on either side."

He nodded, seeming relieved. "That's true. Karen was a lovely woman, and I enjoyed talking to her. When she asked if I'd like to accompany her back to the hotel, we both were clear it would be one night for pleasure."

She smiled. "I'm glad Karen had that with you. Her upbringing made it hard for her to accept doing anything for pleasure."

His intense gaze held hers. "Her upbringing?"

She plunged ahead, deciding to give him a broader

picture of Karen. "She was raised by very conservative parents who didn't let her date. She was only allowed to go to community college and had to live at home. She finally lost her virginity when she met someone she was interested in. We lied and said that she was with me. As crazy as it might sound, she was almost twenty years old, still having to lie to sneak out." Shaking her head as a shiver ran through her, and her features hardened into a grimace. "In truth, Jose, her parents are horrible people. When she discovered she was pregnant, they disowned her. To help make ends meet, I had her move in with me since I had two bedrooms. They didn't even acknowledge Suzette's birth."

Jose's gasp showed his indignation, which made Melanie feel better knowing that Karen would've had someone else on her side.

"I assume they changed their minds when she became ill?"

She slowly shook her head. "No. They never acknowledged Suzette at all. And when Karen became sick, they said it was God's will for her sinful life. They didn't come to her funeral."

He leaped to his feet, and his hands clenched into fists. "What that—"

"Shh!" she said, also jumping to her feet with her hands out, pressing them downward in a *be quieter* motion.

He winced and shook his head quickly. "Sorry," he whispered. Dragging a hand through his dark hair, he stood for a moment, anger radiating off his body.

She gave him a moment to get his emotions under

control while she walked to the sofa and picked up the laundry basket. Carrying it over to the rocking chair, she placed it on the floor, then sat back down. She began folding the blankets and clothes, loving the smell of baby detergent.

He also sat down on the sofa again, a calmer air about him. "I'm sorry. I can't imagine any parent acting that way."

She nodded but remained silent. For a few moments, they sat, neither speaking, yet she didn't feel uncomfortable. She knew he needed time to process everything that she'd had months to be able to understand. Finally looking up, she asked, "What now?"

He rubbed the scruff on his chin. "The chief of my station is married to one of the doctors in town. I hope you don't mind, but he called to find out how to get a paternity test."

Her brows lifted, and she smiled slightly. "I don't mind at all. We both know that's what needs to happen."

"She said it could be done tomorrow, and we'll have the results in a couple of weeks. She also said we could come before the clinic opens for privacy."

"That's very generous of her. If you give me the information on the clinic, then I'll have Suzette there when you want."

He reached into his pocket and pulled out a new phone. With a sheepish expression, he said, "Last Monday, mine dropped into the water while I was on duty. I didn't have a chance to get another one, and that's why I missed all your calls. But I put in your cell number since you'd written it on the envelope."

She chuckled softly as he typed out a text, and her phone chimed on the counter. "I'm assuming that's the clinic's address?"

"Yes, and now you'll have my number, too."

Her lips curved, glad they were having a friendly conversation during a crazy situation.

"May I ask what your plans are, Ms. Landers?"

"First of all, please call me Melanie. And second of all, I'm a teacher. But my school in Alexandria had to make some cutbacks. I had to take time off when Karen got sick to try to take care of her and Suzette, so I knew there was a good chance I might be let go. Even before Karen asked me, I had already decided to come find you. I don't know if you want to have a chance to get to know Suzette... after it's proven that you're her father, of course. But I needed a change of scenery because my townhouse reminded me too much of Karen."

She looked around and chuckled. "Of course, this place is kind of a dump, but it's cheap and clean and serves my purpose for now. I decided to move to Baytown and applied for a job with North Heron County schools. I'd like to be at Baytown High School but haven't heard of the specific school assignment yet."

"That's a pretty big life change for someone who doesn't know if I'm Suzette's father yet."

She stiffened. "Mr. Martinez—"

"Jose, please."

"Okay... Jose. I realize that you only knew Karen for one night, and most of that was, well... let's be honest... it was for sex. But Karen and I were best friends since we were twelve years old. Sleeping around was not something she did. I believed her when she said she hadn't had sex in a long time before you, and certainly not in the few weeks between being with you and discovering she was pregnant. So while the paternity test is needed for you and for legalities, in my heart, I know she was telling the truth that you're Suzette's father. I'm not worried about the paternity test because it'll simply prove what Karen knew."

"Okay," he acknowledged, nodding his head in a conciliatory manner while still wearing a doubting expression. "But it's still a big life change for you, not knowing my response."

"I agree. But as I said, I needed a change of scenery. And a small town on the Chesapeake Bay sounded lovely. My parents now travel a lot, so the timing worked for me to make a move. Once paternity is established, if you decide you don't want to have a relationship with Suzette, that's your right and I'll respect it. And if that time comes, I'll figure out what's next for her and me. I assure you that I'm not asking for anything from you. I have no need for anything in my life other than that beautiful little girl. She and I will be fine regardless of what you decide."

9

Jose sat in his living room, and as the sun set, the room grew darker. He hadn't bothered to turn on a lamp, but the illumination from the kitchen chased away most of the shadows. At least those in his house. On the other hand, his mind filled with thoughts that chased each other around, like Rosemarie's children. Tumbling. Rolling around tangled together. Racing and screaming. Laughing and crying.

He scrubbed his hand over his face, and while never a big drinker, he almost headed into the kitchen to grab a beer. But he tamped down the urge, knowing he needed to think with a clear head. Plus, a few miles away was a woman who had given up her life to raise a baby, and he knew as cluttered as her mind must be, she wasn't indulging in anything to numb the confusion.

He looked around the room, and it hit him that his life had been much different when he'd left his home this morning than when he walked back through the door this evening. Everything was the same in his house, yet nothing was the same for him.

He searched his memory for every recollection of Karen. While he hadn't thought about her since they'd been together, he wasn't with that many women intimately that he couldn't recall her face. Her dark hair had been pulled back, and her complexion was clear with little makeup. Her smile had been shy, and now that he knew more about her upbringing, that trait seemed to fit.

The suggestion that they spend the night together had come from her, and he remembered she mentioned it was something she didn't usually do. They'd both had several drinks, and guilt churned in his gut at the idea that if she had been as unused to alcohol as she was to flirting, maybe she'd relied heavily on liquid courage.

He closed his eyes and leaned his head back, sighing heavily. She'd given every indication that she was not intoxicated. Her words had been clear. When they walked out of the restaurant, her body had been steady. And so, while he couldn't deny the possibility that the alcohol lowered her inhibition to approach him, talk to him, and then ask him to spend the night, it was hard to shake the feeling that he should've just walked away.

But then the image of Suzette came to mind. He'd only gotten a glimpse of her in the station, and her face had been scrunched in distress, with fat tears rolling down her chubby cheeks. Yet he already knew she was a precious life.

As Karen had said in her missive to me, I count it as fate that our night together brought this beautiful child into my life.

The words rang true in his heart also.

After pulling Karen's memory to the forefront of his mind so he could investigate every moment they'd been together, searching for clues that he'd misinterpreted the situation, once his mind was clear, Melanie's face came to mind.

They hadn't met under the best of circumstances. She certainly hadn't dressed to impress but had a natural beauty about her that shone even under her duress. She was a brunette with strands of gold and red highlights. At the station, her hair was pulled back from her face by sunglasses shoved unceremoniously into the tresses. It was not for show but for practicality. Tonight, she'd pulled her hair up in a lopsided bun with haphazard strands falling around her face. Not styled, she was more worried about keeping it away from her face and possibly out of the little grabby hands of her baby.

The baggy T-shirt she wore was not flattering, but the wide neck exposed her collarbones, and now that he thought about it, he realized she was thin. Again, he was struck with a feeling that it wasn't because she dieted or worried about her weight but possibly from stress.

She was my best friend. We've been friends since we were twelve years old. I had her move in with me. I took time off work to take care of Karen and Suzette.

Melanie had changed her life, given her all, watched her best friend become ill and die, and became the legal guardian of a tiny baby. And now, she'd changed her life again in the quest to unite the baby and her biological father.

When he'd stopped by this evening, he'd been surprised to see the apartment building she was living in. Affordable housing in the area wasn't easy to find, but he hated the idea of her living there. He'd seen a few sketchy men loitering nearby and a few teens wandering by when he'd returned to his vehicle.

Jose lurched forward in his chair. His gut clenched as though punched. He didn't regret his caution, and his confusion when he first met her at the station was understandable. But Melanie's sacrifices had humbled him.

And she did all that for my daughter. *My daughter?*

He scrubbed his hand over his face as clarity filled his mind. The paternity test was necessary for legalities and absolute surety. But Melanie's words before he left her apartment were voiced with such strength, they scored straight through him.

I'm not worried about the paternity test because I already know it'll prove what Karen knew.

He pulled out his phone and dialed Ryan. "Boss? Tell Judith I'll come early tomorrow, and Melanie will bring Suzette. But I also want you to explain to Judith what's going on. I'd like her to be informed. While Judith would never be judgmental about anything, I think it would be easier on Melanie if Judith understood the situation."

Offering thanks before his goodbye, he disconnected, then stared momentarily at the new phone in his hand. He shook his head and snorted. If he hadn't dropped his phone into the bay and put off getting a new one, he would have received Melanie's phone messages several days ago. They could've met, talked, and had a private conversation.

And while the situation was no one's fault, he realized it had caused more stress for Melanie. She couldn't get in contact with him, then having to try to see him at work, and then having an audience. And that last was on him. She had asked for a private meeting, and caught off guard, he hadn't responded well.

Now, he wanted Judith to understand what was going on. Besides being a good friend and a good woman, she was a professional physician and would never say anything to Melanie to make her feel bad. But he didn't want anyone to assume Melanie was trying to shake him down when, in truth, she was trying to do the best thing for everyone.

Standing, he checked the locks on the doors and turned off the kitchen lights before heading upstairs to his bedroom. He showered, but the hot water did little to scrub his still-racing mind.

And lying in bed, he looked forward to seeing Melanie and Suzette again the next morning.

Jose waited in his SUV until he spied Judith's arrival at the clinic. Sleep had proven elusive, and unable to stay home and wait, he'd left early to drive to the clinic.

Judith parked on the side and stood at the employee

entrance when he met her. She smiled her greeting and offered him a quick hug.

"I promise this will be quick and painless," she said gently.

"You don't have to promise me anything," he said. "I just want it to be easy on the baby."

Her gaze held his eyes for a moment, and her smile widened and softened simultaneously. She patted his arm and then unlocked the door to enter the clinic.

He hesitated, then pulled in a deep breath and faced her fully. "I assume Ryan explained the situation to you."

She nodded. "Yes. I'm sure this has been a shock."

He waved his hand dismissively. "A shock, yes, but always a possibility. I suppose if most men having sex thought about how a woman can get pregnant even with protection, there'd be fewer casual encounters."

She chuckled softly, still nodding. "You're probably right. I think that's why Ryan and I worry about Trevor and Cindy."

Ryan had two teenage children with his first wife. Judith had become a beloved stepmother, and Jose knew she was very close to them.

"I just wanted to make sure you understood Melanie's part in all this. I know you'd never judge her. She's lost a good friend and taken on a great responsibility. I don't want anyone to misinterpret her situation."

"You're a good man, Jose," she said, patting his shoulder. Inclining her head toward the front, she said, "Why don't you watch out for them and lead them through the side door when they arrive? I'll get everything ready so this can be quick."

He nodded and walked through the waiting room to look out the window. Nerves clawed up his throat as he continually looked down the empty street where only a few cars passed in the early morning by the clinic. Glancing at his watch, he grew restless. Just when he thought he would crawl out of his skin, a small SUV pulled into the parking lot.

He hustled out the side entrance and waved toward her. Not realizing he was holding his breath, it wasn't until she smiled and waved in return that the air left his lungs in a rush. Uncertain she'd want help, his feet acted of their own accord, and he moved straight to her SUV.

He made it to the driver's door just as it opened. Her smile beamed, and he was struck again with the thought that she was not only ready for the paternity test but also appeared confident about the results. His gaze shot to the back seat where the infant carrier was in place, but with it turned toward the back, he couldn't see Suzette. She was quiet, and he was happy that, so far, she wasn't distressed.

"Good morning," Melanie said as she slid from the driver's seat.

"Good morning," he rushed, his gaze taking her in. Her hair was smoothed back into a low ponytail. Makeup was minimal. As fresh-faced as she presented, she was a knockout as a natural beauty. She appeared young, dressed in a light blue top and jeans, and it dawned on him that he had no idea how old she was. *If she's a teacher, she's earned a college degree, so she's at least approaching her midtwenties.*

His eyes darted to the back seat again. "How is she doing? I mean, how are both of you doing? Is everything okay?"

A soft chuckle erupted, and his gaze darted back to Melanie's face.

"It sounds like you're nervous. I assure you that we're fine. She slept through the night and wasn't too fussy when I rushed her a bit through getting dressed this morning."

He dragged his hand through his hair and dropped his chin, nodding. "Yeah, I guess I am nervous." Then thinking about the implication of what he just admitted, he lifted his head and steadily held her gaze. "But in case you're wondering, I'm not nervous about the outcome. I… I have no reason to doubt you or Karen."

Her eyes widened, and she nodded slowly. "Well, this test will lay any remaining doubts to rest. Plus"—she shrugged—"it's needed. I really want Suzette to be able to know. But I do want to thank you for agreeing to this. I'm aware that you did not have to acquiesce so easily."

Before he could respond, baby babbles sounded from the back seat. Laughing, Melanie said, "I think somebody is ready to see something more than the inside of this car."

She walked to the back, and he followed her eagerly. Lifting the tailgate, she reached in and pulled out what looked like a stroller without a seat. His hands naturally reached forward to take it from her, then quickly real-

ized he had no idea what to do with it. Feeling unchival-
rous, he stood to the side as she opened it and locked it
in place. Closing the hatch, she rolled it to the passenger
side and opened the door. She leaned in, obscuring his
ability to see Suzette's face. His fingers twitched, but he
forced his body to lock down and wait patiently.

"Hello, sweet girl!" Melanie cooed. "Are you ready to
get out and meet some new friends?"

Nerves scored through him as she unfastened a
latch, lifted the entire seat from the car seat base, and
then placed it onto the stroller frame. He'd watched his
sister do the same thing countless times, but he was still
amazed at the deftness with which they completed the
maneuver. He had no doubt he would have fumbled and
possibly dropped the baby in the process.

Now that Suzette was in the stroller, Melanie
opened the front passenger door and began pulling out
a diaper bag that appeared large enough to carry everything a baby could possibly want or need. Again, having
been around his nieces and nephews, he shouldn't have
been surprised at what babies need, but somehow, this
was different.

Looking down, he finally had his first true look at
Suzette. She stared up at him with her large, dark eyes,
her fingers tucked into her mouth. With her slightly
olive complexion and dark hair, it reminded him of his
own baby pictures. He felt like all the oxygen had been
sucked from the air and grew light-headed, hoping he
wouldn't pass out. Then Suzette's little mouth widened
into a gummy grin, and his heart tightened in his chest.

He probably would have stared forever if the sound

of the passenger door closing hadn't jolted him out of his trance. Looking over to see Melanie loaded down, he reached out to lift the diaper bag from her shoulder. "Here, let me."

She blinked as though surprised at the gesture. "Thanks. I always feel like I'm packing too much, but I never know what she might need." She wrapped her fingers around the stroller's handle and began pushing toward the clinic. "Which door should we use?"

"This one, here on the side." He led them to the door he and Judith had used, continually glancing down to see the contented expression on Suzette's face. Having seen how quickly she became unhappy the day before, he hoped she wouldn't mind having her cheek swabbed. "I checked into the procedure, and it shouldn't hurt her."

Melanie nodded. "I did too. She'll be fine."

Judith approached from the back and greeted them with a wide smile. "Hello, I'm Dr. Judith Coates. You must be Melanie." She then bent and made a wide-eyed googly face over the stroller. "And this sweetheart must be Suzette."

A shaky breath left Melanie's lips, and Jose realized how nervous she must also be. *Damn, she hides it well.* But it was obvious that Judith's pleasant greeting relieved Melanie, and a new thought struck him. *She's here, surrounded by strangers, and all these people are my friends. No wonder she's nervous.* Wishing he knew what to say to take away some of her anxiety, he remained quiet. *Two weeks until the results come in... can I keep them at arm's length for that long?*

10

Melanie had woken with nerves shooting through her stomach like a Ping-Pong ball. She had been honest with Jose about not doubting Karen's claim that he was Suzette's father. Yet as she lay in bed, unable to sleep, she realized how much was riding on her faith in her best friend. But she wanted the paternity test to fulfill Karen's wishes and give Jose a chance to get to know his daughter if Suzette was his child.

Mornings could be iffy with a baby, and she usually didn't schedule any early morning appointments, never knowing if she'd be able to get out the door on time. But she'd been touched that the doctor was willing to see them before the clinic opened to keep down the possibility of nosy people who might make disparaging assumptions about Suzette.

And thankfully, today, it had not been challenging to get Suzette up, changed, dressed, fed, and out the door.

Pulling up to the clinic, she'd spied Jose waving next

to the side door with a shy smile. Grateful he was there and waving in friendliness, she returned his gesture. While getting Suzette out of the car, she couldn't help but notice that he hovered, and his gaze continually darted down toward the carrier. Her deepest fear had been that he would be angry and resentful, but the man staring at her baby only had a curious, albeit nervous smile.

Once inside the clinic, a sigh of relief passed her lips as the beautiful doctor with a kind smile approached and greeted them sweetly.

I have some forms for you to fill out," Judith said. "They're very basic, essentially just acknowledging that you understand what tests are being done and the results that will be given to you."

She nodded and observed Jose doing the same.

"The test will be a buccal swab on the inside of the cheeks. It's non-invasive and won't hurt," Judith continued.

Once again, Melanie nodded along with Jose. Judith handed the papers to them, and they both read through them, signing at the same time.

Judith said, "I can't accept payment now since my bookkeeper isn't here. Is it alright to just bill both of you?"

"That's fine—" Melanie began.

"Send me the bill for both myself and Suzette." Jose interrupted.

Swinging her head around, Melanie stared, her brows furrowed. "That's not necessary—"

"It's fine," Jose said. "You've gone to great expense to do what Karen has asked you to do. And you certainly haven't asked anything of me other than this test, which I heartily agree to. But please, let me do this."

She nodded slowly and shrugged, looking back at a smiling Judith. "Okay. I guess that's fine."

Judith then looked back and forth between them and said, "Well, since that's settled, who would like to go first?"

It didn't matter to Melanie, but Jose surprised her again when he said, "Can you take us back at the same time?"

Judith nodded. "Absolutely." Looking at Melanie, she asked, "Is that alright with you?"

"Um… yeah… sure."

"Okay, follow me."

He stepped to the side and waved his hand toward Judith's back, indicating that Melanie should proceed. Still not sure what to say, she pushed the stroller down the hall behind Judith, feeling Jose right behind her. They entered the lab, and Judith efficiently pulled out a swab, made googly faces at Suzette, and quickly swabbed the inside of her mouth before dropping it into the tube and sealing it. With a marker, she wrote the identification, then pulled off a printed label with Suzette's identification information and affixed it to the tube.

Suzette's face scrunched, indicating she was ready to squall, but Melanie immediately leaned down and tickled her tummy, eliciting a grin. Grateful a meltdown had been averted for now, she was barely aware that Jose had his cheek swabbed, as well.

Standing, she looked at the two tubes lying side by side on the counter. Sucking in a deep breath, she let it out slowly, realizing that everything about Suzette's future was now in the hands of those two tubed swabs. Glancing to the side, she also observed Jose staring at them. *He's probably having the same thought.*

"I'd like to offer medical services for any time you need, Melanie," Judith said. "We are a fully staffed general practice medical facility. I assume you have Suzette's and your medical records with you?"

"Yes, I do." She glanced toward Jose, pressing, then rubbing her lips together. "Our plans are a little uncertain right now. But we definitely plan on spending the summer here on the Eastern Shore. She'll need her next vaccine boosters in about a month."

"Excellent. You can make an appointment anytime and either have her records electronically sent to us or bring in what you have."

Smiling, she nodded, then followed Judith back out to the side entrance, again feeling Jose right behind her. Sticking out her hand, she clasped Judith's. "Thank you so much for seeing us early. That was very kind of you."

Judith waved away her thanks. "It was my pleasure." Looking down into the stroller, she added, "And I hope to see this little cutie a lot more."

Melanie wasn't sure how to interpret that comment but remembered that Judith was married to Jose's boss. Deciding that another nod would be the best answer, she started to open the door when Jose quickly thanked

Judith and rushed around to hold it open for her. She waved goodbye to the doctor, then pushed the stroller back to her SUV.

Now that the test was over, her nerves dissipated, and she could breathe easier. She clicked the fob of her SUV and unlocked the doors. Turning to say goodbye to Jose, he gently lifted the diaper bag from her arm and set it on the passenger seat. He looked down at Suzette and smiled.

"I would offer to put her in the car for you, but I'm not sure how the seats work."

"I'd never been around babies before Suzette, so I'm learning a whole new set of skills."

"I'm embarrassed to say that with all my nieces and nephews, I've never made the transfer myself."

She laughed as she unlatched the carrier from the stroller and shifted it into the car seat base. "Don't worry about it. Each of these is different, so it took me a while to get used to how things worked." Looking over her shoulder, she asked, "You have nieces and nephews?"

"Yeah. I come from a big family, but I have only one sister with children so far. And she has three."

Jerking around, she stared at him with wide eyes. "Three? Oh my goodness! Sometimes I think I'm drowning with only one!"

Turning toward the inside of her vehicle, she focused on making sure the car seat was properly buckled while realizing that Suzette had three cousins. It had never occurred to her that there was now a whole other family for Suzette. *But only if he wants to share his*

99

life with her.

Sucking in a breath, she closed the door and turned to lift her hand toward Jose. "I want to thank you for making this as easy on me and Suzette as possible. I realize it's… well, we're in a crazy situation that neither of us expected to be in. But I want you to know I do appreciate it."

He reached out and took her hand in his. As his fingers curled around hers and their palms met, a warm current passed between them, starting at their connected hands and moving up her arm. She blinked, her gaze jerking downward and then back up to his face quickly. Deciding she must be overly tired, she pulled her hand back but instantly felt the loss. He looked down, his brows together, as though he possibly felt the same thing. *I'm sure neither of us got much sleep last night,* she thought, trying to find a reason for the reaction to a simple handshake.

"Well, I guess I'll see you in a few weeks when the results come in—"

"Have you had breakfast?"

Her chin jerked slightly as she blinked, his question catching her off guard. "I'm sorry?"

"Breakfast. It's early, and I imagine you rushed to get Suzette ready this morning. I wondered if you'd had a chance to eat yet?"

"Oh, don't worry about me. Once we get home, I can grab a bowl of cereal."

"I haven't eaten and thought about going to a local diner. Would you two like to join me?"

"Oh, well, you don't have to—"

He stepped a little closer and dipped his chin as he looked down at her. "I'm not offering out of obligation, although if I were, that would still be fine. But you're new in town and don't know anyone. We both need to eat. And regardless of how the paternity test turns out, I don't see any reason we shouldn't be able to get to know each other a little."

His dark eyes held a hint of uncertainty, and her fingers itched to reach up and soothe the crease in his forehead. She turned his suggestion over in her mind, searching for a reason she should deny. But, in truth, he was right. She didn't know anyone in town. She planned on being here for at least the summer and hopefully longer with a teaching job in the fall. And if he didn't mind having breakfast with her and Suzette without waiting on the paternity test results, then she couldn't think of a good reason to say no.

Smiling, she hefted her shoulders and nodded. "I wouldn't mind having breakfast." Just then, her stomach growled, and she laughed. "Perhaps I should amend that statement. I *need* to have breakfast." Glancing behind her at Suzette in the car seat, she added, "Since you have nieces and nephews, I assume that you're aware that we'll probably have to eat quickly, and she might pitch a fit in the middle of the meal."

Relief eased the lines on his face as he nodded while chuckling. "The diner can serve us quickly, and they're used to kids."

"Okay, then. You lead the way, and I'll follow."

He led her to a diner north of Baytown near the small town of Easton. As she pulled into a parking spot next to him, he jumped down quickly and was at the back of her SUV as she hit the lift on her fob. By the time she'd walked around, he had the stroller out.

"You'd better check this," he warned. "I'm not sure I did it right."

Glad for his assistance and touched by his enthusiasm, she leaned over to ensure that it was locked into position. "Yep, looks good."

He took the initiative to get the diaper bag while she transferred Suzette. He moved to the front door and opened it so she could push the stroller in.

"Hey, stranger!"

Melanie turned her head to see a pretty, statuesque server smiling at Jose. A quick look at her right hand showed an impressive wedding band and diamond. She barely had time to ponder why that left her relieved before Jose spoke.

"Carrie," he greeted with a slight hesitation in his voice. "I didn't know you were still working here."

"I come in occasionally to help them out." She turned her smile to Melanie, then her gaze dropped to the stroller. "Who do we have here? Oh my, this must be your niece. I swear Rosemarie keeps having the most beautiful dark-headed babies!"

Melanie blinked, and Jose seemed stunned into silence. She blurted, "Actually, this is my daughter."

"Oh, I am sorry! She is beautiful. I'm Carrie, by the way."

"It's nice to meet you. I'm Melanie, and this is my daughter, Suzette." She noticed Carrie glance between her and Jose and quickly added, "I'm new to the area, and Jose and I met through a mutual acquaintance. He just told me this is a good place for breakfast. I'm looking forward to finding out for myself."

"Welcome to the Eastern Shore!" Carrie enthused. "And you're in for a treat. Joe's Diner slings the best breakfast around! Let's get you seated in a booth, and I'll make sure your food comes out quickly. My oldest is a teenager, but I just had a baby not too long ago, so I'm sure you need to eat fast."

"How old is your baby?"

"Beth is six months old now."

"Suzette is three months old!"

She was thrilled to meet another young mother and couldn't imagine Carrie having a teenage boy. They were soon seated with orders given, and she looked across the table at Jose. "Carrie seems nice. I hope the explanation I gave was okay."

He nodded and smiled. "You did really good. I don't know why, but it didn't dawn on me that we might see people here who would wonder who I was with." Giving his head a little shake, he rushed, "Jesus, that sounded bad. I just meant that I hadn't thought about what we would say to people about how we met. But you handled it perfectly."

Shrugging, she said, "I think that sticking as close to the truth without giving away too much information is probably the best plan. Technically, you and I did meet through Karen, a mutual acquaintance."

"Carrie's husband is the county sheriff, and we coach together as part of the American Legion."

The diner was crowded, but she noticed a large table

nearby that remained empty. When the bell rang over the front door and a group of uniformed law enforcement officers walked in and headed straight to the table, she realized it must be their special place.

"Shit," Jose mumbled, then glanced over at Suzette and winced. "Sorry!"

She laughed and waved her hand dismissively. "I don't think she'll remember you cursed." Glancing over at the officers, she was about to ask if that's why he seemed nervous, but suddenly the sounds of greetings met them.

"Jose! Good to see you!"

He smiled and stood, walking over to shake the hands of several of the deputies. Melanie watched as Carrie made her way to a large, handsome man and lifted on her toes to kiss him. The stern man smiled widely and wrapped his arms around her. His eyes warmed as he tightened his embrace, then let her go with a wink. Assuming that was the sheriff, she smiled at their obvious affection. A little sigh escaped, wondering if she'd ever have that kind of relationship. At one time, she'd assumed she would. Glancing down at Suzette waving her arms and legs, she knew that life had changed, and this little one was now her priority.

"Melanie," Jose said, having walked back to the table.

Looking up, she saw a few men with him, smiling down at her.

"I'd like to introduce you to Sheriff Colt Hudson and Hunter Simmons. Colt is Carrie's husband, and Hunter is married to a nurse in the area. You already know that

Colt has a six-month-old, but Hunter also has a year-old baby."

She smiled her greeting as Jose continued, "Melanie is new in town, and we had a mutual friend who wanted us to meet. This is Melanie's little girl, Suzette."

The men greeted her warmly, and she smiled with pride as they welcomed her and Suzette to the area. As Carrie brought the plates of food, setting them in front of Jose and Melanie, the men stepped out of the way and returned to their table.

She looked down and shook her head at the amount of food. "Oh my goodness! I haven't eaten this much food in so long... I can't even remember!"

"I'm sure with everything you've had to do, taking care of yourself has probably been last on your list. So eat up and enjoy," Jose encouraged.

"I'm not going to argue with that. Right now, Suzette seems content, but that could change at any moment!"

The conversation halted as the two of them enjoyed their breakfast. She ate quickly but managed to finish before Suzette began to fuss. She pulled out her credit card and set it on the table before scooting out of the booth and grabbing the carrier. "Use my card while I take her out to the car. She probably needs to be changed, so I'll do that and meet you out there."

She had just finished with a diaper change and was snapping the onesie together when he appeared. He handed her the card as he leaned over to peer down at Suzette.

She looked at her card for just a moment and then

looked over at Jose, her suspicion rising. "You didn't use my card, did you?"

He looked up with a wide-eyed, pretend blank expression on his face. "I'm sure I don't know what you're talking about."

She rolled her eyes and laughed, saying, "Fine, but next time, I'll pay." As soon as the words left her mouth, she wished she could pull them back. While this morning had been special, she didn't want to make any assumptions about seeing Jose again. "I mean..." she faltered.

He smiled and placed his hand on her arm. "There absolutely will be a next time, Melanie."

His words were sweet, but the feel of his hand on her arm captured her attention, making it hard to breathe. *Lordy, girl, get a hold of yourself!*

Staring into his eyes, she watched his expression. And if his face was anything to go by, he felt the warm connection, too. Saying goodbye, she climbed into the SUV and drove back to the apartment. It was time for Suzette to have a morning nap, and Melanie was looking forward to a few minutes alone to process the thoughts that were becoming tangled. Her mind seemed to no longer connect Jose with Karen or Jose with Suzette.

Blowing out a deep breath, she pushed thoughts of him to the side, determined to focus on making the apartment more of a home and getting in touch with the school board office to find out more about the position. The last thing she needed to do was start daydreaming about a tall, handsome, and kind police officer. From what she could tell, she didn't have to worry about Jose rejecting Suzette once the paternity was resolved. But to start daydreaming about something more was a slippery slope she was determined not to fall down. Suzette needed a mom who wasn't suffering heartbreak.

11

Jose had just pulled out on the water with Jared and Bryce when the dispatcher radioed about a stolen fishing boat. It had been docked outside of Bunson Fishing. He steered north, and Jared called out that they were meeting two of North Heron detectives there.

"How big is the boat?" Jared asked, looking over at Jose.

"She didn't say, but aren't all his at least thirty feet?"

Bryce shook his head with his hands on his hips. "There's no way somebody can steal that size boat, then turn around and just use it. They'd have to sell it, and who the fuck would want to buy that?"

"Chop shop," Jose said, sighing. "That's the only answer. These boats have got to be broken down and sold for parts."

"Agreed, but where the hell are they going to take it to do that?"

"If the plan is to start working on it immediately, they could take it to a garage, shed, or barn. Hell, anywhere that once they started getting pieces off it, they could just keep it hidden from view."

They came to the back of the inlet, where the business was located, and eased into the dock. One of the employees came out, and Bryce tossed the rope to him, giving him a chance to secure them to the dock. Alighting from their vessel, they walked toward Hunter and Sam, the two detectives talking to the owner.

Lester Bunson had grown up on the Eastern Shore, working the waters with his dad and granddad. He now owned one of the larger fishing businesses in the area, focusing on rockfish and drum. As Jose neared, the normally calm, soft-spoken Lester was angry.

"I had heard people talking about boats being taken, but I figured we were safe. Who the hell would want one of my boats? Easily identifiable. Not the kind you can change the registration number on to get away with it. I mean, think about it… the lines and nets alone make it much harder to manage unless they know what they're doing!"

Sam offered a conciliatory nod. "I hear you, Lester. When the call came in, we were surprised."

Even angry, Lester politely greeted the VMP officers once they made it to him.

Jose shook his hand and said, "I'm really sorry to hear about this."

"Well, you better tell your daddy to watch what's going on where he works. It looks like whoever's pulling this… this…" he growled, then sighed as he spied his wife near the end of the dock and lowered his voice. "This mess is hitting everybody."

"Do you have surveillance out here?" Hunter asked.

"Yes, sir, I do. I've already looked at it and can tell you that I can see them but can't identify them. But I'll be more than happy to let you see if there's anything you can recognize." Lester looked toward the end of the dock again. "You all come, too. My wife's got some homemade lemonade and will be proud to serve you some."

The gathering made their way down the dock, past several more fishing boats, and into the office. His wife, Arlene, greeted each one with a smile, although Jose recognized the deeper lines from worry on her face.

"Good of you all to come out here," she said, just as polite as her husband. "I've got some lemonade poured, so help yourself." Turning to Lester, she reached out and held his hand. "Honey, don't let this get to you. I don't want to have to worry about my husband having an early heart attack. The boat was taken, but we've got insurance, and nobody was hurt. So while it stings, it's not the worst that could happen." She gave his hand a little jiggle, offered him a soft smile, then nodded toward the men as she walked out.

Turning, Jose witnessed Lester's eyes following his wife until she was out of sight. Then with a little shake of his head, Lester's lips curved into a smile, and his beleaguered expression eased.

"You've got a good woman," Jose said, a strange longing filling him.

Lester turned to look at him and chuckled. "Yes, sir, I do. Makes the bad times not so bad and the good times better."

He and the other officers drank the lemonade since she'd been so kind as to make it, then while Jared and Bryce headed out to the dock with one of Lester's employees to check the area where the boat had been taken, Jose followed Hunter and Sam into the inner office to review the security feed.

They watched as four people dressed in dark clothing, hoods, and face masks slipped onto the dock from a small boat near the very end. Two hopped aboard the fishing boat farthest from the office and disappeared below deck. The other two stood nearby, keeping their bodies turned away from the cameras but obviously on lookout duty.

"Those two standing there, look like lookouts," Jose began. "It's hard to tell because of the poor quality of the camera feed."

They continued to watch as one of the people on the dock started to turn toward the camera when the other one stepped to him, grabbed him by the shoulder, and shoved him to the side. There was no audio, but their body language indicated they were arguing with arms thrown out to the sides. The first one started to turn away again when he was sucker-punched in the shoulder and stumbled to his knees on the dock.

Suddenly, they stopped when one appeared back up onto the deck of the boat, then hopped off. He lifted the rope that had tethered the boat and tossed it over to the deck. The boat pulled away from the dock and started out of the inlet while the three remaining thieves raced back down to the small boat they arrived in and disappeared into the night.

"Coming by water allows them to slip in and out without being seen, as well as not leaving trace evidence from a vehicle bringing them," Sam said.

Jose nodded, sighing heavily. "Making them virtually impossible to catch unless you happen to be right with them."

"While the boat theft looks professional, this just doesn't strike me as the activity of an organized gang. I'd bet my career they're a local gang of thieves," Hunter surmised.

"And from the looks of those two arguing on the dock, they might turn on each other, giving us a chance to root them out," Sam said.

"They're organized. Would a local group be able to pull this off?" Bryce asked.

Hunter shrugged. "Maybe. Depends on who's leading this shit."

"At least one of them knows how to handle a large boat. That's a hell of a lot different from the single-motor boat they came in on," Jared noted.

Jose turned the available evidence over in his mind. "Once you take that security feed, if you can have someone magnify and clarify anything about the boat they came in on, then send that to Ryan. Right now, that'll give us the best information we could have."

"You got it, man," Sam agreed.

As he turned to leave, Hunter stopped him, then asked, "None of my business, but that friend you were having breakfast with at the diner the other day. The one with the baby? Is she someone special? I mentioned to Belle that you were friends with someone new in town who had a baby, and, of course, Belle was ready to call her up immediately." He rubbed his chin and offered a grin. "I just didn't know if she was passing through, planning on staying, or maybe she was someone you're interested in."

Jose knew it wouldn't be long before the word got out about the pretty new woman in town with the baby. When people saw him with her, speculation and gossip might abound. A few days after having breakfast the day of the paternity test, he'd met Melanie and Suzette for a walk in the park one afternoon. Since then, he'd been on duty for the next several days. They still had a little over a week to go before the results were delivered, and he fought an inner battle each day, wanting to go see them and wanting not to become too invested until he knew. But the times he was with them, he'd enjoyed being with Melanie so much that he looked forward to their next visit and loved seeing Suzette.

"We're just friends," he said, then felt strangely guilty. It suddenly hit him that the last thing he wanted was for the news to get around that a pretty *single* woman had moved into town. A strange feeling of possessiveness moved through him when thinking of Melanie and Suzette. "But yeah, she's special." He shrugged, trying to appear nonchalant. "She's uncertain if she's staying, but I'm sure she'd love to meet Belle sometime."

"Well, all right." Hunter smiled. "You've got our number. You're more than welcome to share it with her, and you can expect Belle will call her to meet up soon."

With a chin lift, Jose walked away and headed down

the dock, his mind in turmoil but not on the case. He wanted to spend more time with Melanie to get to know Suzette. And he sure as fuck wasn't ready to share their time with anyone yet. But even as that thought crossed his mind, he knew it wasn't only because of Suzette that he wanted to spend time with Melanie. Scrubbing his hand through his hair, he gripped the back of his neck as he jerked it side to side, hearing the pop.

He needed to talk to his family but had no idea what to say until the results came in. He hadn't planned on telling them anything about the paternity test yet, assuming he'd talk to them if it were positive. But the thought of his mother sniffing out from someone else what was happening sent a grimace across his face.

"Hey, Jose!" Jared called out.

Jerking back to the investigation at hand, he shoved thoughts of the two new ladies in his life to the back of his mind and jogged toward the other officers.

The dock gave no more answers as to who had stolen the boat, so they climbed aboard their vessel, called in to dispatch, and headed back out onto the bay. The afternoon continued with routine fishing and license checks, and by the end of the day, he was grateful for no emergencies.

"How are you doing?" Jared asked.

Jose snorted. "I assume you're talking about Melanie and Suzette and the question of paternity?"

Jared held his gaze, then looked out over the water before shifting his eyes back to Jose. "Yeah, I was. But I have to admit it's interesting to hear you call them by name."

"Why would I just say the woman and baby?" he asked, tilting his head to the side.

Jared threw his hands out in a placating motion. "No offense, man. Honestly. I just thought maybe you were trying to maintain some separation until you found out the results. But hearing you say their names makes me think you've already built a connection."

"Yeah, I've seen them a couple of times."

"That's cool, man. I'm sure she could use a friend right now. I guess I just want to make sure you're taking care of yourself, too. I mean, this was a huge boulder that just got dropped on top of you."

The tension in his shoulders relaxed. "I'm not offended, Jared, and I appreciate the concern. But the reality is that I've got friends all around here that will support me if it turns out that I'm not her father, and if I am, they'll rally around all of us. But Melanie has no one. She's staying over at the Wilder Apartments, north of town, and it's only one bedroom. I've gone by a couple of times, and she's handling everything beautifully. Hell, she's decorated, the place is clean and as nice as it can be, and she's devoted herself full-time to Suzette. But with her life on hold right now, she's got no one. So whether Suzette is mine or not, I've enjoyed spending time with them. I figure I can be a friend if nothing else."

"The women around here would love to pull her into their camaraderie."

"You're right. I'm just nervous about how to introduce her. A friend? That would make sense, but what if I'm Suzette's father? Then how do we let people know?" He sighed. "Jesus, I look at them, and all I see is sweetness and beauty. And then I think about other people's possible reactions and hate to think animosity will touch them."

"When will you find out for sure?"

"Hopefully, in less than a week, but it could be a little longer."

"Then I would just wait until you're sure. Then you and Melanie can decide what comes next and what to tell people. I know it seems like a long time, but maybe it's better that way. But once she decides to stay, whether or not the baby is yours, you can believe the women around here will swoop down and befriend her."

He nodded. He knew Jared was right and looked forward to the time when Melanie wouldn't be so alone. As he stood and looked over the bay's crystal-clear water, the feeling remained that Suzette was his. But as much as that excited him, he knew that would change everything. For Melanie and for him. Because either way, he wanted them to stay.

12

Melanie sat on a rickety folding chair Trey had pulled out of the trash cans at the end of their building. She sat just outside her cracked apartment door. Suzette slept in her crib, and Melanie had the infant monitor in her lap along with one of her biology books. Trey and Ricky sat on the concrete breezeway near her.

"You know what got me, Ms. Landers?" Trey asked. "That photo stuff."

"Photosynthesis, shithead," Ricky said, kicking Trey's foot with his own.

"Yeah, yeah, that!" Trey agreed, shifting his feet over without breaking his enthusiastic response.

"How about you, Ricky? Was that one of the areas you had a problem with?" Melanie asked.

He shrugged his heavy shoulders. "Nah. I got that."

"Ricky's smart," Trey said, grinning while he nodded. "Like he's really smart."

Melanie observed the two boys, as different in personality as they could be. "I'm sure you're both very intelligent. Grades and intelligence often don't go hand in hand."

"Huh?" Trey leaned back against the railing.

"She means that some smart kids don't get good grades because of other shit going on, and some kids that aren't so smart do get good grades 'cause they do extra work or maybe just suck up to the teacher."

She laughed and nodded. "You're exactly right, Ricky."

"So if I'm not smart but I do extra work or suck up, I can pass?" Trey asked, his eyes bright with hope.

"How about we just study what we know you have to learn, and then I'll bet you can pass?" she said.

They worked for most of the next hour, and she was impressed with both boys. Trey was funny but also could apply himself when he tried. She imagined he spent a great deal of time in the classroom being a clown to hide that he was bored or didn't like the subject. But she discovered that when he reviewed notes several times, he was able to grasp the concepts. And Ricky was smart but there were layers to him that she'd yet to uncover.

Just when they were almost finished, the apartment door three down from her opened and a large man walked out in a stained wifebeater and baggy pants. He lit a cigarette before he looked over at them. He scowled, then began coughing.

"Boy, get me a beer."

Ricky had already gotten to his feet and murmured his thanks to her, but she watched as a curtain fell over his expression as he ambled toward the man. Just as he got to the door, he ducked in quickly. The man looked at her and sneered before following Ricky inside.

"Is that his father?" she asked, not liking the way the man spoke to Ricky.

"Nah. That's his uncle. He lives with him 'cause his parents are gone." Trey leaned closer and lowered his voice. "I try to stay out of Cory's way. He likes to pop us on the head. Ricky ducks better than I do."

The sound of approaching footsteps on the stairs caught her attention, and a woman appeared at the top, walking toward them.

"Mom!" Trey called out, a wide smile on his face.

Standing, Melanie met her with an outstretched hand. "Ms. Blevins, hello. I'm Melanie Landers."

"I'm Rita Blevins. Nice to meet you. I got off work a little early and saw y'all sitting up here. I wanted to say thank you for helping these boys." She smiled as she looked up at her son. "Trey, honey, can you get the groceries out of the car? I got some ice cream that we don't want to melt."

He whooped and raced down the steps, calling out his goodbye.

Melanie laughed. "It's my pleasure to work with them."

Rita shook her head and laughed. "Not a lot of people would consider sitting in the hot sun, teaching a couple of teenagers without getting paid to be a pleasure, but I'm glad you got it in you to do so. Means a lot to me and Trey. And I know it means a lot to Ricky, although he might not say so."

"Ricky lets me know in his own way."

Rita nodded. "My Trey lost his dad in a car accident when he was only six. That's a hard time to lose a father, but we've done all right. And his memories are good ones. Plus, he's got all his grandparents and a couple of aunts and uncles to be good influences. But Ricky's got no one. So anything you can do is appreciated."

Just when she was about to ask more, Suzette began to stir from her morning nap. Rita smiled and said, "Sounds like you've got a little one to get to. Just wanted to say thanks."

Melanie waved goodbye and headed inside. She was glad she'd had the opportunity to talk with Trey's mom but now was excited for the excursion she'd planned once Suzette was fed.

Melanie pushed the stroller into the high school an hour later, glad the students were already out for summer vacation. She entered the office, smiling at the secretary, who returned her smile with one of her own.

"Hello. I'm Melanie Landers. I'm here to see Principal Watkins."

"Oh yes, Ms. Landers. I'll let her know—"

"I'm here!"

Melanie saw a woman in a bright blue T-shirt with Baytown High School emblazoned across the front walking toward her with the confidence of someone used to being in charge.

"I'm Ellen Watkins, the principal here. Come on back."

Besides the school T-shirt, Ellen was dressed casually in slacks. Glancing down at her own attire of khaki capris, sneakers, and a pink top with little cap sleeves,

Melanie breathed a sigh of relief, knowing she hadn't underdressed for the summer meeting.

She glanced down at the stroller and said, "I hope you don't mind if my daughter comes, too. I haven't been in town long enough to know anyone to use as a babysitter yet."

"Not at all!" Ellen said, waving her forward.

With another smile sent toward the secretary, she moved around the counter and pushed her stroller into the principal's office. Praying Suzette continued to snooze, she took a seat in front of the desk.

"I was informed by the school board office that I had a job offer with the county for the fall, but at the time, they weren't sure what the position would be. And to be honest, my situation was a bit fluid, so I wasn't even sure if this was going to work out. But I received an email yesterday that a biology position was open here at the high school and I should come in to see you."

"Yes, and thank goodness! We had two people retire from the science department, and I've been desperate to get someone. Getting quality teachers to move out to the Eastern Shore is so hard. Housing can be difficult to find, and there's certainly no nightlife for younger teachers to enjoy, so turnover can be high." She glanced toward the stroller and asked, "You said your plans have been fluid. I have to ask—are they any more settled?"

"Yes, Ms. Watkins." She hesitated for just a moment, then decided to confide. "Suzette is not my biological child. My best friend gave birth to her and was diagnosed with cancer only a month later. And a month after that, she passed away—"

"Oh my God!" Ellen said, her eyes wide as her hand pressed against her chest. "Poor little baby." She lifted her gaze and peered at Melanie. "And you now have guardianship?"

"Yes, she didn't have any family, and the father was unaware."

"I see."

Ellen's voice held no judgment, for which Melanie was thankful.

"And what brought you out to the Eastern Shore?"

"I needed a change of scenery, having grieved the loss of my best friend. My parents have to travel with my father's job, and... well, I chose this area for some personal reasons. And once here, it seems like a peaceful place to live."

Ellen smiled softly. "I moved from South Carolina to get away from an abusive ex many years ago. I found peace here and even met my husband. It was a great place to raise our children, and I hope it's the same for you."

Tears stung the backs of her eyes at the understanding coming from Ellen. "Thank you. That means a lot."

"Now... down to business. As all new teachers do, you will be expected to start a week before the other teachers. You'll be sent a packet, not only from the school board office but from our school, as well. You can leave your address, email address, and phone number with the secretary out front. The position will be as a biology teacher. I've already looked at your references from your last school, and they were exemplary, so we're lucky to have you."

"Thank you. That's nice to hear."

"We have seven periods during the day, and you will be expected to teach five of those, have one for planning, and meet with your science department team at least one day a week. And then the other will be a duty period such as lunch duty, hall duty, or a study hall."

"That sounds like the school I just came from, so I'm familiar with that type of schedule."

"Excellent! You will probably teach two classes of regular biology and two classes of advanced biology, both for sophomores. We desperately need an advanced biology seminar class for juniors and seniors, and since you've taught that before, our science department chair and I agree that that should be offered to you."

"I would love that, thank you."

"We were uncertain if we'd be able to offer it, and there might be enough students for two of those advanced biology seminar classes. If so, then we would take away one of your sophomore classes. But those decisions will be made by myself, our educational coordinator, and the department chair."

Melanie nodded, then glanced down as Suzette began to squirm. "I have had the chance to meet a couple of teens that live in my apartment building. They've mentioned failing the biology state test. I wonder if I could borrow a textbook? I'm tutoring them this summer before school starts."

Ellen smiled widely. "Absolutely!" She walked out of

her office and returned a moment later carrying a large biology textbook. "Here you go." Settling behind her desk again, she asked, "May I ask the names of the students?"

"Trey Blevins and Ricky Montgomery. I actually met Trey's mother today."

"Oh yes, I recognize those names well. Trey will be a junior and should be able to graduate on time if we can keep him settled enough to focus on his classes. Ricky will be a senior but has serious family issues that make his situation more tenuous. His father is in prison for armed robbery, and his mother died years ago. He lives with his uncle, I believe. And I'm not sure his uncle's actions are far removed from his brother, Ricky's dad. But if you can help either of them, that would be a huge bonus in their lives."

As the meeting concluded, she pushed Suzette's stroller back to the car, excitement filling her. It didn't take long to drive to the apartment, and Suzette was ready to get out of the carrier. After a diaper change, she placed her in the playpen, where a few toys surrounded her. Melanie heated a bottle while making herself a peanut butter and jelly sandwich. Between bites, she fed Suzette.

She loved their rocking and cuddle time and watched Suzette's eyes grow heavy. Grateful they were having a good morning, she placed Suzette down for another nap. The timing was perfect when her phone rang, and she saw her mom's number.

Speaking softly, she answered, "Hey, Mom! How are you and Dad?"

"We're fine, and I have to say from the sound of your

voice, Suzette must be sleeping, and you're in a good mood."

She quietly chuckled. "You're right. Suzette is a dream, and I met with the high school principal this morning. The full-time position at the high school came through. I really like her, and I'm going to teach biology to sophomores and some advanced biology classes to juniors and seniors."

"That is good news!" There was only a moment of hesitation before her mom continued. "Have you heard anything about the paternity test yet?"

"We should have the results in just a few more days. I suppose it could come in a little bit earlier, but then, on the other hand, it could come later. Ugh, I hate waiting."

"How are you handling the new place? I hate the idea of you and Suzette being there alone, feeling like you're in limbo."

"We knew it was going to be this way, Mom. But I haven't been completely alone. I've seen Jose a couple of times. After the paternity test, we had breakfast together. And then, the next day, since he had it off duty, he met us at the park in town, where we strolled her around."

"How do you feel about that?"

She looked down and scratched her fingernail along one of the stains on her shirt from Suzette's spit-ups. "I'm glad?"

"That sounds more like a question instead of an answer."

"I guess it is. It's been nice to feel like after our initial and unpleasant introduction, which, let's be realistic, was never going to be anything but unpleasant, he's been nice."

"Well, for that, I'm pleased."

"It was kind of weird because the server at the restaurant looked at Suzette and made a comment that she thought she was looking at one of his nieces. I guess that really hit home that when the paternity test comes back positive, then there's the whole issue of how other people will perceive our situation."

"Sweetheart, your dad and I have talked about that, too. But you need to worry about yourself and Suzette first."

"And Jose," she added softly.

"Yes," her mother agreed. "Him, too."

"He's given every indication that he wants to be involved in Suzette's life, but until the test comes back, we haven't really discussed particulars."

"That's what I mean. You two will have to figure out co-parenting. You need to get settled and get her settled in the new place, and you've got a new job to start. Other peoples' thoughts about your situation don't matter. If people are going to be rude, there's not much you can do about it other than hold your head up high and know that you are sacrificing everything for Suzette. Which already makes you the best mom you could be and is exactly why Karen chose you."

Tears stung her eyes, and she squeezed them shut as one dripped down her cheek. She'd stayed so busy taking care of Suzette that she hadn't allowed herself a chance to grieve recently. "Thanks, Mom. I really needed to hear that. I guess I've just been kind of lonely."

"Well, if I know you, you'll soon have lots of friends."

They talked for a few more minutes about the trip that her parents were on, happy to find out that her dad's work was going well. Disconnecting, she tossed her phone onto the sofa and leaned back, letting her thoughts drift. She looked over to the wall where she'd hung a picture frame filled with a collage of photographs. There were several with Karen when they were younger and one the day Suzette was born. As always, her heart squeezed a little at the sight.

"I'm trying, Karen. But I miss you. And God, I hope I'm not messing everything up."

"You're doing great, Melanie. She's happy and healthy."

"And she's beautiful. Just like you were."

"But she looks like her daddy."

Melanie pressed her lips together. Now that she'd met Jose, she could understand why Karen *said* that. Before she had time to think more of Karen, the infant monitor indicated Suzette was stirring.

Suddenly filled with a desire to get outdoors, she hurried into the bedroom, her smile widening as it always did when it landed on Suzette. "Let's go strolling, sweet girl. And maybe, we can find some other little ones and their moms out today, too. I think we both need to find some friends!"

13

The Baytown Park was not crowded, but as she strolled around, she saw a small group of women gathered near several benches, and many of their children appeared to range from toddlers to infants. She'd never been afraid of making friends, but she suddenly felt nervous, wondering when the deeper questions would start after meeting someone. It had seemed easier to offer her explanation to the group of deputies she'd met at the diner. *Because men often don't continue to ask probing, personal questions.* She snorted slightly, realizing her comment was sexist, but women tend to be more intuitive. *And can sniff out inconsistencies faster than the detectives can!*

She didn't want to do or say anything that might make things more difficult for Jose, but she was desperate for a chance to talk to other moms. She wondered if she was doing so many things right. Blowing out a breath, she marched forward, the nerves in her stomach settling as she was met with smiles as she approached.

"Hello!" The calls and smiles from multiple women all rang out at the same time.

She offered a little wave in return. "Hi."

The women gathered quickly around her as she pulled her wide-eyed daughter out of her stroller. Bouncing her lightly on her hip, she said, "I'm Melanie, and this is Suzette."

"I've wanted to meet you!" a pretty, dark-haired woman said, moving closer. "My husband, Hunter, met you at the diner. I'm Belle."

Soon, the others called out their names, but she knew she'd have trouble remembering them right away. Tori, Katelyn, Jillian, Maddie, Jade, Rose, and Sophie. And trying to remember their children's names was going to be next to impossible. But with her heart lighter, she didn't care.

"So you're new in town?"

"Yes, we've just moved here. I'm going to be teaching this fall at Baytown High School—"

Several women's cheers startled Suzette, and Melanie quickly grabbed the pacifier to keep her from crying.

"Oh, I'm sorry," Belle said. "It's just that some of us are from here and graduated from that high school. The sports games are still a huge draw for the community."

"I'm a teacher, also," Jade said. "I teach at the elementary school."

"Your daughter is beautiful," Katelyn said. "Is she your first child?"

"Thank you, and yes."

"You look more rested than I did with my first," Maddie said.

"Well, she's a dream, but I confess, I have no idea what I'm doing most of the time."

"Oh, honey, no mom does!" Tori laughed. "Even with nine months to prepare and read all the books."

They smiled at her expectantly, and suddenly, the urge to explain rushed through her. "Actually, I didn't have nine months to expect motherhood. She's the daughter of my best friend who became ill a month after Suzette's birth and died—"

The gasps and wide-eyed, dropped-mouth expressions of horror filled each face staring back at her. As she pressed her lips together, her chest depressed, and she wished she'd kept her mouth shut.

Belle rushed over and pulled her and Suzette into a deep hug. "Oh, Melanie, my heart breaks for you."

Swallowing deeply past the massive lump forming in her throat, she nodded.

"And you're her guardian?" someone asked.

Nodding her head in short jerks, she didn't bother looking at their faces, choosing instead to just breathe in Suzette's sweet baby scent. No one asked about the baby's father, for which she was grateful.

They ushered her to sit with them, and soon the conversation turned to feedings, night schedules, brands of formula and diapers, various teething toys, and a plethora of other topics that she'd worried about. Hearing these mothers' struggles mirror her own made her feel so much better. They also filled her in on the best places to shop and eat in the area.

"I know she's too little, but Rose's Ice Cream Parlor is a must to visit even for a mom pick-me-up!" Maddie said, nodding toward the blushing Rose as the others agreed.

"Anytime you want, please come in," Rose invited.

"And Jillian's Coffee Shop can't be beat," Tori threw out.

Jillian laughed and said, "No false modesty here! Come in and let me prove that my coffee is the best!"

By the time she was ready to leave, the names and numbers of all the other moms were programmed into her phone.

Waving goodbye, she strolled Suzette back to where she'd parked her SUV. Taking a chance that Suzette would stay in a good mood, Melanie decided a trip to the grocery store might work. Thirty minutes later, she was sure she had descended into the seventh level of hell.

Suzette had been perfectly happy when they entered the store, and Melanie had made it through the fruits and vegetables, deli, bakery, and almost a third of the aisles. But by the time they came to the pasta, Suzette began to squirm, her face scrunching. When Melanie had made it to the canned goods, Suzette was no longer whimpering but starting to cry. She rushed through the frozen foods, desperate for something quick she could throw into the microwave, but Suzette announced in no uncertain terms that she was no longer amused at the grocery store.

She hustled to the checkout line with everyone looking as though she must be pinching her baby. She was grateful when an older, kind-faced woman, just getting ready to start placing her items on the conveyor, motioned for her to proceed. Barely able to express her gratitude over Suzette's screams, she hastily plopped her grocery items in front of the checkout cashier. The young girl stared at her wide-eyed, practically tossing the items through the scanner in an obvious rush to get them out of the store.

Finally paying, she hastened to her SUV, where she left her groceries in the cart resting by her vehicle. She opened the back door and managed to wrestle a new diaper on Suzette, who was now in a full-blown, five-alarm meltdown.

Sniffling back her tears of frustration, Melanie cuddled her against her shoulder, rubbing her back while bouncing her. After a moment, Suzette hiccuped as her crying subsided. Breathing a sigh of relief that her child was no longer voicing her displeasure at the world for all to hear, she snapped her back into the car seat.

All the goodwill and confidence she felt after meeting the mothers at the park had dissipated with one short trip to the grocery store. She quickly unloaded her cart, careful to move out of the way of the shopper next to her.

"They're so hard at this age, aren't they? Precious, but hard."

She turned to see the woman who'd so kindly

allowed her to go ahead in the checkout line. Embarrassed, she swiped at her tears and nodded.

"I raised five children and now have grandchildren. Believe me, I understand."

Melanie managed a small smile. "I didn't have a chance to thank you properly for letting me go in front of you."

The woman waved her hand dismissively. "I'm sure you'll do that one day for another new mom."

Melanie hadn't taken the time to think about it but vowed she would do just that.

The woman looked past her and smiled at Suzette. "My goodness, she looks so much like my youngest granddaughter." Still smiling, she said, "I'll give you a little hint that used to help me. As much as my husband hated going to the grocery store, after a few meltdowns when I had two children, I finally told him if he wanted to eat, then he had to help." She laughed and shook her head. "So we planned our grocery trip, grabbed two carts, and divided and conquered. At least it might not keep our baby from screaming, but somehow, we managed to get through things faster."

Smiling, Melanie nodded. "That sounds like a good plan, but I'm afraid I'm a single mom."

"Oh, I am sorry," the woman said, a specter of sadness passing through her eyes.

Melanie couldn't tell if the woman was disapproving, disappointed, or just disheartened that she was alone. Suddenly overcome with fatigue, she thanked her again and hustled to get behind the wheel while Suzette was still calm.

Driving back to her small apartment, she sighed, more tired than she could remember being. Once there, she began the multiple trips to get all the groceries up the stairs and inside. Not willing to leave Suzette alone in the apartment for even a few minutes, each trip had her carry Suzette in her arms. By the fourth trip, tears were streaming down her face. Suzette had picked up on her mood and was starting to wail again.

Barely aware of her name being called, she turned around to see Jose jogging toward her, his face dark with what looked like worry or anger or an emotion she couldn't discern.

"What's going on, Melanie?" He reached out to take the grocery bags from her arm, but they were twisted in a way that didn't come off easily.

Just when she was about to say, "I've got it," he shifted his reach and carefully plucked a screaming Suzette from her arms. He pulled her against his chest, gently patting her back.

Suzette stopped crying but continued to sniffle and hiccup as she batted her dark owl eyes at the new person holding her.

If Melanie wasn't so exhausted, she might have been jealous. But as it was, just not having the baby scream in her ear gave her a modicum of peace.

As they went up the stairs, he asked, "Is there more?"

"No, this is the last trip."

"How many trips did you make?"

"Well, for the first one, I had her carrier, my purse, and the diaper bag. Then I had to carry her in my arms for the next two trips to get the groceries in. So this is technically the fourth trip."

She fumbled with the apartment key, and with his free hand, he pulled the keys from her grip and unlocked her door. Once inside, he looked around and then asked, "What would be easier? For you to take care of her and me to put up the groceries, or for you to deal with groceries while I entertain Suzette?"

Suzette was still fascinated with him, making her decision easy. "I can put the groceries away quickly since I know where they go. If you don't mind holding her just until I can—"

"Go, Melanie."

"Are you sure?"

"Absolutely."

Without giving any more thought as to why Jose was jumping in to help with Suzette without knowing if she was his child, Melanie realized that the truth was staring her in the face as the words of BettsAnn came back. *He's a good man.* Considering that Karen had had a one-night stand with very little experience, it would not be much of a stretch to think she might have picked up a man who would not be standing here holding her daughter right now.

"Melanie? Groceries."

She jumped at Jose's reminder and shook her head. "Sorry," she mumbled as she turned to the kitchen counter and quickly put the groceries away, tossing them into the cabinets and the refrigerator. Once that chore was done, she looked over to see Jose in her rocking chair, murmuring softly as he rubbed Suzette's back.

Needing a quick break, she darted down the hall and into the bathroom, grateful to relieve her bladder. Washing her hands, she went back into the kitchen to prepare a bottle. Once it was ready, she walked into the living room, the sight before her easing her stress. "I've got her bottle ready."

He nodded and resettled Suzette in his arms. Lifting his hand, he reached for the bottle.

"Oh, I can do it."

"Yes, I'm sure, but I can, too. Give me the bottle, and you settle on the sofa to rest."

She hesitated, but without a good reason for denying him, she handed the bottle to him. Suzette quickly latched on, sucking greedily. Melanie did as he suggested and moved to the sofa. Plopping down, she closed her eyes, intending to only rest for a moment.

14

Suzette finished her bottle, and Jose set it on the end table before shifting her up onto his shoulder. He patted her back the way he'd seen his sister and brother-in-law do so often. In fact, when his mom had been babysitting for Rosemarie, he'd often seen her do the same. After a moment, the most adorable baby burp emitted, and he grinned, feeling as though he'd passed a test.

He looked toward the sofa, and his grin widened as he observed Melanie with her head back, eyes closed, now asleep.

He cast his gaze around the room, spying a frame on the wall that held a multitude of photographs. It was easy to see from where he sat some were of Karen with Melanie, and one where she was holding Suzette. As he stared, he recognized that Karen had been pleasurable company for an evening. But that was all.

He turned to look at Melanie again. With her sleeping, it was nice to have a chance to really look at her. She was dressed in khaki pants that came to just below her knees, sneakers, and a pink top with little sleeves. Even exhausted and with a tearstained face, she was a beauty.

A strange thought darted through his mind, and a touch of guilt followed. But the truth was, if both Karen and Melanie had been at the bar that night, his interest would have settled on Melanie. Glancing down at Suzette, he winced as though his thought was somehow traitorous. *Jesus, what a mess.*

With Suzette now fast asleep as she lay curled up on him, he wondered if he should try to lay her in her crib. He continued rocking for several minutes, debating the merits of putting her down and possibly having her wake up screaming. That would undoubtedly wake up Melanie, so he continued to rock Suzette, letting both sleep.

He settled in, finding the rocker to be more comfortable than he'd assumed. He slowed the motion, not wanting to wake Suzette. It was the first time he was with them when there wasn't talking, crying, or all the busyness that goes on with caring for an infant. In the quiet, he began to process her space as he looked around. Without putting in a small dining table, Melanie had used the area for a playpen, an infant swing, and a changing table with diapers and toys underneath. There was only one stool at the counter, but since she was the only adult in the home, she kept the furnishings to a minimum.

He remembered Melanie mentioning that she had to take the last several months of the school year off to care for Karen and Suzette when Karen became ill. He now wondered if Melanie had been paid during the time she'd been off work.

And in the quiet of her small apartment, the importance of what Melanie was doing truly hit him. She'd put her life on hold, first for Karen and now for Suzette. If anyone wondered if she'd come here to try to get money from him, they'd only have to look around. She hadn't asked him for anything. Even if the paternity test was positive, he felt she still wouldn't ask him for anything. All it seemed Melanie wanted was for Suzette to know who her father was.

He had known them for only a week and hadn't been with them each day. He couldn't say that the initial shock of finding out that his one-night stand had possibly resulted in a child still seemed real. But these two females had taken root and were never far from his mind.

Another thought slammed into him—if Karen hadn't had such a good, loving, and reliable friend as Melanie, he might never know about Suzette. Even though the paternity results weren't in yet, it was hard to imagine not knowing them.

He resettled Suzette on his shoulder, her little soft sniffing breaths sweet against his neck. With one hand on her diaper bootie and the other still gently rubbing her back, his mind let the cares of the day drift away. In this tiny apartment, he could forget that there were boating accidents, citations to give, or boat thefts to investigate.

He shifted his gaze to the side toward Melanie as she slept. Just staring at her eased the tightness in his chest.

He now wished that he was sitting on the sofa next to her. He glanced down at the baby in his arms and wondered if she would be disturbed if he moved so that he would be close to both. But Melanie was so exhausted when he'd arrived that he didn't want to disturb either of them.

There was a basket of clean laundry on the floor, and it dawned on him that he hadn't seen a washer and dryer in the apartment. Realizing she had to haul the baby and the laundry back and forth to either a laundry room in the apartment or a laundromat, he grimaced. Neither of those options made him happy. *Hell, I've got a washer and dryer. I need to offer to let her come over.*

He tried to think of how he could help her situation, acknowledging that he wanted to be in their lives regardless of the paternity test outcome. That thought gave him pause for a moment. Used to careful analysis of situations, he wasn't known to make hasty decisions.

But the more he thought about it, the more he realized it made sense. He liked Melanie. Undoubtedly, he was attracted to her, but he liked getting to know her. If he wasn't Suzette's father, then there would be virtually no way to discover who was since Karen was now gone, and it appeared she'd only ever considered him to be the father. And that would leave Melanie to raise Suzette alone.

She could use a friend. He chuckled loud at the thought of only being a friend and wondered if he could ignore his attraction for her. The movement of his chest jiggled Suzette, and she squirmed. He held his breath until she finally settled again.

Just then, Melanie stirred as well. She blinked for a few seconds before her eyes popped open wide, and she gasped. She bolted forward, her head swinging to the side, searching. Then a huge rush of air left her lungs when she saw Suzette safely tucked in his arms.

Whispering, she exclaimed, "Oh my God! I can't believe I fell asleep!"

"I think you needed it."

"That might be so, but I should never have fallen asleep like that."

"Why not? I was here, and you knew she'd be safe."

A disconcerted expression crossed her face as her brows crinkled and her nose scrunched. "It wasn't my intention to use you like that."

"You had no idea I was coming over, so you could hardly be accused of using me. I'd like to think you knew she would be okay, and that's why you were able to rest."

She held his gaze, and the intense look sent warmth throughout his body as well as made him want to squirm, wondering what she was thinking. She slowly nodded. "You're right. I knew she'd be fine with you." Standing, she walked over and reached her hands out. "I'll take her and put her in her crib."

He stood with Suzette still in his arms. "Lead the way, and I'll carry her."

Again, she hesitated but then slowly nodded. He followed her into the bedroom, giving her a moment to make sure the baby monitor was working. He laid Suzette in the crib and then stepped back, giving

Melanie a chance to make sure the little one remained asleep. Finally, they walked back into the living room.

She stood awkwardly, clasping her hands in front of her as uncertainty filled her eyes. It would make sense for him to leave since he'd just stopped by to see how they were doing, but he didn't want to go now. He'd loved feeding and rocking Suzette to sleep, but now wanted to spend more time with Melanie.

"Tell me about your day," he asked. "I know you were overwhelmed by the time you got back from the grocery store, but I'd like to hear about it."

An incredulous scoff slipped out, and she shook her head. "I'm not sure you want to hear about my tales of woe in the grocery store." Suddenly, her face brightened, and a smile curved her lips. His eyes snagged on her mouth, loving the smile and wanting to see more of them.

"I do have to admit that before the grocery store, I had a really good day!"

"Yeah?"

She hesitated, glancing toward the kitchen. "Would you like a hot dog and some chips? I'm hungry, and as embarrassing as this is, I never have time to fix much for dinner. Since it's just me, I don't really want to spend time cooking, so I just buy things that are easy. So it's not much, but I can offer you a hot dog."

"I love hot dogs, but only if you let me help."

She laughed. "Well, my kitchen isn't very large, and all I'm going to do is boil the wieners. But while I'm doing that, if you want to get the hot dog buns and grab the chips, I've got paper plates in the cabinet."

It didn't take long for them to have their plates filled. She suddenly looked at the single counter stool and blushed.

"Don't worry about me," he said. "I can stand, and you have a seat."

"It doesn't seem like I'm being a very good hostess."

"You don't have to be a hostess for me."

She held his gaze, and her brows lowered slightly. "What am I, then?" As soon as the words left her mouth, she grimaced, and it was evident she wished the question had never slipped out.

"Friends." There was so much more he wanted to say. Friends. Good friends. Close friends. Friends with an attraction. Maybe more. But for now, his single-word answer would have to do. It seemed to suffice as she smiled and nodded.

It didn't take long to devour their simple meal, but he had to admit that standing at her kitchen counter eating a hot dog off a paper plate with her was a lot of fun. It sure as hell beat eating a meal alone at his house.

Finally wiping his lips with a torn paper towel that they'd divided between them, he reminded, "You were going to tell me about your day."

A smile returned in full force, and it was hard for him to drag his gaze away from her face. Taking a long drink of the cool ice water, he could finally focus on her without feeling like a leech.

"This afternoon before the grocery store, I went back to the park, and there was a group of women with babies and toddlers. It's always hard for me to approach a group when it seems like they're all friends and I'm an outsider. But I was desperate. So I walked over, and they were so sweet!"

"I knew you'd start making friends here. Do you remember any of their names? I might know some of them."

"Well, they all sort of ran together, but I remember Tori, Katelyn, a woman who also runs an ice cream parlor. Um, her name is Rose. There was one who has a coffee shop, but I can't remember her name."

"Jillian," he supplied, and Melanie's eyes lit.

"Yes! And then there was Jade, who is also a teacher but is at the elementary school, and a real sweetie named Belle, who said she was Hunter's wife. There were a couple of others, but I'm afraid I forgot some of their names."

He nodded his encouragement, his heart light at the idea that she'd met some of the best women he knew. "I'm really happy for you, Melanie. All those women are wonderful. They're all married to men I'm friends with, and I think most of them belong to the American Legion Auxiliary. That would be a really good group of people for you to become involved with."

"I got their phone numbers, and they said they'd give me a call the next time they get together at the park. We also just talked about being a mom. I always feel like I'm messing things up because I don't know what I'm doing, but they assured me they feel the same way."

He shook his head emphatically. "How can you think that? You take such good care of Suzette!"

She shrugged and sighed. "It's just that sometimes I feel so out of my element. After Karen first died, I could barely get through the days." She scoffed. "I remember when I was little, my parents signed me up for swimming lessons. All the kids were sitting on the edge of the pool, but I just wanted to get in. So I jumped in and had no idea what to do, but I furiously worked my arms and legs to get back to the side."

"What happened?"

"The teacher swam over and got me the rest of the way out of the pool, but I'd gotten fairly close to the edge on my own. They were fussing, but I just wanted to jump in and start even though I could have drowned. This feels a little like that. I had to jump in, but I don't know what I'm doing."

"I'm not sure anyone does when they have a child."

She nodded. "Those ladies today helped me see that." Her chest heaved with a heavy sigh. "I'm still not sure I've grieved properly. My parents put off a trip for Dad's work so they could help me. I can't imagine what I would've done if it wasn't for them."

"When I look at Suzette, I see a beautiful little girl who's thriving. And that's all on you, Melanie." They were silent for a moment, but he wanted to hear more from her. "So you went to the park and the grocery store this afternoon. Did you do anything this morning?"

Her smile widened once again. "This morning, I tutored a couple of teenagers who live in the building. When they found out that I was a teacher, they said they needed help, so I volunteered."

He could see her excitement but was unsure about

who lived in her building. "You didn't have them alone in the house with you, did you?"

She rolled her eyes. "No, of course not. Suzette was sleeping, so I had the baby monitor with me. We just sat in the doorway so I could make sure she was okay. But I'm not stupid, Jose. I'm just getting to know Trey and Ricky, so I wouldn't put myself or Suzette at risk. Sitting outside was fine."

He nodded but still planned to check them out. "Trey and Ricky? Do you know their last names?"

"Yeah. Trey Blevins and Ricky Montgomery. Why?"

"Oh, I just wondered if I knew them or their parents."

"Trey lives with his mom. I met her briefly. She was nice and grateful for the help. But Ricky lives with his uncle. I saw him from a distance, but Trey said he was a jerk."

He just nodded but was determined to check them out. If she was suspicious of his questions, she didn't react. Instead, she rolled right into her next story, with equal enthusiasm.

"And then, I went to Baytown High School. I met the principal, and she told me I would teach biology. That's my favorite subject to teach and is my specialty. She was nice, and it seems that I will not only be teaching biology to the sophomores, but she's giving me one or two classes of an advanced biology seminar class for the juniors and seniors. That might not sound like a lot to you, but it's a big deal for me. And while I met with her, Suzette was an absolute doll, so it went easily." She

150

reached out and grabbed his arm, giving it a little shake in her excitement.

He loved watching her face light, but the spark he felt on his arm from her touch caused his lungs to expand as though there wasn't enough air to fill them. Trying to focus on her words, he heard the confirmation that she planned to stay in the area. His heart pounded a rhythm that he was sure she'd be able to hear. "That's fabulous, Melanie."

"I know! She also gave me a biology textbook to use when I tutor Trey and Ricky."

He wasn't sure if it was the excitement on her face or the jolt of electricity he felt from her touch that kept his heart racing.

"Not only is it great to be employed in my field, but a steady paycheck and getting back on health insurance will be huge. That will take so much stress off me."

His pleasure tripped over her last statement. He jerked, and his brows lowered in a scowl that he could feel and knew she could easily discern. "Wait. You don't have health insurance right now?"

She sighed, her eyes losing their sparkle. "Jose, I'm not sure how that could be a surprise to you. I had to take a leave of absence *without* pay when Karen got sick. It didn't fall under emergency leave because she wasn't my immediate family. I was already caring for Suzette when Karen became so ill, but I was truly a full-time mom when she died. My paycheck dried up, and so did my health insurance. When I got the letter from the North Heron school board that said that they could offer me a position in the fall, I knew I'd only have to go

MARYANN JORDAN

a few more months before I'd finally get a paycheck and health insurance again."

"But what if something happens to her? What if something happens to you?"

She crossed her arms around her middle, pulling them tight, but he ignored her obvious sign of self-protection. "I don't know, Jose. I don't have all the answers. If something happens, I'll pay. I've got some savings, and my parents will help."

His jaw tightened, and his molars felt like they were going to crack. He wanted to rail at her— tell her she was taking a huge chance with her health and Suzette's.

"I'm doing the best I can, Jose."

She'd spoken so softly that the words barely penetrated his ire. But then the sound of her voice curled around his heart, wiping away some of the tension. *None of this was her fault.* She *was* doing the best she could. *And doing a damn good job.*

He nodded as regret and guilt hit him in the gut. "You're right. You are. I'm sorry." Slowly, a heavy sigh pushed the air out of his lungs. She was a woman caught in a situation no one could've planned. He glanced up at the photos on the wall. *Well, almost no one...*

He'd been struck with a thought but dared not give voice to it, fearing Melanie's anger. The last thing he wanted to do was give her a reason to push him away. So they sat in silence for a few moments as the evening shadows deepened in the room.

Finally, in a voice so small, she whispered, "Is it horrible that sometimes I'm conflicted?"

He had no idea what she was referring to but could feel the tension pouring off her body. Wanting to tread very carefully, he kept his voice soft and even. "I don't think anything you feel is horrible. You have a right to your own emotions."

He gave her a moment for those words to sink in until she gave an almost imperceptible nod. Pressing forward, he prodded. "And your confliction?"

She swallowed deeply, dragging her tongue over her bottom lip. "I've thought it, but I've never said it aloud."

"Then who better to unburden yourself than with a friend?"

She stared at him, unblinking for so long that he wasn't sure she would speak. He wanted to hear her thoughts, especially whatever was creating such angst. And truthfully, he was curious to see if her thoughts had followed along the same trail as he had. But if she was going to confide in him, it would have to come from her and not because he begged.

Her fingers now clutched together and twisted until her knuckles were white. He reached over and placed his hand on her, stilling the motion while noting the warmth between their connection whenever they touched.

She stared down at their hands for a moment, then lifted her chin, and pinned him with her intense gaze again. Sucking in a deep breath, she let it out slowly, then said, "I wouldn't give up Suzette for the world. I've said it before, Jose, and I'll say it again. Regardless of what the paternity test reveals, she is my daughter."

He nodded his agreement but gave the words she

obviously needed to hear. "Yes. She'll always be your daughter." He knew that the paternity test results would make a difference for all of them, but he was already determined to be in their lives no matter what. But her statement had not revealed the confliction, so he waited, still gently rubbing her fingers.

"But sometimes, I wonder how things would have been if Karen had told you she was pregnant. It was your right to know, and while a paternity test was needed, that would've already been done. And you could have chosen to be involved in the pregnancy and birth if you'd wanted. And when Karen got sick, you would've been involved in decisions for Suzette." She squeezed her eyes tightly shut as a tear dropped off her cheek and onto her shirt.

He stared at the wet spot for just a moment until another one joined it. He shifted closer, wrapping his arm around her and pulling her into his chest.

"And I hate saying that because it would mean that you would have custody of Suzette instead of me, and I can't stand the idea that she wouldn't be considered my daughter. And maybe if you and Karen had spent more time together, you would have fallen in love." She shook her head as though to dislodge the thoughts filling her mind as she pressed in tighter to his chest. "Sometimes, those thoughts get tangled up with my love for both of them. I'd begged Karen to tell you, but if she had, then I wouldn't have the life I have now." She peered up at him, tears hanging on her lashes. "Does that make me a horrible person?"

With both arms now wrapped around her, he rested

his chin on top of her head. He rubbed one hand up and down her back in a motion similar to how he'd calmed Suzette. At first, the desire to offer quick platitudes and denials were on the tip of his tongue, but he could tell that Melanie wasn't looking for a fast answer. And there was no denying that her conflicting thoughts had burrowed deep inside.

"Nothing about you or what you feel is horrible. You're real, gutsy, and strong. You can't change the past, so you just have to live with the present. Karen made her decisions, forcing them on you. And you're making a life built on what you've been given. And you're working toward a future that will be good for everyone involved. I think that's the definition of *not* a horrible person."

Then he reacted instinctively and pressed his lips against her forehead, kissing her lightly. She didn't move other than to tighten her arms around him. They sat together, drawing strength from each other, without speaking until the evening shadows deepened more, and the two of them were cloaked in darkness.

The infant monitor indicated Suzette was beginning to stir around, and Melanie pushed away slightly, wiping her face and smoothing her wayward strands from sticking on her wet cheeks. "You must think me a complete nutcase," she said, shaking her head. "Is there a chance you can forget I said any of this?"

He brushed a tendril back, tucking it behind her ear. "No, only because it makes me respect you more."

Her head jerked, and she stared into his eyes.

"With everything you've been through, if you didn't

have conflicting thoughts, worries, anxiety, doubts, and even anger, I would think something was wrong with you. But everything you've said just makes you normal. Everything you do makes you amazing."

She jumped up as Suzette began to cry, and he stood, as well. He still hated to leave and was grateful when she started down the hall and looked over her shoulder, calling out, "Do you want to see her?"

He rushed after her, a smile curving his lips when he peered down at a babbling Suzette who grinned up at both of them. Melanie changed her, fed her again, and then when it was time for her to have a bath, he said, "I should leave."

She nodded, and he was glad to see a smile on her face again. With Suzette in her arms, she walked him to the door. He placed his hand on Melanie's waist, leaned over and blew raspberries on Suzette's neck before kissing her chubby baby cheek. Without thinking, he then kissed Melanie on her cheek, just on the corner of her mouth.

He hadn't planned the kiss but felt her body stiffen for only an instant before she relaxed into his embrace again. Refusing to analyze why it felt so right, he gave her a squeeze. Then before he chickened out, he whispered, "I would have wanted a place in Suzette's life, but I wouldn't have been with Karen. She was a lovely and sweet woman, but there was no spark, Melanie. We would have co-parented only."

She leaned back and peered up at him, her eyes searching his. He didn't look away, wanting her to see the truth and consider what he was implying. "I've got to work tomorrow, but how about I take you two out to eat on my next day off?"

She smiled and looked at Suzette. "What do you think, sweet girl? Want to go out with a handsome man?" Her cheeks turned pink as she peered up at him again.

He just laughed and said, "I'll take that as a yes. I'll call you tomorrow, and then we'll plan on eating out on Thursday." With that, he walked out the door and headed down to the parking lot. Driving home, his mind filled with spending time with his two girls in a few days. And thinking of them as *his* two girls didn't scare him at all.

15

Jose walked into the station early the next morning, a smile on his face and his steps light. With the time he'd spent with Melanie and Suzette the night before, he felt like there had been a breakthrough. They were no longer just waiting on the results of the paternity test to see if there was going to be an ongoing relationship. Melanie was doing a fabulous job in a difficult situation, and he wanted to do whatever he could to help.

He hadn't planned on the simple kiss that was more of a peck on the corner of her mouth, but he'd felt the way her body responded after her initial surprise. It seemed as though the beautiful Melanie might want to explore the possibility of more than friendship.

But he didn't want to move too fast or ruin what they had, so he was determined to go slow. At least until the results came in. And if indications were right that he was Suzette's father, he didn't want to take it slow after that.

His thoughts were so firmly entrenched in Melanie

and Suzette that he almost walked past the workroom until his name was called out. He did an about-face and hurried inside. Seeing Sam and Hunter sitting with Ryan and Callan in front of a computer screen, his thoughts jumped to work, and he hustled over.

"What have you got?"

"Even with enhancing the security video, there's very little that we can discern about identities, but some interesting inferences can be made," Hunter said.

Before anything else was discussed, the other VMP officers walked in from the back, all crowding around.

"As far as the boat they came in on, it was a small, single engine, and from the edge of the camera view, we can see they used oars to bring it silently to the dock."

Callan shook his head in frustration. "So we've got nothing from that. Any one of them could have the skills to steer one of those."

Sam pointed at the screen, and Jose was instantly on alert. "Watch these two fighting. Note the body language."

Leaning closer, he stared at the zoomed-in figure. They were both in black pants, shoes, jacket, hoodie, and facemasks. The guy closest to the camera appeared uncomfortable as his posture hunched. His hands were jammed into his pockets, and he seemed to want to disappear. "There's no bravado about that guy," Jose said, pointing at the screen. "The other guy is walking around, chest out, and this guy gives off the image that he doesn't want to be there."

"Inference? My guess is that he was coerced. A gang member who wants to prove himself would be cocky as shit to be there. Even if this is a bunch of locals, they want in on the action. This guy… he's not happy to be there," Hunter commented.

Jose added, "If he's coerced to be there or not all-in with what they're doing, he may be someone you can turn if he can be identified."

Sam said, "Keep watching. Look at his cap under the hoodie, and you'll see the edge of a logo."

The entire group leaned forward in unison, eyes trained and strained on the computer screen as Hunter enlarged it as much as he could. The logo was half obscured, but the half that was visible was clearly an eagle in the exact mascot logo of Baytown High School.

The collective exclamations were heard around the room.

Ryan was quick to remind them, "This, in and of itself, doesn't mean anything. As most of you are aware, clothing items with a Baytown Eagles logo are sold at the school bookstore, the parents' athletic website, and every sporting event. Hell, even the local dollar store and grocery store sell these items. Chances are, most of us in this room have a hat with the logo. So this in no way indicates that this person is currently, or has ever been, a student at Baytown High School."

Jose knew Ryan was right, and his frustration rose again. On one hand, it was the closest piece of evidence that they had. On the other hand, it literally meant nothing.

"I hate to ask a question that I probably should know the answer to," Bryce said. "But if it doesn't mean anything, how does that affect our investigation?"

"It does lead credence that they might be local," Sam said. "Someone coming from Norfolk or Baltimore probably wouldn't have a local high school cap. It will be easier to catch a local gang than someone coming in from another place and then going right back there."

They continued to watch the two lookouts as they argued. "Both guys are big, but one of them is definitely more in charge. The one with the logo cap getting punched and yelled at, could easily be a teenager, just by their demeanor," Jose noted as he continued to watch the video play again.

"Shit, they're coercing teens?" Andy groaned.

"Do you remember a few years ago when we had a gang of teenagers breaking into elderly people's homes and stealing some of their medicine?" Hunter asked. "Some of you weren't around then, but it ended up involving Colt and Carrie's son. He overheard one of his friends getting pressured to do this, and then, when his friend was kidnapped, their son jumped in to save the day." Shaking his head, he said, "I still remember Carrie nearly having a shit fit, but Jack really showed what he was made of that day."

Joseph grinned. "Now that he's dating my adopted niece, Rachel, I couldn't be prouder of him."

"So someone could be using a local kid?" Jose asked.

A low growl came from Ryan. "I hate the idea of teens being used. Back then, a couple of adults ran a Fagin-like gang of teens to do his dirty work. But the lure of money, or just being coerced, can be strong. This county has a lot of kids who live in poverty." He leaned back in his chair and scrubbed his hand over his face. "Damn."

"This kind of operation might have some teens assisting, but they're not organizing it. They don't have the know-how or the resources. No way," Callan said.

"Plus, adults were at this scene, so they might just be using a few teens. Or maybe just this one, if he is a teenager," Jose commented. "Could be just an adult who isn't into what they're doing."

"Okay," Ryan said, standing. "Keep your eyes out, talk to the people you see on patrol. Someone will see something that catches their attention."

As the others left the conference room, Jose stopped Hunter and Sam. "Hey, can I ask a favor?"

"Sure," both men said in unison.

"Melanie is tutoring a couple of teens that live in her apartment building. One of them is Ricky Montgomery. He lives with his uncle, and she spoke to the high school principal, who told her his dad was in prison. Is there any way you can check on this for me? I'd just like to know who is living near her."

"Absolutely," Sam said as Hunter reached out and took the paper from Jose with the address on it.

"I appreciate it," he said, walking them out of the station. With that, he headed out to the vessels with the other officers to begin patrols.

By the end of the day, they pulled into the harbor, and he, along with Joseph and Bryce, restocked and readied their vessel for the next day. As he walked to the station, he looked up to see Zac Hamilton, the captain of the Baytown rescue squad and fellow Legionnaire. An idea struck him, and he jogged over.

"Hey, Zac. Can you spare a minute?"

"Absolutely. What do you need?"

"For reasons I don't want to go into right now, I need to purchase an infant car seat. I went online, but there are a fuck ton of them! You and Maddie have a little one, but since you work at the fire station, you're responsible for installing them for a lot of the people around here."

He held his breath for a few seconds, wondering if Zac was going to ply him with questions or react with shock. But he should've known his friend would do neither.

Zac simply nodded and said, "Sure thing. Can I ask the age of the child it's for?"

"She's three months old now."

Again, without skipping a beat, Zac nodded. "If you want, I can email you a list of some of the top brands we recommend. And once you decide, come by the station, and I'll make sure it's installed properly."

Thanking him, he walked back to the station. The idea of having Suzette in his SUV sent a smile across his face. Then the reality of a crying, pooping, spitting-up Suzette in the back seat caused his feet to stumble. *How the hell does Melanie do it?*

Melanie was surprised at the nerves that twisted in her belly. She tried to focus on Suzette but kept walking to the window that overlooked the parking lot, waiting to see Jose drive up. She'd been surprised when he wanted to take them to dinner, but then everything about him had been a surprise.

Looking back, she realized that she and Karen had never really talked about Jose. Not in any real terms. He'd simply been the person Karen had found attractive, talked to enough to be comfortable with, and decided to take a chance to proposition him. Shaking her head, Melanie knew what a huge step for Karen that had been. Something wild. Something different. Perhaps, even something rebellious. Now that she thought about Karen's parents and upbringing, she had no doubt that it was largely something rebellious.

But other than that, Karen had never talked about the man she'd slept with, and Melanie had never asked. It struck her that she knew him so much more than Karen had. Granted, she hadn't slept with him, but that was only physical knowledge. A tiny sliver of envy moved through her at the idea that Karen had had a part of him that she didn't and probably wouldn't, but she tamped that down. She felt the need to think of him as Suzette's father. *We have to co-parent. There's no reason to make this more difficult on myself than it needs to be. And unrequited interest would make it more difficult.*

Picking up Suzette, she snuggled her close, walking over to the window again. *Yes, I definitely know more about Jose.* She knew his expression was often serious, but when he smiled, it was all the more special. She knew his dark eyes were attractive and stayed focused on her when she talked, giving his attention completely.

She knew that he could have walked away the minute she'd shown up at his workplace with Suzette or told her that he'd talk to her after the paternity results came in. And he would've been well within his rights to do so. But instead, he'd seen her struggle and wanted to help. And in doing so, he opened himself up to the possibility of friendship, regardless of paternity.

Before she had a chance to ponder more about the man who filled her mind in ways that went beyond Suzette's father, she recognized his SUV pulling into the parking lot. Smiling, she snuggled Suzette again, saying, "Look, sweet girl! He's here!"

He climbed out, and her breath caught at the sight of him. Dark slacks. Blue button-down. Tall, wide chested, muscular, fit and trim. *"He's a tall drink of water on a hot, summer day."* She laughed, remembering the words her grandmother used to say when she'd see a handsome man. "Oh yeah, Grannie Landers. You were so right."

With Suzette still in her arms, she grabbed her purse and diaper bag, and had just stepped outside her door when he appeared. Smiling, she greeted him with enthusiasm. "Hello!"

He smiled warmly in return, his eyes on her as he bent and kissed her cheek before turning to Suzette and nuzzling her nose, eliciting a baby giggle. Melanie's heart melted a little more.

"Are my girls ready for dinner?"

As she handed Suzette over to him, she couldn't help but notice the way he'd used the words *my girls*. Terrified to read too much into that, she simply nodded. They walked down the stairs and headed straight to her

SUV. Once Suzette was buckled, he held out his hand for the keys. She didn't hesitate to drop them into his palm. Jose didn't strike her as having a bullshit macho attitude declaring he had to drive. But since she didn't care, and he knew where the restaurant was, it simply made sense for him to be behind the wheel.

As soon as they were on the road, he said, "I was hoping on my next day off that we could run up to the Superstore, and you could help me buy a car seat for Suzette."

Her chin jerked slightly as she looked to the side, seeing his focus on the road. "Um... sure."

"I talked to a friend of mine who's the Baytown Rescue captain. I think you met Maddie, his wife at the park. Anyway, I wanted to get a list of approved infant car seats. He emailed me the list this morning."

"Sounds good," she said, turning to face the front again as she failed to keep the smile off her lips, noticing her heart pinging inside her chest.

"I'm not ready to go solo with her yet," he confided. "In fact, I feel like I've got a long way to go before I'm comfortable doing that. But if I've got a carrier in my vehicle, then we have a choice on what to drive. And certainly, I'd be able to take her in an emergency."

Once again, it hit her that Jose was making plans without waiting on the paternity results. Whether or not he truly believed he was the father or simply wanted to be with them no matter what, she wouldn't worry about his motives.

They pulled up to the Seafood Shack, and he said, "When you said it was best to eat at a time that was less crowded, I thought this would be good. We're hitting it between lunch and dinner, so we should have no problem getting seated. They're a family restaurant, so they're used to kids."

She patted his arm and smiled. "I trust you, so you don't have to explain. But just remember that dining out with a three-month-old can be unpredictable!"

He laughed and nodded. "Consider me forewarned."

He carried Suzette in her carrier after they decided not to use the stroller. With a diaper bag in tow, they were soon settled into a booth. Grateful the server hustled over to them, they ordered their food at the same time they ordered drinks. "It saves time if I give the meal order as quickly as possible. I know restaurants like to have a little extra time, but with a baby, I'm desperate to make every moment count."

His brows lifted as he nodded. "Smart woman."

She laughed and shook her head. "More like I've learned things from mistakes I've made out of ignorance."

He leaned forward and placed his hand over hers. "Then I repeat what I said. You're a smart woman."

She tried to laugh, but it came out as more of a strangled chortle as her focus was on the tingle from where their hands touched. Afraid he would notice her blush, she turned toward Suzette and made a face, eliciting gurgles and coos. The server brought the food quickly, and they both dug into their meals before Suzette became wiggly.

She and Jose managed to carry on part of a conversation between eating and entertaining Suzette. She had asked about his job duties, and he'd told her about the recent thefts.

"Someone is stealing boats and taking them somewhere to be dismantled?"

"That's what it looks like."

"Is that profitable?" She shook her head. "I guess that's a dumb question. They wouldn't do it if it weren't profitable. But boat parts?"

"It's a lot more profitable than you'd think," he said. "Just like with car parts, boat parts are in high demand. Boaters, especially people who make their living with boats such as fishermen, need parts for repairs, and getting them used is a helluva lot cheaper than getting them new."

She sighed and shook her head again. "I so admire what you do, Jose. I can't imagine investigating crimes and saving people on the water."

"Well, I could say the same thing about you. You teach teenagers. Not only the ones who really want to learn but the ones that are convinced that school is the last place they want to be. I think the patience you have and the dedication you have is admirable."

"Teenagers are great to work with. They are old enough that you can have an adult conversation with them and still young enough to feel like I have the opportunity to make a difference in their lives."

He held her gaze without speaking, and she cocked her head to the side. "What are you thinking?"

"I want to—"

Suddenly, his attention was drawn to the side, and his eyes widened slightly. She turned to see what captured his attention. A middle-aged couple walked toward them, and she recognized the woman who'd allowed her to go in front of her at the grocery store. Thinking the woman was coming over to say hello, she was stunned when Jose stood and greeted, "Mom. Dad."

Jose had a smile on his face, but it didn't reach his eyes. Even calling out their names, she heard a thread of tension in his greeting. Now, unease slithered through her, and she kept a smile on her face although the expression felt painted on instead of real.

The couple stopped at their table, and his father greeted them heartedly while his mother's gaze darted between Jose and her, and then down to Suzette.

"Jose, aren't you going to introduce us to your friends?"

"Of course. Mom, Dad…this is Melanie Landers and her beautiful daughter, Suzette. Melanie, these are my parents, Carlos and Mary Martinez."

"Your mother and I've actually met."

Jose's head jerked around, his brows lowered. "Really? When?"

"She was kind enough to allow me to go in front of her at the grocery store when Suzette was having her meltdown." Turning toward Mary, she said, "Thank you again for that kind gesture."

Mary offered a smile and nodded, but just like Jose's smile, Melanie didn't think it reached her eyes.

"What a pretty little girl," Carlos said, smiling and wiggling his fingers toward Suzette.

"Thank you."

"Well, Jose," Mary said. "Make sure you come for

your nephew's party on Sunday after work." She smiled at Suzette. "It's my daughter and her *husband's* child."

Melanie blinked, wondering if she had imagined that Jose's mom had emphasized the word husband.

"I'll be there, Mom," he assured.

"We've got to go," Carlos said. "We were just picking up takeout. Melanie, it was lovely to meet you and your daughter."

Everyone said goodbye, and when they left, Melanie turned to Suzette, focusing her attention on her wiggly daughter, hoping Jose didn't notice how self-conscious she felt.

"Melanie?"

Without looking up, she opted for a nonchalant, "Uh-huh?"

"Will you look at me?"

Guilt slithered through her, and she turned to see his pensive expression.

"Are you okay? I didn't expect my parents to be here, so they caught me off guard. Are you upset that I didn't tell them about—"

Shaking her head, she rushed, "No, no! I would never expect you to explain now. In fact, what you decide to tell them at any time is up to you." Her gaze dropped, and her shoulders slumped. "I just felt a little awkward, that's all."

"I would hope my family would never make you feel awkward. I didn't realize you'd already met my mom."

"It was when I was at the grocery store, and Suzette was screaming as I was trying to get to the checkout line. Your mom was just ready to move forward when she turned and looked at me with such sympathy. She let me go in front, and then I ran into her in the parking lot and thanked her. She was lovely, really. When she mentioned how her husband used to help with the shopping, I mentioned that I was a single mom. I suppose it just seems like today she was wondering why her son was out with me... a single mom."

"She's always trying to set me up with someone, but there's never once been a spark with anyone. I told you there wasn't a spark with Karen, but that is the same for any other woman I've gone out with." Laughing, he shook his head. "Not that there's been that many." He held her gaze. "But with you, it's different."

The restaurant's noise faded into the background, and his words penetrated, sending warmth throughout her. She smiled, then suddenly Suzette cried out, jerking their attention over to her.

"It looks like the princess has spoken." He chuckled. "Let's get her back to her castle."

Hating the moment was lost, she nodded, then turned to Suzette, making another silly face. Grabbing the diaper bag, she stood to the side, knowing that Jose would carry Suzette. And while it all might seem make-believe, walking out of the restaurant together, it wasn't hard to imagine they were a real family.

16

The drive home was quieter than Jose would've liked. It seemed the easy camaraderie he and Melanie had developed had taken a giant step backward with the introduction to his parents.

When he'd seen her standing outside her apartment door, his breath had caught in his lungs. Her hair glistened as the blond and red highlights caught the sunlight. Her dark pink dress hung to her mid-calves, giving her room to move while still managing to show off her curves with its fitted top. And when he'd spied Suzette in a dark-pink baby dress, his heart warmed at the sight of them dressed alike.

Now, it seemed as though the joy of the date had ended abruptly. If he wasn't driving, he would've closed his eyes and banged his head on the steering wheel in frustration. As it was, he could only focus on the road and try to rein in the desire to throttle fate for having them run into each other, and his mom for her barely-hidden dig when she emphasized Rosemarie's husband.

But more than his frustration was his surprise. His mom was one of the kindest people he knew, and he couldn't imagine why she might have something against Melanie just for being a single mom. When he glanced to the side, it was evident by Melanie's slumped shoulders that she was still bothered by the encounter.

He opened his mouth to offer assurances, then snapped it closed, realizing he had no idea what to say. And that only added more frustration to him. Glad when they finally pulled into Melanie's apartment parking lot, he was shocked when she said, "Thank you for dinner. It was lovely."

He didn't want to be dismissed so easily, especially leaving things unsaid between them. "Let's get her in." He could tell his suggestion was unexpected, but Melanie was quick to agree, which he took as a positive sign.

Once inside, he set the carrier on the floor and unbuckled Suzette. Pulling her up into his arms, he snuggled her close. Every time he was with her, he fell more in love with the little girl. He would be disappointed if the results came back negative, but that had nothing to do with the way he felt about her. He wanted in Suzette's life no matter what. And in Melanie's.

A whiff of something caught his attention, and with brows raised, he looked over at Melanie. "I think someone needs a change. And probably a bath."

Melanie laughed and shook her head. "She got a little fussy at dinner, and then had such a pleasant expression settled on her face. I wondered if she had gas or pooped!"

"Do you mind if I stay? I wanted to anyway, but I'd love to see bath time." Once again, he held his breath as he awaited her response. But like with everything so far with Melanie, she was easy.

"Sure, if you'd like."

He followed Melanie down the hall, murmuring to the little one in his arms. "I still think you're a sweet girl, even if you are a little stinky." His sing-song voice elicited another gummy grin from Suzette.

Melanie laughed as she turned on the water and checked the temperature. She laid a towel on the floor and had him lay Melanie on top of the towel. She deftly unsnapped the little pink dress and pulled it off, allowing the smell to infiltrate the entire room.

"Whew!" he exclaimed. "How on earth did she manage to poop so much?"

Melanie giggled. "Just be glad it didn't explode out of her diaper and all over her clothes and carrier!"

He choked back a gag. "That happens?"

Melanie looked up and laughed. "Duh…" She tossed the clothes to the side and then pulled off the dirty diaper, wrapping it up tightly. Cleaning her with the baby wipes, she then scooped her up and placed her in the bathtub seat.

He watched in fascination as Suzette kicked and splashed while smiling and babbling. He didn't remember his siblings when they were babies, and even though he'd been around his nieces and nephews when they were tiny, he'd never been involved in something as mundane as bath time. But now, seeing Melanie and

Suzette enjoying their time together, he felt a tightness around his heart.

Wanting to be helpful, he snagged the folded dirty diaper from the floor and took it into the bedroom where he'd seen Melanie dispose of diapers into a special container. "Do you have certain clothes for her to sleep in?"

"Look in the top dresser drawer," Melanie called out. "That's where I keep her sleepers. You can pick any one."

He pulled open the drawer and stared in awe at the selection. Finally, choosing one that was pale yellow with little pink bunnies on it, he started into the bathroom when she called out a reminder that she needed a clean diaper. Seeing a stack of them on top of the dresser, he grabbed one and headed back into the bathroom.

By now, Suzette's dark hair was covered in suds, and her face was scrunched in displeasure as Melanie gently washed the baby shampoo out. "I take it she doesn't like that part?"

"That's why I save it till the end. At least she can enjoy bath time and then only gets fussy at the very end."

Stepping over Melanie, who was kneeling next to the tub, he maneuvered as though they'd worked together since the beginning, not just knowing each other less than two weeks. Bending so he was in Suzette's line of sight, he called out, "Hey, pretty girl! Who's got suds in their hair? I think it's you! Is it pretty Suzette with suds in her hair?"

Melanie rinsed the shampoo while Suzette stared wide-eyed at Jose, distracted from what her mom was doing. As soon as Melanie finished, she started letting the water out of the tub and plucked the wet, slippery baby up into her arms, kissing her cheeks. "What a good girl!" Laying her down on the towel, she wrapped her tightly, drying her off carefully.

Again, Jose was fascinated with how Melanie made everything look so easy. Once Suzette was in her sleeper, Melanie picked her up and handed her to Jose. "You guys go snuggle while I clean up in here and prepare her bottle."

Walking into the living room, he sat in the rocker and cuddled the sweet-smelling little girl who had stolen his heart. Her mom walked into the kitchen a moment later to heat the bottle. Staring at Melanie as she moved with ease around the tiny kitchen, he knew she'd stolen another piece of his heart.

She walked over with the bottle in her hand, then stopped and looked at him. "What are you thinking?"

He startled. "Oh, nothing. Just waiting on the bottle, that's all," he lied, reaching his hand out.

Shifting Suzette around in his arms, she grabbed at the bottle, patting her hands against the side as she sucked eagerly. Once again, he stared at her, fascinated. By the time she finished, her eyes were droopy, and he shifted her to his shoulder, patting a few little burps out of her tummy.

Repeating their actions from the other night, he carried her into the bedroom, lay her gently down, then stepped back while Melanie kissed her good night and grabbed the infant monitor. As they walked back into the living room after closing the door almost shut, his hand rested on Melanie's back as they made their way over to the sofa.

If she was surprised that he was staying, she didn't say anything. Once again, they twisted their bodies to face each other.

"I suppose we need to talk about your mom's reaction, don't we?" she began.

The more time spent with Melanie, he recognized that she didn't shy away from what she was thinking. In his few past relationships, he always hated trying to figure out what they were thinking, especially if he could tell they were upset or angry. But Melanie was open and honest, a trait he admired. "Yeah, I guess we do. I want you to tell me whatever you're thinking, and don't hold back just because it's my mom."

She shook her head emphatically. "I don't have anything bad to say about your mom. It's just I had the distinct impression that she was surprised to see you out with someone... well, with a single mom and her child."

He nodded slowly and sighed. "To be honest, Melanie, I can't tell you exactly what my parents thought. My dad's an easy-going guy, and he would be thrilled just knowing that I was out having a good time with someone I enjoy being with. My mom's reaction? Well, I'm not really sure what her reaction meant. My mom can be pretty intense, but she's always had a big heart and a kind spirit. So why it seemed to throw her that I'd be having dinner with you, I don't know. I'd like to chalk it up to her just being surprised."

Melanie nodded, her gaze shifting to the side, and she chewed on her bottom lip, obviously deep in thought. He gave her some time, not wanting to pressure her into speaking before she was ready. But after a moment, he was crawling out of his skin, wanting to pull her into his arms and tell her what he was feeling.

Finally, she looked up and said, "I've said this before, but I feel like our relationship has changed in subtle ways. I don't want there to be any misunderstandings. Taking me to dinner tonight was lovely. Staying after Suzette goes down and chatting with me is also really enjoyable. But I need to emphasize, Jose, that I know you're going to be a part of Suzette's life. You don't have to be with me for that to happen."

He jerked back slightly, holding her gaze. "You think that I'm spending time with you just to ensure that I'll be able to be with Suzette when it's proven that I'm the father?"

"Please don't be offended. I just want to lay everything out." She blew out a long breath before scrunching her face as though all the jumbled thoughts going through her mind caused pain.

He reached over and pulled her hand over onto his lap, linking their fingers. Her eyes opened, and her gaze shot down to their connection.

"Okay, Melanie. I'm going to lay things out for you, too, because I don't want there to be any confusion. There's no doubt that the way you and I met was unusual. And believe me, if there had been no spark between us or interest in anything more, we wouldn't be sitting here right now other than just discussing Suzette. And that would be fine. It hasn't been proven yet, but I believe she's my daughter. And I would be determined to find a way to co-parent with my daughter's legal guardian in any way we needed to make it work."

Her gaze hadn't wavered, and he shifted a little closer before he continued. "But I did feel a spark. Granted, when we first met, there was doubt, disbelief, some frustration, and a whole lot of what the hell. But that quickly passed when I spent time with you and Suzette. I've already fallen in love with that little girl. She pulls at my heartstrings in a way that I never thought possible. And if, by some wild chance, I'm not her biological father, I'll still love her."

Tears welled in Melanie's eyes, and his grip on her hand tightened.

"And I realize that some people would assume that our feelings might not be real because of our unusual meeting and situation. Or that our relationship might be forced. Or might be misinterpreted. Whatever. All I know is that I feel a spark with you, not only as Suzette's mom, but with just you... Melanie... all on your own. When we're not together, I wonder what you're doing. I think of you and can't wait to see you again."

"So it's not just because I'm Suzette's mom?" Her voice held a touch of uncertainty, but he could see the hope blooming in her eyes.

"No," he said, shaking his head and tightening his

grip on her hand. "Let me ask you a question. Are you interested in me just because I'm Suzette's dad?"

Her hand twitched as her body jolted. "No. Absolutely not. I'm interested in you because I feel the same spark when we're together."

"While we might not have met if it hadn't been for Karen and Suzette, that doesn't matter because we *did* meet."

"And if people think I just came after you to get a baby daddy?"

"They would be the same people who think I just came after you so that I could be with the baby mama."

At that, she laughed and shook her head. "So you're saying that I shouldn't worry about what anyone else thinks about us? Including your mom?"

"The people who care about us are going to see that there is something between us. And that includes my mom. Anyone else who just speculates that it's only because of Suzette, then they don't matter."

She was quiet again, chewing on the bottom of her lip. His gaze snagged on her mouth, and he leaned closer. "I can think of something better for you to do with your lips than what you're doing."

Her gaze jumped back up to his, her eyes wide. Then with a little flirty smile, she asked, "Yeah? And what would that be?"

He wrapped an arm around her back and pulled her closer. She threw one leg over his legs, straddling his lap, sliding her hands to his shoulders. He pulled her closer and, tucked in his embrace, whispered against her mouth, "This."

He erased the distance and lightly pressed his mouth to hers. He pulled back for a few seconds as a little sigh escaped her. That tiny sound was all he needed to know she missed his touch. Angling his head, he sealed his lips over hers, taking the kiss deeper. If he thought the connection of their hands had caused a spark, he was caught entirely off guard by the jolt of lightning that struck his body as her tongue glided over his. He explored her mouth as their tongues danced, pulling her closer until her breasts pressed against his chest.

As her hips rocked, her core rubbed against his erection, and he wondered if she even knew what she was doing. Instinct had taken over for both, and all other thoughts fell away. What started as a delicate caress soon became a raw passion. Barely aware of her soft skin against the stubble of his jaw, he knew she'd wear the mark of their kiss, and that filled him with a primal eagerness to claim all of her.

With Melanie's honesty, and his need to act on his feelings, he now celebrated their newfound relationship. Seconds turned into moments, and then he had no sense of time as their bodies pressed tightly and their mouths continued to plunder and explore.

She pushed against his shoulders, separating from the kiss. He bit back a groan but realized that instead of stopping, she simply gasped for more air. He grinned, giving her a chance to catch her breath as their gazes stayed locked on each other. Her hands slid from his shoulders to clutch his jaws and then planted her lips over his again.

Like two teenagers dry humping on the sofa in a lip

lock, they gave in to the feelings they'd declared. He only prayed that whatever came with the paternity test would make them closer, giving them the chance to see where this relationship could go.

If the baby monitor hadn't alerted them to Suzette moving around, he wasn't sure they would have stopped, and they might have broken in the small sofa in a way neither had expected. But they jerked apart, neither moving as they stared at the monitor camera. A collective sigh of relief escaped as Suzette settled back to sleep.

Staring into each other's eyes, they smiled. Then chuckled. Then laughed. She clutched his jaws as her mirth slowed. "Wow."

He leaned into her palm as his hands gripped her hips. "Yeah, wow."

They blew out long breaths simultaneously, then smiled again. He leaned forward and kissed her lightly, murmuring, "I need to go. If not, I won't be able to leave you. As it is, I'm going home to take a cold shower."

Her top teeth landed on her bottom lips as her eyes stayed pinned on him. Mirth had morphed into a shadow of doubt.

Lifting a hand, he rubbed the reddened flesh of her lip with his forefinger. "Don't doubt. Don't doubt what's happening."

"It's scary," she admitted.

He nodded slowly, his finger still tracing her lips. "Yeah. But I'm not going anywhere. Your days of all giving are over. I promise, I'm here."

It took every ounce of willpower to stand, setting

her feet onto the floor. Adjusting his hard-on, he groaned as she pressed tightly to him, fireworks exploding throughout his body. Finally, linking fingers with her, he walked to the door, then bent to kiss her goodbye. "Lock up. I'll call you tomorrow."

Stepping outside, he waited to hear the click of the locks before jogging down to his vehicle. Once home, he flipped on the lights and stared at his house. What used to be peaceful silence now just felt lonely. With a grin, he couldn't wait to have Melanie and Suzette come over. They would make the house feel like home.

17

Jose turned at the sound of Ryan's voice. "Yes, sir?"

"Sam wants you to meet him at the old Bakersfield farm. Do you know where it is?"

Nodding, he said, "Yeah. Up past Easton, near the inlet?"

"That's right. Someone reported to the sheriff's department that they noticed a truck going in and out of the lane, and the only thing out there is an old barn. When the deputies investigated, they found some boat parts. Sam wants you to come. I'm sending Bryce along also."

Invigorated at the idea of making headway on the case, he turned to see Bryce ready to go. Bryce may have been new to the VMP, but he had been in the Navy for several years and had the best marine mechanical background.

Taking a smaller vessel, they climbed into the twenty-four-foot, single-engine Contender, and headed out of the harbor. Twenty minutes later, they docked at

MARYANN JORDAN

the back of the Bakersfield farm. "This farm hasn't been in use for a number of years," he explained. "After his wife died, and his two daughters went off to college and married, and moved away, Mr. Bakersfield kept it going for a little while. When he died, I heard that neither of the daughters wanted to come back and run the farm, but they also weren't ready to sell. As far as I know, it's just been sitting here for about five years. The fields would've been grown over by now, and the barn has probably sat empty."

"For a place to be so run-down, it looks like some activity has happened near this dock," Bryce noted.

"I was just thinking the same thing. Not fixed up enough that somebody coming by would wonder why, but enough that you could dock and move something around." As they climbed onto the wooden pier, they took pictures before heading through the closest field to the barn.

Once there, they met Sam on the inside. Pulling off his sunglasses, he gave his eyes a few seconds to adjust to the darker room, then looked around with interest. A long wooden shelf was built into the back of the barn and contained a few old engines. The dirt floor, which should have been packed and unspoiled in the last several years, had fresh oil spills, and several deep ruts indicating various heavy objects have been dragged around.

Looking over at Sam, he asked, "I'm assuming your people have already investigated?"

"Yes. It's clear for you to look around."

He and Bryce walked slowly around, studying the

interior. Stopping at the back shelf, he recognized the engines as parts of single-engine boat motors. "Fingerprints?"

"Some, and we'll run them to see what we get."

"These are from small boat motors, not any larger ones that have been reported stolen. But there have been enough small boats stolen that could have easily come from any of them. If the stolen boats are brought into the inlet, they can haul them along the path to where they're dismantled."

"What's the value in some of these?" Sam asked.

"Selling used outboard motors can bring in ready cash, but not enough to make a big profit. My guess is that it's the boats themselves that make a difference. When we were busting that drug running gang not too long ago, the big gangs have serious money to buy the best. But this seems smaller scale to me. Although, the theft of the big fishing boat is way different from this. I wonder if this was from the early days of learning how to chop up a boat to re-sell parts?"

Bryce walked over, shaking his head. "This looks like my old uncle's place. He worked on boat engines down in North Carolina. I used to hang out at his place, and he'd use old outboard motors and teach me how to take them apart. Said I needed to know how to dismantle them and then put them back together if I ever wanted to join him."

"Is that why you chose mechanics as your specialty in the Navy?" Jose asked.

"Yeah. I was going to get trained and then come back and work for him." Bryce sighed, his hands on his hips as his gaze moved around the old barn. "He died before I was barely in basic training. His wife sold the business, so I just stayed in the Navy. Had no reason to go back."

Jose rubbed his chin, moving around the barn. "This doesn't look like someone who has a big chop shop going on here. So could this be a copycat, or is this just part of a larger scheme, where multiple locations are used?"

"Could be. It'd be nice if some prints came back with a hit." Sam said, rubbing his chin. "By the way, you asked about the teenager, Ricky Montgomery?"

"Yes." Turning to face Sam more fully, he gave his full attention to him. "What did you find out?"

"His dad is Curtis, doing time in the state prison for armed robbery. He's been in for four years and has about three more to go unless he gets out early. His brother, Cory, was also arrested but was never brought to trial because it was never proven that he was part of the robbery. He's the uncle that Ricky lives with because there's no other living relative."

Jose's fingers curled into fists but nodded slowly. "Hate like hell hearing it but thanks for the confirmation." He started to turn away, then asked, "Does he have employment?"

"Not officially. He probably does odd jobs to bring in some money, but nothing he reports taxes on."

Offering a chin lift, Jose said, "I appreciate you looking into it." Then he turned and joined Bryce as they headed back to their boat.

Jose stood on the VMP vessel as Bryce pulled them alongside the forty-foot yacht. His eyes were focused on the deck, seeing several people standing around, drinks in hand, glaring back at the two VMP boats that had called out for them to stop.

"Excuse me," one man called out. "What are you doing? You can't just board us!"

No one answered him until they had secured the VMP boat to the side of the yacht. The protestations rang out from the gathering.

"I'm an attorney!" "If you cause damage, I'll sue." "What the hell are you doing?"

Jose and Andy boarded the yacht, ignoring the continued protestations. "Who owns this vessel?" Andy asked.

While Andy ordered the owner to provide his identification and license information, Jose cast his gaze around the others, seeing three women, two men besides the owner, and three children running around the deck. The children were not wearing life jackets.

"I demand to know why you have stopped us!" one of the women said, teetering forward, her bikini covering little as her martini splashed over the rim of her glass.

"We are from the Virginia Marine Police—" Jose began.

"You can't just stop us. That's against the law and is harassment!" one of the men said.

"We have the right to board any vessel in the waterways—"

"You do not have probable cause to board us. I'm an attorney and—"

"Sir, if you're an attorney, then you should know that the Code of Virginia, Article Three, Boating Safety, clearly states the Virginia Marine Police shall have the authority to stop, board, and inspect any vessel subject to this chapter after having identified himself in his official capacity. We identified ourselves when we called for you to stop."

The man opened and closed his mouth several times, giving a fish-like appearance while his friends clambered to ask more questions.

Jose inclined his head toward the children who were now standing near one of the women, eyes wide. He hated for them to be scared but cared more about their safety. "The children are not wearing life preservers," he stated.

"This is a yacht, not some little fishing boat," one of the women sneered. "They wouldn't have a lot of fun if they were having to wear lifejackets every minute of the day."

"They're required by law to be wearing life preservers while on the water." Glancing over at Andy, he caught the slight nod given. Tapping his radio, he softly said, "Breathalyzer needed."

Callan, Joseph, and another officer, Marty, had approached their vessel, and while Jose busied himself writing a citation, Calen came on board and stood close to Andy.

Jose looked at the woman standing closest to the children. She was the only one that didn't have a drink in her hand, and with the children clinging to her, he stepped closer. "Who are the children's parents, ma'am?"

"I'm the mother of these two," she said, looking down toward the two little boys. "And this is my niece, who's with us for the day."

"Do you have children's life preservers on board, ma'am?"

Her gaze jerked toward the man who had announced that he was an attorney and had currently walked over toward the boat owner. "Um... my husband..."

It appeared he was more concerned about his friend than his children and niece. Repeating the question, Jose asked, "Are there life preservers that fit the children?"

"I told Jeff that we needed to have some, but he insisted that as long as the children were playing in our sight, they wouldn't need them. I honestly don't know if George, um... the owner, has any, but I bought some before we left. They're still in the bags below deck."

As though just realizing that Jose was speaking to his wife, her husband turned and stormed over to them. "What are you doing?" he asked, looking at Jose. Then glancing at his wife, he bit out, "What are you telling him?"

"I asked if there were children's life preservers," Jose replied. He continued to write the citation. "I need to see your identification."

"You absolutely will not!"

"Sir, you are in violation of the law by not having the children in life preservers."

"That's ridiculous! Look around you! There are

plenty of adults supervising, and the kids were below deck playing video games most of the trip."

Tired of listening, Jose snapped. "Federal regulations state that a child, age thirteen or under, is required to wear a US Coast Guard-approved lifejacket while underway. While they do not have to wear it when they are below deck, the children were playing up here when we approached. You were also seen by several fishermen, who reported to us that the children were playing on the deck without lifejackets."

"So they are expected to take them on and off every time they run up and down on the deck?" the man argued.

"I would think that the safety of your children and your niece would be of utmost importance to you. But yes, if they are running up and down, then you, as a responsible adult, you need to make sure that they have the life preservers on when they are on deck. So again, I repeat, I need to see your identification."

"Fine, we'll do that from now on. But I'm not accepting that citation! You'll get nothing from me."

"Then you'll be placed under arrest."

Several gasps were heard, and the third man looked over. "Jeff, for Christ's sake, give him your information! Martha and I told you earlier that the children needed to be in life jackets, so stop acting like you're above the law. Just give them your information!"

A commotion was occurring with Andy, Callan, and the owner, George. He finally agreed to the breathalyzer and was found to be legally intoxicated.

It took another thirty minutes to sort through the

situation. George was placed under arrest and transferred over to Callan's vessel. The children were placed in life preservers by their parents, with the other couple assisting. Jeff finally stopped arguing and accepted the citation while still grumbling about filing a lawsuit, but since he was the only one who could legally operate the yacht besides the owner, agreed to follow them back to Baytown.

Jose stood tight-lipped as Bryce steered them back to the harbor, his gaze pinned on the yacht traveling behind them, making sure the kids were still in their life jackets.

An hour later, he was in the workroom as they wrote up their reports. So focused on what he was doing he barely heard Andy ask, "You okay? That was a fucking nightmare waiting to happen, but you looked at those kids, and I could tell you were really pissed."

"I just don't see how someone can be so cavalier about a child's safety."

Callan nodded. "I know, man. It's fucked up, isn't it?"

They were quiet for a moment before Joseph spoke. "Can I ask how things are going with you?"

He looked around, discovering every eye on him. "If you're wondering if I've heard officially about the paternity test, no, I haven't. It should come in the next day or two. But I've been spending time with Melanie and Suzette and, truthfully, have gotten close to both of them." If he thought his words would cause shock or dismay, that wasn't what happened. The smile that greeted his statement eased the nervousness that had snaked through his chest.

"And if you find out that… um… well, that…" Andy stumbled.

"That I'm not her biological father?" Jose provided, finding all his friends' gazes directed at him. "Then I still plan on being in their lives. The relationship I've built over just the past two weeks will keep moving forward."

The men grinned and nodded before everyone returned to their tasks. Jose glanced at his watch, and his mind filled with Melanie and Suzette.

18

Melanie clapped as Trey managed to remember the parts of a cell. "Good for you." Even Ricky managed a smile as he watched Trey dance around.

When he'd stopped celebrating, he said, "I just need to pass the state test. Won't need this for after high school."

Melanie leaned forward. "What do you want to do when you graduate?"

"I want to be rich," Trey announced, munching on the apple slices she'd brought out.

"Okay, but what do you want to do to get rich?" she prodded.

"I'm taking a tech class this coming year. I'm going to learn about auto mechanics. Mom says I can make good money fixing cars."

"Good for you," she exclaimed. Turning to Ricky, she asked, "And you?"

He shrugged, but she pressed forward. "I can't imagine you don't have any ideas."

"Tell her, Ricky," Trey encouraged.

Ricky rolled his eyes. "Navy."

"You want to join the Navy?"

"Oh yeah," Trey jumped in. "We had recruiters come to school this past year. Ricky liked the idea of the Navy."

"That's wonderful."

He shrugged again. "It's a chance to get away from here. There's nothing here for me but just the same old sh—um, stuff. I gotta get away. Plus, they pay you while you learn a trade. I thought about learning mechanics, also."

"Me on cars and you on boats. We'll be rich!" Trey shouted.

"The first step is having a goal, and both of you have great goals," she said. Suzette cried out over the monitor, and the boys jumped to their feet.

"Thanks for the apples and the help!" Trey shouted, already racing down the steps.

Ricky followed more slowly. "Thanks, Ms. Landers," he said. He hesitated as though he wanted to say more, but then just threw up his hand in a wave and followed Trey.

***

Melanie looked around her living room at the gathering and wished she had more room while enjoying her company. Judith had stopped by with her stepdaughter, Cindy, and her friend, Rachel. Cindy's dad was Ryan,

Jose's boss, and Rachel's adoptive dad, Joseph, also worked with Jose.

"Whenever you want a babysitter, we're available!" Cindy enthused while sitting on the floor playing with Suzette.

Rachel, a soft-spoken young woman, smiled at Melanie. "We thought you might be more comfortable with the two of us watching her."

Melanie was thrilled with the proposal. Rachel and Cindy co-babysitting sometimes when she needed a break or when tutoring would work out well.

As Rachel joined Cindy on the floor to entertained Suzette, Judith joined Melanie in the kitchen as she poured glasses of lemonade. She cast a glance toward the living room before whispering, "I don't suppose you know when we'll hear?"

Judith offered a soft smile as she shook her head. "I won't get anything. The results will be sent to Jose."

Melanie nodded, the answer expected.

"How are things going?"

She hesitated for only a moment, desperate to unburden herself. With her parents not around and having no one to talk to who knew her situation, she desperately wanted to confide in Judith. "Really good, to be honest. Jose comes around often. He's not waiting on the results to spend time with us. He says it doesn't matter what the results say. We're getting closer, which is nice. Although, we're not sharing anything with anyone yet."

"That makes it difficult, doesn't it?"

She sighed heavily and nodded. "I knew my friend

Karen like a sister, and she would never lie, so I know that Jose is the father. And regardless of our need to co-parent, we're building a relationship. But I worry about if it seems like we're rushing things."

"Because of how the relationship got started?"

She nodded, nibbling on her bottom lip, and she thought of Jose's family. "Yeah, it's not exactly a boy meets girl kind of story, is it?"

"Around here, getting together in strange ways isn't exactly unusual."

She tilted her head to the side, and her brows lowered. "I have to admit, I'm curious!"

Judith glanced toward the living room, but the two teens were happily chattering as they played with Suzette, not paying any attention to the adults. "I knew Ryan when we were teens, but he married his high school sweetheart, and I left for college a few years later. It wasn't until last year that I returned to town and discovered he was divorced. He and I met up again when his kids came into the clinic to see me, but let me just say that we did *not* have a sweet reunion. At least at first." She smiled and added, "But it got better!"

Melanie smiled at Judith's honesty. "And there's more?"

"Rachel's aunt, who is her guardian, is with one of the VMP officers. Joseph and Shiloh met when he tried to use his charm on her, and it backfired. She didn't want to have anything to do with him for a while. And a few of the other VMPs have equally strange stories. Andy got with Ivy after he rescued her when she fell off the Chesapeake Bay Bridge. When they first met, Jared and his fiancée, Billie, hated each other. And don't get me started with some of the people in town. I know you met some of the other women with little ones, and I assure you, many of their relationships started just as strangely."

"I'm glad you told me those stories. It makes me feel better! I just assumed people would think that I was trying to trap him into helping out or that he was only with me out of an obligation."

Judith waved her hand dismissively. "If anybody thinks that, then they're not worthy of your time."

Melanie chuckled and nodded. "Jose said the very same thing."

Judith grinned. "I knew I liked him!"

She reveled in unburdening herself to a newfound friend. Then looking toward the living room at Cindy and Rachel playing with Suzette, her spirit felt lighter.

———

Jose jogged up the staircase to Melanie's front door. He hadn't planned on coming over this evening. He was going to pick her and Suzette up tomorrow to go to his parents for his nephew's party, but what he needed to do couldn't wait. As soon as he arrived at her door, he reined in his nervous impatience and knocked softly.

The door opened, and his gaze landed on Melanie's wide eyes. With his hand on her belly, he gently pushed her back into her apartment and stepped inside, closing the door behind him. His gaze immediately followed the sound of Suzette babbling in her swing, and his emotions skittered all over the place. Gut clenched. Heart leaped. A lump formed in his throat.

"Jose? What's going on?"

His head swung back to her, his gaze raking over every detail. Hair pulled into a sloppy bun. Leggings and a T-shirt. Bare feet. Concern moved through her eyes. Beautiful.

Blowing out a long breath, he reached inside his pocket and pulled out an envelope, trying to keep his hand from shaking. For an instant, her brows lowered before her eyes flew open wide as her whole body jerked.

"The results?" she squeaked.

He nodded slowly. "I didn't open them. I wanted us to do it together. Is that okay?"

Her head bounced up and down, giving her agreement. "We didn't talk about how we were going to do this. But it's all I could think about for the last couple of days," she confessed.

"Me, too."

"I feel like we should sit down. Or maybe just rip it open. Or... I don't know. It seems so monumental, yet it's just an envelope."

He reached out and put his arms around her, pulling her close. The subject of Suzette's paternity had been how he and Melanie met and, whether they talked about it or not, had been with them every day. "Before I open the results, I want to reiterate once again," he began. "I don't plan on going anywhere, regardless of what this says."

She leaned back and held his gaze with a tremulous

smile dancing over her lips. Sucking in a deep breath, she let it out slowly. "Okay. Let's do this."

His hands continued to shake as he ripped open the envelope, and they pulled out the sheet of paper together. The top part was filled with columns and rows of various tests, codes, and numbers that meant nothing to him. "Thank God Judith told me what to look for," he muttered.

Melanie's finger pointed at the words near the bottom, and he read out loud. "Statement of results: The alleged father cannot be excluded as the biological father of the tested child. Based on the analysis of STR loci listed above, the probability of paternity is 99.9999999 percent."

"You're her father," Melanie breathed, her voice barely a whisper.

Even though it was what he'd grown to expect and hoped for, it took every ounce of his strength not to drop to his knees. Melanie's arms slipped from around his waist, and she stared up at him, eyes wide.

Their gazes remained locked on each other before he turned slowly to see Suzette swinging back and forth, kicking her legs and slapping a little tray in front of her. *My daughter.*

"Yes, your daughter," Melanie said.

He hadn't realized he'd vocalized his claim, but looking back at Melanie's face, which still held concern, he whooped as he picked her up with his arms around her waist and twirled her in the middle of the room. "She's my daughter! We have a daughter!"

Melanie laughed, holding on tight. When he finally

set her feet on the ground, he released her waist, clutched her cheeks, and kissed her soundly. Then he rushed over to the infant swing. He hesitated, and Melanie anticipated the reason. She showed him how to slow the swing and then unbuckled Suzette.

He gently pulled her out of the padded swing seat and held her against his chest, nuzzling her hair and breathing in her scent. Pressing her tight against his heartbeat, he closed his eyes as he rocked back and forth, memorizing the feel of his daughter at this moment.

Opening his eyes, he directed his gaze on Melanie, standing close by, her face lit by her beautiful smile.

Lifting one arm, he readily accepted her as she rushed forward, and the three of them formed a trio in the middle of her living room. They stayed like that for several minutes until Suzette decided she was tired of being held and let her displeasure be known. Chuckling, he shifted them to the floor, where the baby blanket was spread out with several toys.

For the next hour, he allowed himself to memorize every detail of her, almost as though he were seeing her for the first time. Besides focusing on Suzette, his awareness of Melanie was heightened. Their relationship had been evolving, growing closer. And what he told her before was true. It didn't matter how they met… they had as much right to build a relationship as anyone else. But now that they knew he was Suzette's father, he knew they'd have a lot to discuss.

"A line has formed along your forehead," she stated, her eyes roaming over his face.

"Is that like the crinkle that forms between your brows?"

She laughed and nodded. "I think so. I've already come to realize that when a crease forms on your forehead, you're thinking hard about something."

He shook his head. "Right now, I just want to enjoy my two girls. There will be lots of time for heavier discussions later." As soon as the words left his mouth, he spied the aforementioned telltale crinkle between her eyes. Laughing, he said, "Now you need to stop overthinking. I just mean, we have many things to discuss, but it's all good."

It amazed him that he already understood Suzette's routine in such a short period. He helped with bath time, then gave her a nighttime bottle. Melanie gave cuddles and snuggles, and then they put her down in her crib before they slipped back out to the living room.

She yawned widely, and he could feel her fatigue. She'd already told him earlier about the good visit with Judith, and how Cindy and Rachel volunteered to babysit.

Wrapping his arms around her, he rested his chin on top of her head. "Are you ready to meet the rest of my family tomorrow?"

"As ready as I'll ever be," she said, and he didn't miss the little sigh that left her lips. She leaned back and held his gaze. "Are we telling them?"

He wanted to scream *"Yes!"* but could tell she had some trepidation. He nodded slowly and said, "I think we should. I don't want to force you into anything you're not ready for, but now that we're certain, I can't imagine being around my family, especially with you and Suzette, and not telling them."

"You're right. It would be very disingenuous to do that. So far, the only people who are aware that it's even a possibility have been the people you work with and Judith." She sighed again. "It's weird, Jose. We got the results that I expected, purely based on my knowledge of Karen's character, and what I've told people about Suzette has all been true, only leaving off the part about the possible father. It'll be strange enough as people find out, but starting with your family is the best thing to do."

He bent forward and kissed her, losing himself in the gentle warm pressure of her lips against his. He wasn't sure he'd ever believed in love at first sight, and certainly, he hadn't fallen in love with Melanie the first time they met. But it hadn't taken long for feelings to begin. And he wanted to give those feelings every opportunity to grow.

He slowly nibbled her lips as the kiss eased. She walked him to the door, and he said, "I'll pick the two of you up tomorrow. We'll spend time with my family, and then we'll go celebrate on our own."

Her wide smile let him know she was good with his plans. As he headed back to his SUV, excitement mixed with nerves about his next day's plans. But then, thinking about spending the day with Melanie and Suzette, he knew they could face anything together.

19

As soon as Jose pulled into his parents' driveway and spied several vehicles, the nerves he'd felt all morning came rushing back. He'd gone to bed last night with thoughts of Melanie and Suzette in his mind, but by morning, he was rethinking his plans.

While he had no doubt that his parents would be thrilled, he also knew that his news would be shocking and surprising. It probably wasn't fair for him to plan on announcing his news without talking to them privately first.

Scrubbing his hand over his face as he put Melanie's SUV in park, he shouldn't have been surprised when she asked, "Are you ready?"

He rolled his head to the side and stared at her. Light makeup highlighted her features. Her hair was pulled back with a headband, the waves falling about her shoulders. Blue modest-length shorts and a navy top. With sandals on her feet, she was the epitome of a summer beach beauty. A babble from the back seat sent a smile across his face. Melanie had dressed Suzette in a blue outfit also. When he'd arrived at her apartment and seen them together, he thought they were adorable as Melanie gave Suzette a little twirl and called out, "We're twinsies!"

Smiling, he said, "I'm ready. I'm ready to announce our news to the world."

The Martinez house was modest, but they walked around to the backyard, where he knew the picnic tables would already be set up, along with the webbed lawn chairs his dad would repair every few years when the webbing wore out. His mom, Rosemarie, and Katy would already be making trips back and forth from the kitchen to the tables with food. His nieces and nephews would run around, chase each other, and have fun.

He carried Suzette against his shoulder and linked fingers with Melanie as they entered through the gate and into the backyard. Greetings were called out as they approached. But it didn't miss his attention that there seemed to be wide-eyed expressions of surprise between Rosemarie, Stanley, Bethany, Jimmy, and Katy.

His mom stepped out of the kitchen, her eyes bugging at the sight of him. "Jose! I... didn't know you were bringing... *visitors*."

He stiffened at the word visitors but didn't have a chance to respond before an attractive, smiling young woman came out of the kitchen. Her gaze took him in before landing on Suzette and then dropping to his hand linked with Melanie's. She stopped suddenly, her eyes opening as wide as his sisters'. Instantly, he realized that his mom had invited a woman he didn't know to come to a family gathering as a potential blind date for him.

Hearing a slight gasp from Melanie, he could tell she was also reading the situation. Livid for them all to be put in this embarrassing circumstance, his fingers tightened, and he kept her hand clasped with his.

His mom appeared nervous as her hands fluttered and her gaze darted between Melanie and the young woman behind her, but Jose was too angry to care. She rushed to explain, "I invited Joanne to join us so that you would have a chance to meet her. You hadn't mentioned bringing a... um... friend."

The tension was thick, and if it hadn't been for the children playing on the other side of the yard, he wasn't sure what he would've said. As it was, he smiled politely, nodded to the young woman, then turned to the gathering and said, "I'd like to introduce my girlfriend, Melanie, and daughter, Suzette."

His siblings and their spouses moved forward, all greeting Melanie and Suzette warmly. His dad walked over, shot a sympathetic glance his way, then turned to Melanie. "I've been holding Rosemarie's youngest, but I'd love to have my hands on this sweet little girl. Would you mind?"

Carlos had addressed the question to Melanie, and Jose battled the urge to roar that he didn't want to give up his daughter. But Melanie gently pulled Suzette from his arms and walked toward Carlos.

Everyone drifted over to the chairs, leaving Joanne and Jose standing near Mary. Deciding that honesty was the only way to move forward, he smiled at Joanne and said, "I'm afraid when my mother invited you, she wasn't aware that I already have someone in my life."

Mary opened her mouth to speak, but he sent her a glare and shook his head. "Mom, I think you should check on Rosemarie's kids."

She pressed her lips tightly, then sent an apologizing half smile toward Joanne before walking farther into the yard.

Joanne's eyes crinkled as she smiled and shook her head. "You don't have to apologize, Jose. Believe me, my mom's been trying to set me up with anybody and everybody since I've been back in town."

"I am embarrassed, though. I don't want you not to feel welcome."

She waved her hand dismissively. "Please, don't give it another thought. I felt awkward coming to a family party anyway and then finding out it was an ambush with you makes it even more awkward. But as nice as your invitation is, I think I'll grab my purse and head out."

"Are you sure?"

"Absolutely. And no hard feelings. In fact, this is now giving me the impetus to tell my mom to stop trying to set me up."

He chuckled and nodded. "I completely understand how you feel."

She reached out her hand, and he curled his fingers around hers in a gentle goodbye shake. But it was impossible to ignore that there were no sparks. Not that he expected to feel anything special, but it was nice to note that there wasn't any. She was an attractive woman, and he was sure that she would find her own dates her way.

She waved goodbye and left the backyard. He turned and walked over to the others, ignoring his mother's pinched lips and glare. Melanie glanced up at him, her wide eyes indicating she was feeling the nervous pressure of not knowing how to handle the bizarre situation. Deciding that beating around the bush or ignoring the facts was not going to work, he leaned forward and gently pulled Suzette back into his arms. Kissing the top of her head, he held out his hand for Melanie, wrapping his arm around her shoulders when she joined him.

Turning toward his family as all their eyes landed on him, he blurted, "I have an announcement. And while you'll have a lot of questions, I need to let you know that Suzette is my biological daughter."

Shocked silence met his announcement, and he was just about to continue explaining when Suzette scrunched her face and started crying. With wails and screams soon following and fat tears rolling down her cheeks, she threw up all over her outfit.

———

Melanie grabbed the diaper bag and, making bug eyes at Jose, scooped her daughter into her arms. Casting a half-apologetic glance around the group, she said, "I'll just slip inside and get her cleaned up and changed. You can chat with your family while I take care of her."

She hustled through the back door, desperate to escape. Never having been to the Martinez's house, she was uncertain which way to go. She discovered a large laundry room just off the kitchen that included a wide counter, perfect for a diaper and outfit change.

As she pulled the little dress over Suzette's head, glad that the cries had turned to sniffles, she cooed, "You had a tummy ache, didn't you, sweetheart." She sighed. "So does Mommy. You probably picked up on my mood."

The sound of voices from the backyard met her ears, and she turned, discovering the window over the washer and dryer was open. Pressing her lips together, she felt strange eavesdropping but justified her listening because they would be talking about her daughter. And occasionally peeking out seemed justified, as well.

"What do you mean, your biological daughter?" Mary asked, her hands on her hips.

"I didn't know about Suzette until just a couple of weeks ago," Jose began.

"And that woman in there didn't tell you? She was pregnant and never told you?" Mary's voice grew louder.

Carlos intervened, "Mary, hush. Let him talk."

"Thanks, Dad." Jose dragged his hand through his hair. "As I said, I just found out two weeks ago about Suzette and just got the paternity test results in yesterday—"

"Paternity test?" Mary all but yelled, then jerked her head around toward Rosemarie's kids, before swinging back toward Jose. "She didn't even know who the father was? And you show up here at our family's get-together holding hands with that... that... that woman?"

Jose erupted, but the cacophony around him almost drowned him out.

Rosemarie turned to Stanley and said, "Honey, take the kids to the very back part of the yard and keep them busy."

Her husband nodded, then called out to his kids, moving them away from the adults.

Jimmy had stepped closer to Jose in a show of brotherly support. Katy stayed rooted to the spot, her eyes wide as her head jerked amongst the others standing around.

"Jose, son, what's going on?" Carlos asked. Then turning back to his wife, he added, "And you need to be quiet and let your son speak."

"A year ago, I met a woman who was visiting." Sending a quick glare toward his mom, he added, "And, no, it wasn't Melanie. It was Melanie's best friend. I'm a grown man, and my choices are my own, but suffice it to say that we spent a night together. She left the next day, and I never heard from her again, nor did I expect to."

By now, Melanie had finished changing Suzette's diaper and put her in a clean outfit. Her eyes were still drawn to the scene outside like a moth to the flame. Attracted, enticed, yet unlike the moth, she was completely aware that she could get burned. She was terrified of Jose's family's rejection, knowing their response would affect her and her daughter's lives. Picking up Suzette, she held her tightly against her chest, bouncing and trying to keep her entertained while watching out the window, listening to every word.

"Two weeks ago, Melanie came to town to inform me that her friend Karen had given birth, then became ill and died. Karen gave custody to her friend, Melanie. And Karen's

211

deathbed wish was that she finds me to let me know that I was the father."

The family's response was one of shocked silence as they stood with their mouths falling open.

"Melanie knew I'd want a paternity test, so we met the next morning to have one. Since then, we've been talking and getting to know each other. I had already decided that I wanted to be part of this child's life regardless of what the paternity test said. Then last night, I found out that I am Suzette's father. Considering that I've already fallen for Suzette and Melanie, that news made it better."

"You've known this woman less than two weeks," Mary said. "I'm having a hard time wrapping my mind around the fact that you have a child... Oh my God, I have a grand-daughter. But you have no reason to tie yourself to this woman."

"Why do you insist on calling her this woman? Her name is Melanie!"

"Yes, yes, Melanie. But you can't be in love with her after only two weeks. And this works out very well for her, doesn't it? Her friend leaves her with the baby, and that's sad and can't be easy on her. So getting the baby's father to fall for her just makes her life that much better."

"Jesus, Mom, can you hear yourself? Melanie hasn't asked me for anything. Not a dime. Which, by the way, considering I am Suzette's father, she and I will have that conversation. But I feel incredibly lucky to not only find out I have a child, but I have feelings for the child's mother!"

"But what if it doesn't last? She's not the baby's real mother. You're the biological father. You're the one who should be in charge and making the decisions. What if you *and Melanie break up? What if you find a woman you want to marry? Wouldn't you want that woman to become your daughter's stepmother?"*

At those words, Melanie's heart dropped into her stomach, but a blinding rage filled her vision. Only the sweet baby in her arms kept her from turning into the Tasmanian devil and screaming her head off. Shoving everything into the diaper bag, she slung it over her shoulder, and with a kiss on Suzette's cheek, she left the laundry room and started outside.

Stomping toward the group, Jimmy saw her first, and she heard him mutter, "Oh, shit."

The others turned and stared as she stormed toward them. Ignoring Jose, she looked straight at Mary and said, "Make no mistake, Mrs. Martinez. Suzette *is* my daughter. I have legal guardianship and have loved her since the day Karen told me she was pregnant. And while I will co-parent with Jose no matter what happens in the future, no one... I repeat, *no* one will take this child from me. I will fight to the death for anyone who tries."

Her voice choked, tears threatening, but as Jose reached toward her, she stepped back. "I'm going for a drive."

"Melanie, I'll go with you—"

"No. This has been a disaster for your poor nephew, and you need to spend time with your family. Quite honestly, I need some time alone with my daughter. I'll take the car if you can get somebody to drop you off back at your place." She could sense that Jose did not want her to go, but with her insides quivering and her heart threatening to pound out of her chest, she looked at him and begged, "Please, I need this."

Without giving him a chance to answer, she turned and walked through the gate, heading to the SUV. Buckling Suzette in, she climbed behind the wheel and backed out of the driveway.

Her phone dinged an incoming message, and she pressed play.

"Melanie, please be careful. I'm going to give the present to my nephew, and then I'm coming. Do not let what my mother said bother you. Remember our trio. You, me, Suzette. Nothing has changed."

She bypassed her apartment and drove into town. Sending a message to tell him where she was, she clicked the carrier into the stroller and pushed Suzette out onto the Baytown pier.

"Come on, sweetie, let's take a walk. Mommy needs some sunshine, a cool breeze, and the bay to make my day better!" Looking down, she felt her heart lift as she added, "Well, all of that and my pretty girl. You make every day better!"

20

Jose stood with his hands on his hips, anger pouring off him as he watched Melanie and Suzette walk away. He wanted to run after them, but his dad clamped his hand on his shoulder.

"Son, give her a break. I didn't realize that the back windows of the house were open, but I have a feeling she just heard everything. She knows your feelings, and she knows you defended her." He turned and looked toward his wife. "Unfortunately, she also knows your feelings, too."

Mary closed her eyes and shook her head slowly. "I'm sorry, Jose. All of this caught me by surprise. I still don't understand."

Heaving a heavy sigh, he grimaced. "I understand this caught everybody off guard, and that's my fault. I should've come over by myself and explained the whole situation before bringing them along. That's on me, that's my mistake."

"Jose," Rosemarie said, "Tell us more. I think Mom will understand better if you give us the whole story."

He looked over at his sister, recognizing her gentle way of always being able to step inside the family rifts and bring peace.

Sucking in another deep breath, he stared down at his boots for a moment, then lifted his chin and held the gazes of his family, noting the gentle expressions on their faces. His mother's face was conflicted, but he could see she was horrified that Melanie had overheard her.

"While it might be embarrassing to admit to a one-night stand to my parents, it happens. Not often, but it did. And while it's equally embarrassing to mention protection to my parents, yes, I used protection. Karen was a lovely woman, but it was nothing special, so we both knew it was one night only."

With another sigh, he continued. "I've learned from Melanie that Karen had parents who were very controlling and did not give her unconditional love. When they discovered she was pregnant, they disowned her and cut her out of their lives."

"Oh no..." Mary breathed.

"Her best friend was Melanie, and you need to hear this, Mom. Melanie allowed Karen to move in with her, helping to take care of her during the pregnancy. They'd been friends since they were quite young. Melanie's parents also helped, as well. Melanie begged Karen to find me and tell me, but Karen didn't. Melanie can only assume that having been rejected by her parents, Karen didn't want to be possibly rejected by her baby's father, as well. So Melanie was the one at the birth and was going to help raise Karen's baby."

"And then Karen became ill?" Jimmy asked, wrapping his arm around his wife.

"A month after she gave birth to Suzette, she became ill. They discovered an aggressive brain tumor—"

Gasps were heard among his family again, these given in heartfelt shock for the young mother.

"Melanie took an *unpaid* leave of absence to help care for Suzette and Karen. But one month later, Karen died."

Tears formed in Mary's eyes, and as he looked around, Bethany, Rosemarie, and Katy were also blinking back tears. Carlos cleared his throat and said, "God bless her."

"Near the end, Karen contacted an attorney and gave full guardianship over to Melanie. She also gave a letter to Melanie and had one addressed to me. Her last wish was that Melanie find me, give me the letter, and let me know that Melanie was willing to work with me to determine that Suzette was mine."

He looked around his family again and then settled his gaze on his mom. "Now, do you understand? My child's biological mother made her own choices based on her own life. Whether we agree with them or not doesn't matter. She's gone, having done the best that she thought she could do. Melanie has done nothing but sacrifice for her best friend, putting her own life on hold and taking care of her ill friend and her newborn baby. And when her friend knew she was dying, she promised to raise Suzette and be her mother. She might not be Suzette's biological mother, but she has proven over and over what kind of mother she truly is. And that is the best kind of mother there is. So if you're wondering if Melanie is worthy of me, I'd have to laugh. Melanie has proven her worth every day."

"And you've fallen for her," Carlos said, his dark eyes warm on his son.

He noticed his father had not asked a question but made a statement. "You don't have to know someone for years before you fall for them. I realize that the way we met was unconventional, but that doesn't affect our feelings. I wasn't very nice to Melanie when I first met her because I was shocked. But she's done nothing but be gracious and accommodating to me, acknowledging that she knows our situation is unique. And while I only met her a little over two weeks ago, I can tell you, truthfully, that my feelings are real and growing."

Mary hung her head and wiped her eyes. Looking up, she held Jose's gaze as she walked forward and pulled him into a hug. He was stiff for only a few seconds, then wrapped his arms around her.

"I'm so sorry, Jose," she said. "My only excuse is that I, too, was shocked. I didn't realize you had somebody special in your life, and that's why I invited Joanne to come. And when you showed up with Melanie and Suzette, I was rude to them because I was embarrassed. I'm ashamed of how I've acted. Hearing the story, I'm humbled at Melanie's sacrifices for her friend and that little innocent baby. I also cannot judge Karen's choices. We can't understand what makes a person do something if we haven't walked in their shoes."

He leaned back and stared into his mother's eyes and smiled. "There she is."

"There who is?" his mom asked, her head tilted slightly.

"My mother. The one who always tried to understand people and had one of the biggest hearts I've ever known."

She pressed her lips together and wiped another tear away. "I've made a horrible mistake."

"You always told me that mistakes can be rectified," he said. His phone buzzed in his pocket, and he pulled it out. Seeing the message was from Melanie, he tapped it quickly. Looking up, he said, "She's letting me know she went to the Baytown pier."

"Jose," his mother said. "You stay here with the family for now. I have a mistake I need to rectify."

Melanie had reached the end of the pier, smiling at a few people leaning against the railing with the fishing poles in the water. She walked back halfway, where there was a covered area with a bench. Grateful it was empty, she sat and stared out over the water while Suzette snoozed in her stroller.

The bay was beautiful. Diamond reflections twinkled on the surface of the water as it gently undulated in the breeze. Children laughed and played on the beach nearby as families gathered to enjoy the day.

She closed her eyes for a moment, sucking in a deep breath before letting it out slowly. Fatigue pulled at every muscle, and she knew if she was home, she would've put Suzette down for a nap and then crashed on the sofa for a nap herself. The sound of the water splashing against the rocks underneath the pier camouflaged the sound of anyone approaching.

"It's lovely out here, isn't it?"

Her eyes jerked open at the sound of a woman's voice close by, and she was surprised to see Jose's mother standing alone at the edge of the covered section of the pier.

Uncertain why Mary was here or what she should say, she simply responded to her comment. "Yes, it is lovely. I haven't been out here before, so I was pleased to find the benches to sit on."

Mary nodded, then inclined her head toward the bench. "Would you allow me to sit with you?"

Without hesitation, she nodded. "Yes."

The tension in Mary's face relaxed as her lips curved hesitantly. She sat, not too close, but where she would be able to peer into the stroller. Melanie's gut clenched, and she remained quiet. Regardless of how Mary felt about Melanie, she was Jose's mother and Suzette's grandmother. But Melanie's mama bear was awake, so she stayed alert. But Mary only smiled, her eyes gentle as she watched Suzette sleep.

Finally, Mary turned her gaze toward Melanie. "I've made a terrible mess of things. I'm ashamed of myself. And when I told Jose and Carlos that I was coming here, I told them that I was coming to rectify my mistakes. But now that I'm here, my shame is overwhelming."

"You love your son."

Mary's body jerked slightly, and her brows lowered. "Yes, I do. But that's not an excuse for my rudeness."

"Maybe not an excuse, but it is a reason."

"I'm sorry, but I'm not sure I understand what you mean."

Melanie looked down at Suzette and smiled, seeing her daughter's face scrunch slightly in sleep. "I sometimes wonder what she's dreaming when she makes such faces."

Dragging in a breath before letting it out, she turned back to Mary. "It was hard for me to understand why Karen didn't want to contact Jose to let him know she was pregnant. But whenever I brought it up, she refused. I told him…" She choked as memories flooded her mind. "I told him that I think Karen had faced rejection from her parents for most of her life. And when they kicked her out and disowned her when she was pregnant outside of marriage, even though she was an adult, the rejection cut her deeply. The idea of telling Jose about the pregnancy would have exposed her to more possible rejection. It was just easier for her to decide that she was going to handle everything herself."

Mary nodded slowly. "I don't understand how parents can reject their children."

She scoffed. "They refused to see her when she gave birth to Suzette or when she became ill. And didn't come to the funeral. They said it was because of her sinful life."

Mary's mouth dropped open, and a look of pain and rage crossed her face. "Oh my God!"

"My parents and I made sure that neither Karen nor Suzette wanted for anything."

"Jose said you gave up your job. You changed your life for them."

Shrugging, she said, "It doesn't feel like a sacrifice."

"Spoken like a true mother," Mary said.

Those words scored straight through Melanie, and a gasp escaped as she held Mary's gaze. After a moment, she said, "I came to Baytown to fulfill Karen's last wishes. To be honest, I would have done it anyway. But I want you to believe I didn't come here to trap him. If he wanted nothing to do with Suzette, that was fine. I just wanted him to know she existed. But you raised such a good man that he wanted to be around us to ensure we were cared for even before he knew positively that he was Suzette's father. And then, during that time, we've grown closer."

"There were sparks, right?"

Her smile widened, matched by Mary's, who continued, "When I met Carlos, there were sparks from the minute he held my hand. I knew that Jose would never settle for anything less. Ever since he came back from the Navy and has been around, I've tried to set him up with one woman after another. But he always said there were no sparks. So when he told me he was with you, I should've known you two felt sparks."

Melanie laughed and nodded. "Yes, there were sparks." They sat quietly for a moment as Suzette snoozed, occasionally jerking in her sleep. "I had plenty of time to get used to the idea of Suzette and even finding Jose. Believe me, when I first told him, he didn't trust me, and he was not happy. So it's not surprising that his family would feel the same. We didn't handle things right today. He should've come and spoken to you in private. Prepared you. Explained to you. Allowed you to ask questions. It was unfortunate that we didn't give you a chance to have your natural reaction without an audience."

"You're being very generous, Melanie. It's true, I was caught off guard and made assumptions that I shouldn't have. But I have never treated a guest in my home in such a way, and I'm ashamed. I ask for your forgiveness."

"It's already given, Mrs. Martinez."

Suzette squirmed a little more, then blinked, opening her eyes. As soon as they landed on Melanie, she grinned, waved her arms, and kicked her legs. She leaned over and tickled Suzette's tummy. "How's my sweetie? Did you have a good nap out here in the fresh air? I'll bet you're getting hungry."

Then looking toward Mary, seeing her face light up as she peered at Suzette, she asked, "Would you like to hold her?"

Mary sucked in a hasty breath, blinking back the moisture hanging on her eyelashes. "I would be honored to hold my granddaughter."

Melanie leaned forward and unbuckled Suzette, pulling her from her carrier and giving her a kiss. Reaching into her bag, she pulled out the bottle and, gently placing Suzette in Mary's arms, handed the bottle to her. Mary rocked Suzette and fed her with the practice of a mother and grandmother.

A slight blush crossed Mary's face after a few minutes as she cast a side-eyed glance toward Melanie. "I'm a very good babysitter."

"I'm sure you are. And in case you're wondering, as long as Jose agrees, I'd love to have you babysit sometime."

"And I was thinking... that perhaps you and Jose would like to go on a baby-free date. You two need time together just for uninterrupted conversation and... well, adult time."

Melanie blinked, the blush now rushing over her cheeks. "Mrs. Martinez! Are you offering to keep Suzette so that Jose and I can—"

"Please, call me Mary. And let's just say that you two deserve to enjoy all the sparks."

Laughter rang out as she threw her head back. The idea of a date with Jose that didn't include diapers and feedings sounded wonderful. As her mirth slowed, she spied the grin on Mary's face.

As they sat quietly, Melanie looked back over the water and smiled. *She's going to have a wonderful family, Karen. A big, loving family, just like you would've wanted.*

This time there was no reply to be heard. But a gentle breeze lifted her hair and kissed her face.

21

The atmosphere in the vehicle was vastly different as Melanie and Jose drove away from his parents' house from the first time they had visited. The unease had nothing to do with his parents, but it would be the first time she'd left Suzette with anyone other than *her* parents.

Carlos and Mary were going to babysit Suzette while she and Jose had their first alone date. She'd reviewed Suzette's likes and dislikes, feeding schedule, and favorite toys. Pulling out the diaper bag's contents, she double-checked to ensure plenty of diapers, wipes, and extra outfits. Her nerves were palpable as she fiddled until Suzette began picking up on her mood and started to fuss. Ignoring the looks shared between Jose and Carlos, she started the whole process over again as she dug in the diaper bag for a pacifier.

Finally, Mary took her hands and held them tight while leaning close. "Go. I promise she'll be fine."

Tears had pricked Melanie's eyes, and she looked

down at Suzette, now babbling contentedly in Carlos's arms. Mary hugged her and whispered, "You deserve this evening. Let us give it to you."

She'd nodded as Jose gently took her hand in his and ushered her outside. Halfway to his vehicle, he wrapped his arm around her, and she wasn't sure if he just wanted her close or to keep her from turning to rush back inside.

Now, in Jose's SUV with the new car seat empty in the back, she blew out a long breath. Looking over at the little smile playing about his lips, she sighed. "You think I'm ridiculous, don't you?"

Turning, he shook his head as his dark-eyed gaze roamed over her face. "I think you're a good mother. I think you give your all to everything you do." He leaned across the console and kissed her lightly. "But tonight is about me giving to you. So buckle up and enjoy the ride."

As he started the engine, she forced her body to relax and had to admit she was excited. *Date night.* She rubbed her hands along the skirt of her dress, butterflies dancing in her stomach. Jose reached over and linked fingers with her. "So you never told me where we were going."

"It's a secret." He grinned.

It didn't take long for them to turn down a rural road dotted with older small houses with large yards. He pulled into the driveway of a two-story house, the white paint peeling in a few places. The grass was mowed, and the few shrubs near the porch were trimmed, but it was evident by the green stains on the porch posts that the shrubs had once been overgrown.

A separate garage was just to the right, and newer construction built a room that connected it to the house.

"Is this your place?" Her gaze swung back and forth, trying to take it all in.

"Yes," he admitted, his voice sounding unsure. "I know it's not much to look at, but I'm working on the place bit by bit. I haven't worried about the outside painting because I'm going to take the old clapboard off and install siding that will last for years. So I've mostly focused on the inside."

She looked over and saw his anxiety in how he shoved his hand through his hair. "I can't wait to see your home."

He grinned, and if she wasn't mistaken, a little sigh of relief escaped his lips. Once out of the vehicle, he linked fingers with her again, and they walked toward the front door.

"I want to hear all about what you've done," she said, excitement spearing through her.

"The front bushes had grown so tall that you couldn't even tell there was a front porch. Dad and Jimmy came over one day, and between the three of us, we managed to dig out some of the oldest ones that looked the worst and then trimmed back these. Right now, there's so much work to do on the inside that I just needed something functional on the outside."

They stepped on the front porch, and she clapped her hands at the sight of the porch swing. "A swing? Oh my God, it's perfect!" She turned toward him, her eyes bright. "Does it work?"

His smile dropped as his brows lowered. "Um... work? It's a swing, so... you have to sit on it and use your legs to make it swing..."

Laughter burst out as she felt her face heat. "God, that was such a dumb way for me to phrase my question, but I wish you could see your face!"

His chuckle joined hers. "Okay, so what exactly did you mean?"

"I just wondered if it was usable. Safe? If we sit on it, it won't fall down, will it?" She shook her head and groaned. "I think sometimes mommy-brain has sucked my ability to speak!"

"Come on," he said, tugging on her hand as he walked to the swing. Sitting, he gently pulled her down next to him and wrapped his arm around her. Pushing off with his foot on the wooden porch, he set the swing in motion.

She dragged in a breath before letting it out slowly as she peered over the yard, trying to blink away the threatening tears before he could notice. His arm tightened on her shoulder.

"What's the matter?" he asked.

Swallowing past the lump, she said, "My grandmother had a porch swing. I always used to sit on it with her and found that when I swung back and forth on it, all my troubles seemed to disappear. She and I would talk about everything. Stories of her growing up. Remembrances of my dad when he was little. What I wanted to be when I grew up. It was as though that porch swing was magical."

"Maybe it was the combination of the swing and the people on it," he said, drawing her gaze to his face.

She nodded slowly. "This is so peaceful, just like at her house. I'd never really thought about where you lived. But this place? It's a home."

He leaned over and kissed her lightly again, then pulled back and grinned. "Come on, let me show you the rest of the place." Standing, he once again guided her to the front door. Unlocking it, he ushered her inside.

She had expected small rooms in keeping with the house's era. But he had removed some walls, so she was impressed with how spacious it appeared. The refinished, original wooden floors flowed between the living room and dining room, taking up the entire front of the house. A wide arched doorway led from the dining room to the kitchen. He didn't have an excess of furniture, but the few pieces looked comfortable. An image of Suzette having a place to run and play hit her.

"I had an old coffee table in here but stored it in the garage. I thought it would be better for Suzette to have more space when she was here."

She bit her lip at how his thoughts had aligned so perfectly with hers. Turning toward him, she wrapped her arms around his waist and squeezed. "I think that's a great idea."

After a long hug, she loosened her arms so they could explore more. She could see where he was still working as they moved into the kitchen.

"The kitchen was small, and there was no family room. Upstairs, the three bedrooms were also small, with only one bathroom. I've extended the back of the house so that the kitchen would have a breakfast nook that overlooks the backyard, and there's room for a family room. Then that allowed me to expand the upstairs owner's bedroom and put in a separate, larger bathroom."

"Wow, I'm so impressed!"

"There's still a lot to do, but the space is closed, insulated, and drywall is hung. The electric outlets are in, and the HVAC system was upgraded for the extra space. But I haven't painted, and the enlarged bathroom has a working toilet, shower, and soaker tub. I just don't have it all finished yet."

"And the room between here in the garage?"

"That contains a laundry room, space for coats and boots, and makes it easier to bring items in, such as groceries from the vehicle and into the kitchen without being in the weather."

She turned around, eyes wide, then flung herself into his arms. "Jose, you're amazing! You saw this place, had a vision, and worked hard to make it your own."

Holding her tight, he peered down at her. "So you like it?"

"I love it!"

"Do you see it as a place where you and Suzette can be happy?"

She startled at his words, pushing away from him slightly. Her breath caught in her throat. "What exactly are you asking?"

He ducked his head, offering a nervous chuckle. "Let's eat first. There will be plenty of time to talk once I've wined and dined you."

She looked over at the kitchen counter, and the scent wafting from several bags had her salivating. "Oh, wow! If that's Chinese food, then I'll probably say yes to anything you ask."

Barking out laughter, he nodded as he led her over to the counter. "Good to know. I'll keep that in mind for future reference."

They took the food to the table and spread out the bounty. "I went for easy takeout tonight, but I really can cook. Mom made sure that was something all of us knew. She might seem old-fashioned at times, but she was adamant that Jimmy, Jonas, and I knew how to cook, clean up our messes, and do laundry. She also made sure that Rosemarie and Bethany knew how to mow the grass and change a tire."

She filled her plate with all her favorites and sat at his table. "Tell me about Jonas. He's in the Army, right?"

"Yeah. Probably will make it a career. It was me, as oldest, then Rosemarie. Jonas came next, followed by Jimmy, and then Bethany is considered the baby."

"Such a big family. I was an only child but always wanted siblings." She raised her eyebrows. "Although, five kids? Whew! I don't see how your mother did it!"

"As the eldest, sometimes I got tired of having to look after my siblings, but now I realize it wasn't so bad."

"Did you want to have kids?" The question slipped out even though she knew it was loaded.

He nodded slowly, his gaze pinned on her. "Yeah. I always figured I'd get married someday and have a family."

She pressed her lips together, nodding also. "Me, too."

They continued to eat, keeping the conversation lighter, but she couldn't help but notice the way his gaze lingered on her, lust occasionally flaring in his dark eyes.

Finally, she pushed her plate back and sighed in contentment. "I should feel guilty that I just ate my fill and didn't have to jump up once to take care of Suzette."

"No, you shouldn't," he admonished. "You've spent so much time taking care of others. You needed some time just for yourself." He sucked in a deep breath before letting it out slowly. "Speaking of doing for others, we need to talk about money."

She opened her mouth to protest, but he shook his head. "We don't have to dig into details now, but just know that I want to look at your expenses for Suzette, and we need to figure out how I can start paying for things. And that includes looking at health insurance."

She looked down, her thoughts crashing into each other. While it seemed strange to think of someone else being responsible for helping with the costs, she couldn't deny that the assistance would be good. Lifting her chin, she nodded. "You're right. But not tonight. I want tonight to be just for us and not for business."

"I wholeheartedly agree." He reached over and slid her hand in his as he stood, drawing her to her feet. She glanced down at the table, and he shook his head.

"There's time later to take care of the leftovers. I haven't finished showing you the house yet."

With their palms connected, he guided her to the staircase, then led her upward.

"Originally, there were three bedrooms and one bath. On one side of the house were the two smaller bedrooms. At the very back was the bathroom that was not much bigger than just room for a tub, a toilet, and a single cabinet and sink.

"This is the owner's bedroom," he said, opening the door on the left. She stepped inside, amazed at the spacious room. Glancing at the floor, she could see where the original wood floor met the not-yet stained new wood covering the expansion. A king-size bed was centered on the back wall, with a comfortable leather chair in one corner. The tall chest of drawers sat on the wall next to the closet, and there was still wall space for another dresser to be added in the future. The closet door was open, and she could see it had also been expanded.

Continuing to follow him, she stepped into the owner's bathroom and gasped. "This is as large as my apartment bedroom!"

A large shower filled the back corner. It had been tiled and appeared functional, except it was missing the glass doors. He had fashioned a shower curtain to make it usable, but she imagined it would be beautiful once the glass doors were installed. The soaker tub was modern, and a vision of her sitting in a tub filled with bubbles almost made her want to insist she try it out right then.

The double sink cabinet was in but still awaiting the counter and sinks.

"This room should be finished in about two weeks," he said. "Until then, I've been using the hall bathroom."

She walked over and wrapped her arms around him, pressing close while leaning her head back to hold his gaze. "Your house is beautiful, Jose. Absolutely beautiful."

She kept her eyes open so she could see his face until it blurred when his lips met hers. The sparks only took a second to flame, and the kiss deepened. She tasted the wine and spices as his tongue danced with hers, and he pulled her tighter against his chest.

At this moment, nothing mattered except the connection they had and were building. No interruptions. No worries about Suzette. No trying to analyze the past or being afraid for the future.

Her fingers grasped his shirt, and she lifted on her toes. He was so much taller than her, and she gasped when he scooped her up into his arms, carrying her carefully out of the bathroom and into the bedroom.

She hoped he would go straight to the bed, but he stopped in the middle of the room and lowered her feet to the floor. Their mouths now separated, and a small groan escaped from her. He lifted his head and peered down, his dark eyes almost black as his gaze roved over her face. She could feel his erection pressing against her stomach as their bodies remained tightly aligned.

"There's too much at stake for me to fuck anything up," he said, his voice low as the words seemed pulled from deep inside. Swallowing audibly, he glanced over her shoulder toward the bed. "I want you. I want this... tonight... between us. But if you're not ready or think we are not at the right place for this, then all you need to say is—"

"I want you," she rushed. Desperation filled her at the idea that he was talking himself out of what she needed and hoped for.

His brows lifted, and she pushed forward. "I don't want to talk about the past right now. I don't want to think about any other woman you've ever had before me. I don't want you to think about my life before we met. Our past relationships and friends will always be part of us. We can't escape that fact. But right now, I just want to be the woman you're interested in. The woman who could be more than a one-night stand. The woman who's more than Suzette's mom."

"Oh, Melanie, baby. I'm not interested in just one night with you. Not just a physical release. Not even close."

"Then what are we waiting for?"

He grinned and shook his head slowly. "All I was waiting for was the confirmation that you felt the same way I did."

Laughing, she lifted on her toes again. "Then you've got it. You, me, and that king-size bed over there. I can't think of anything else I need right now."

"Thank God," he murmured against her lips as he picked her up again.

Prepared to be tossed onto the bed, she gasped as he twirled her in the center of the room instead. Laughter erupted in the middle of their kiss as she clung to his shoulders.

As he slowed his movements, she was unaware they had made it to the edge of the bed. Instead of lowering her feet to the floor as he had earlier, he bent forward, still holding her body with one arm, and planted the other on the mattress. Ever so gently, he laid her back, the kiss never breaking. Rolling to the side, they faced each other, feasting on the knowledge they were finally ready to take their relationship further.

At first, they focused on their kiss, with their arms wrapped around each other and their legs entwined. But her breasts grew heavy, and her core began to ache. She felt the pressure of his erection digging against her mound. As her need increased, she wanted more action and fewer clothes.

He'd worn a dress shirt, and while one of her arms was trapped underneath his head, she fumbled with her free hand until his shirt was unbuttoned. She tried to drag the material over his shoulder, but his body kept it trapped.

She groaned in frustration as she angled her head to keep their tongues exploring together but was unable to remove their clothes.

His hand drifted down to cup her breast, and she felt his thumb drag over her nipple. Her wrap dress had a deep V, and his fingers slipped underneath the material, tracing the top of her bra. Excitement and the cool air made her nipple pebble even harder when he tugged the bra cup down. He kissed along her jaw and neck, sucking and nibbling before dragging his tongue over the plump flesh, then latching onto the nipple, pulling it deep into his mouth.

Sparks had fired with the simple touch of their hands, but the sensation seemed dim compared to what she now felt with his mouth on her breast. If lightning were striking the room, she wouldn't have been surprised.

He lifted his head and peered down at her, eliciting a sad mewl at the loss of his mouth on her tender flesh.

"I really want you out of this dress, but it looks complicated."

Grinning, she separated from his arms and slipped from the bed. Standing, she bit her lip and peered down, seeing his dark eyes pinned on her. She pulled the tie at the side of her waist, and the front of her dress fell open, exposing a small snap on the inside. Popping it loose, she shrugged, and the dress fell off her shoulders and puddled onto the floor.

Eyes wide, he grinned and shook his head. "I swear that dress is magic. You barely did anything, and it fell off."

Laughing again, she said, "Do you like it?"

"Hell, every man in the world would like that dress on the woman they're trying to strip."

His hot gaze raked down her as she stood in a demi bra and satin panties. They weren't a set, but she'd never worried about matching lingerie before. She knew they both fit beautifully and showcased her curves, something he seemed to appreciate.

He sat up on the bed, and when he reached for her, she stepped back ever so slowly, wagging her finger in front of him. With a deft move, she unsnapped her front-clasp bra and shrugged it off as well. Lifting her thumbs over the elastic of her panties, she dragged them down her legs until she stood completely nude in front of him.

With sex partners in the past, this was always the moment when she felt the most vulnerable. When a man looked at her naked body, she wondered if her breasts were the size he liked or if her ass was tight enough. She'd lost a little weight since becoming a full-time mom, but it never seemed to drop from the parts of her body she thought needed it the most.

His gaze seared a path over her, and he slid off the bed, standing in front of her. "You are so fucking beautiful, Melanie. You are the most beautiful woman I've ever seen. Inside and out. Absolutely beautiful."

She smiled, his words chasing away the insecurity and strengthening her desire. Cocking her head slightly, she stepped closer. "You're overdressed."

"Do you plan on doing something about that?" he asked as she grabbed both sides of his shirt and pushed the material back.

Now unencumbered, the material easily fell behind him and dropped onto the floor. "Oh, hell yeah!" Her fingers went to his belt buckle, but her eyes remained glued to his naked torso.

Jose didn't have bodybuilder muscles upon muscles, which she'd never found appealing anyway. He was tall with lean muscles that gave evidence of his strength.

Diverted by the temptation, she ran her hands over his ripped abs, giving new meaning to the idea of a washboard. Going back to her original plan, she finished unbuckling his belt, barely able to drag the zipper of his pants down over his erection.

"You keep licking your lips like that, and I'm going to give you something to do with them."

Her gaze jerked up to his face, and she blushed. She hadn't even realized she had licked her lips, but it seemed he didn't miss anything.

Grinning, she now hooked her thumbs in his pants and started dragging them downward, careful not to snag his erection, but as soon as his cock came into view, her eyes widened.

He chuckled and said, "While you look, I'll take it from here." He toed off his shoes and finished shucking his pants and boxers, making quick work of his socks at the same time.

Standing straight again, they stood completely naked, their eyes devouring each other.

"You're gorgeous," she said. "Lean and muscular and tall, and your eyes feel as though they can see straight into me."

"You're gorgeous, too," he said, grinning. "Smooth, taut muscles and soft curves. And when I stare into your eyes, I feel as though all the goodness in the world looks back at me."

Her grin met his as the scant space between them erased, and she jumped into his arms. He twisted toward the bed, laying her back down again. Only this time, he crawled over her. With his hands planted on the mattress on either side of her head and his knees on either side of hers, his long cock pressed at the apex of her thighs.

He lowered his body while tilting his head and sealing his mouth over hers. Once more, the room crackled with the lightning she'd felt earlier. He slowly moved down her body, kissing, nipping, sucking, teasing, and tantalizing over her breasts and down her stomach until he lifted her legs over his shoulders and buried his face against her sex.

Gasping at the sensation rocking through her body, she clutched the bed covers until the desperation to feel him sent her fingers into his hair. He worked her body as he licked and sucked, and a coil deep inside tightened. Filled with the need for tension to ease, she lifted her hips as she urged him on. He slipped a finger deep inside as he sucked on the bundle of nerves. That was all she needed for the coil to spring and her release to rush over her. Crying out, she couldn't believe how hard she came from just his mouth.

She floated on the cloud for a moment as he licked her folds and finally kissed his way back up over her body. Her eyelids were heavy, but she was determined to open them. And when she did, his dark eyes stared down at her with an intensity she always felt from the moment she'd met him. The warmth now threatened to consume her. And she was happy to go up in flames.

22

Jose could not believe how responsive Melanie's body was or, for that matter, how much his body craved hers. Going down on a woman had not been something he usually did. For him, it was an intensely personal act that he wasn't willing to give for a one-night stand. And previous girlfriends had had varying responses, finding that some women loved it while others seemed just to endure it.

But with Melanie, he didn't hesitate, and her uninhibited response had fired his blood, making his cock even harder than he thought possible.

He reached for a condom that he'd stored in his nightstand, hoping they would have the opportunity to use it. But he also hesitated, the fact that they aren't one-hundred percent effective against pregnancy slamming into him.

He rolled it on, but his jaw was tight, finding the words choked in his throat, not wanting to do anything to remind Melanie that he'd been with her best friend a year earlier.

But like everything with Melanie, she was easy and honest. And intuitive. Her fingers gripped his forearms, drawing his gaze to her face.

"It's okay. I understand. But to ease your mind, I'm clean and on the pill. I have pretty rotten cramps, so I've been on the pill for years to help with them."

The tension around his chest eased, and he stared down at the most beautiful woman he'd ever seen, humbled and awed that she was here with him.

Smiling as he bent and kissed her again, her hands slid up his biceps and curled around his shoulders. She opened herself to him, and he reached down to guide the tip of his cock to her entrance before slowly sheathing himself. Her inner muscles were tight, but as he continued to thrust slowly, he was struck with a feeling... it felt like coming home.

Her eyes stayed open, shining as a smile played about her lips. She groaned her encouragement, and he began to thrust, slowly at first, and then, as her breath hitched, he moved faster and faster. She wrapped her legs around his hips, urging him with her heels pressed against his ass. Her breasts bounced slightly, rubbing against his naked chest.

His movements increased until he was pounding into her. Barely aware of anything but his own need firing his blood, he kept his eyes on her. But her smile widened, and her fingers dug in deeply as she cried out for more.

He shifted his body so that one hand could cup a

breast, lifting it so the nipple was presented like a gift he wasn't about to refuse. He began to suck in time to his thrusts, and with her body shattering underneath his, she cried out her release. He let go of her breast and kissed over her jaw to her mouth again as she dragged in air.

Sparks turned into flames.

Then with his eyes closed and his body tight, his own orgasm hit him as he continued to slam into her until every drop had left his body.

Flames turned into an inferno.

He collapsed on top of her with no finesse, shifting his arms enough to link his fingers with hers but unable to do much else. After a moment, he realized he must be crushing her and rolled to the side. She sucked in a deep breath and then laughed.

His eyes flew open, and he said, "Shit, babe, I didn't mean to crush you."

"It's okay," she said. "I love the feel of your body pressing into mine."

"Yeah, but I didn't want to suffocate you."

"Well, first of all, what a way to go. And second of all, I promise I would've said something if you were too heavy."

They lay side by side, more words failing as they simply focused on breathing while their hearts pounded.

And the inferno slowly became smoldering embers.

Eventually, when consciousness returned, he gently pulled out, kissed her deeply, then mumbled, "I'll be right back."

He headed off to take care of the condom, then returned to find her sitting up in bed. The sated smile on her face was soft, and he longed to do whatever he could to keep that very same expression on her face often.

"I would love to do nothing more than lay here in bed with you, making love all night long," she said.

He sat next to her and pulled her into his arms. Resting his chin on the top of her head, he nodded. "I was just thinking the same thing."

They sat together for a while, their bodies cooling. Finally, as though they both knew their date night was slowly ending, they stood and dressed.

"You never told me what you meant by your question earlier," she said.

He walked over and stood in front of her, lifting his hands to cup her face. With their gazes locked on each other, he said, "I asked if you could see you and Suzette being here in this house."

She pressed her lips together, rubbing them gently, before speaking. "It's easy to say yes, I can. You have a beautiful home. You have enough rooms that Suzette could have one all to herself. You have a fenced-in yard and a porch swing. You have a garage that would allow us to get her in and out of a vehicle in bad weather without her getting wet." She pressed her lips together again. "I guess the question doesn't quite make sense to me. Because, of course, I could see us being here. But what I don't know is exactly what you're asking. Are you looking for a way for us to co-parent by you having room here for Suzette to spend the night sometimes and have a place to run around and play?"

He was filled with many emotions he wanted to convey but was uncertain how to say them correctly. "What about you? Could you be happy here?"

Their bodies were pressed together, yet all he could focus on were her eyes peering up at him. He waited, anxiety sending his heart pounding almost as much as his release had.

"Yes," she said, nodding against his palm still holding her cheek. "I could be happy here. It seems too soon, but I don't feel rushed. I can't imagine what other people would think of us doing that after knowing each other for barely a month. Yet I'm certain I want to be with you."

The breath rushed from his lungs, and his smile widened. "You don't have to make any promises now, Melanie. I just wanted to know if this is going in the direction that I see it going."

"You, me, and Suzette. Together. That's the direction I want us to focus on. And not because you're her biological father. And I don't want the offer to be because you feel I need to be thrown into the bargain for you to be able to be with her."

He shook his head. "I think you and I are beyond that, now, don't you?"

She grinned and nodded. "Yes. I want you, for you."

"And I want you, for you." He released her face but pulled her in tighter so that her cheek was against his heartbeat. He looked around the room and knew more work still needed to be done. "Let's go downstairs. I have dessert in the refrigerator, and we can talk some more before it's time to pick up Suzette."

A few minutes later, they were in the kitchen, and she squealed in delight as he pulled out a chocolate cake. "My mom brought this over earlier," he said.

Taking a huge bite, she moaned, licking her lips. "This might just be better than sex—ow! You pinched me!"

"Do you want to amend your previous statement?" he asked, one eyebrow lifted in mock anger.

She tapped her finger on her chin, pretending to think. "Okay, fine. Sex with you is the best. But your mom's chocolate cake is definitely in the running as one of my favorite things."

"Duly noted." He laughed.

Once they finished eating and put away the dishes and the leftovers, he wrapped his arms around her again. "Here's the deal, babe. I still have some work on this house to make it the kind of place that I feel would be safe. I have a few outlets that don't have the covers on them. I need to stain the floors upstairs in the main bedroom, and I don't want Suzette around those fumes. I also need to finish painting upstairs, the counters and sinks are supposed to come in, and I also don't want her around when I've got tools and friends here that might end up leaving something out, like a nail or a screwdriver."

She nodded with emphasis. "Absolutely agree! But I also don't want you to work yourself to the bone. She and I are fine in the apartment for now. That also gives us a chance to keep spending time together as a couple and a family before moving in."

"Well, I won't be willing to have this last much longer. I figure in about two weeks at the most with friends and family helping, I'll have everything done well enough that you guys can move in."

She smiled as her arms tightened around his waist. Tilting her head back to hold his gaze, she asked, "So, Jose Martinez, are you officially asking me to move in?"

He barked out a laugh. "Absolutely, Ms. Landers. You're already in my heart, and so is Suzette. So now I want you both in my house, and *you* in my bed."

"I like the sound of that."

"I know we've got to go get her, but how about another kiss for the road?" Bending, he thought to keep the kiss gentle, but the sparks erupted once more, and he devoured her mouth. Finally, they separated, chests heaving as they both gasped for air. "Damn, girl. We keep kissing like that, and I'll change my mind and move you guys in tonight."

Laughing, she danced out of his arms, giving them the space needed to cool off. "Come on, let's get back and rescue your parents. She's probably fussed the whole time."

"If I know my parents, we'll be rescuing Suzette from them. They probably haven't set her down all evening."

With arms wrapped around each other, they walked out to his SUV. It took extra minutes to collect Suzette because it seemed as though everyone had a good time.

Suzette was snoozing in Mary's arms, and Carlos plied them with tales of how much fun they'd had.

It was late, and as much as Jose hated to say good-bye, he managed to get them back to her apartment, get Suzette into bed without waking her, and then kiss Melanie goodbye at her door.

Sitting in his SUV, he looked up to see the curtain flutter in the apartment three down from Melanie's as though someone was looking out at him. With his gaze trained on them, the curtain dropped. While that was nothing sinister in and of itself, he wanted to get them out of this apartment building as quickly as possible.

Driving away, he felt he was leaving his heart behind and was determined to finish his house as quickly as possible. Because if there was one thing he knew... until they moved in, his house wasn't really a home.

23

Melanie stepped outside her apartment when she heard the sound of the rickety folding chair scraping along the concrete breezeway. She didn't want to keep the older chair in her apartment, afraid Suzette might get hurt even though she wasn't crawling yet. Throwing open the door to greet Trey, she was surprised to see Ricky's uncle standing just outside her door.

"Oh!" She startled. "I'm sorry. I thought you were Trey."

"Nah. I saw him get this chair, so I've been watching to see what he was doing."

She knew that was a lie, considering this man had stood outside smoking and scowling at her several times when she'd been working with the boys. But from the size of him and the glare he cast her way, she wasn't about to call him out on his fib. "Well, thank you for setting it up for me."

"What are you gettin' out of this?"

She blinked, uncertain of what he meant. "I'm

sorry?"

"You ain't doing this for nothing. Uppity bitch living in a place like this. I just wanted to know what your game was."

"I assure you I don't have any game other than living my life."

He took another drag of his cigarette. "You're a teacher?"

"Yes. I'll be at the high school this year."

"I don't want you filling his head full of shit."

Anger fired through her, but with her daughter asleep in the bedroom, she wasn't about to poke the bear of this large man who looked as though he not only could break her in half but was thinking about it. "The last thing I want to do is fill anyone's head with *shit*. But to graduate from high school next year, he needs to pass the state exam in biology. I'm helping him to obtain that goal."

The man snorted, then looked out over the parking lot before turning his scowl back at her. "You're just making him think he's got a shot in life."

"Ricky's smart. He does have a shot in life—"

"He ain't going to be nothing other than what he needs to be."

She waited, afraid yet sure that he was going to say she could not work with Ricky anymore. She remained quiet, trying to steady her breathing in a failing effort to calm her anger.

Suddenly, a noise from the steps sounded, and she looked over as Trey came bounding up the steps. Ricky followed at his usual steady pace. As soon as they got to the top, they smiled at her, then their gazes swung over to Ricky's uncle. Anger flashed through Trey's eyes, along with a healthy dose of fear. She prayed he wouldn't say anything to make the tense situation worse. Trey was smart, but his enthusiasm sometimes got in the way of discretion. But in this case, it appeared self-preservation prevailed.

He avoided Ricky's uncle's glare and moved over to her, picking up the book before sitting on the steps. He busied himself, flipping through the pages, but she could feel his nervousness.

"Good morning, Trey. Good morning, Ricky," she greeted, hoping her voice was not as shaky as it sounded. Ricky stared at his uncle, and, seeing them together, she realized that Ricky was as tall and broad as his uncle. And while his uncle had appeared so intimidating, Ricky had never used his size to do so.

Ricky's face showed no emotion as he continued the stare down. Finally, his uncle tossed the cigarette butt over the edge of the railing to the parking lot. "Bunch of pussies," he muttered.

He turned and went back into his apartment, then Ricky swung his gaze over to her. She forced her lips into a smile she'd practiced many times before. She'd only been a high school teacher for a few years, but this wasn't the first tense situation she'd ever been in. She'd occasionally had to wade in to stop a fight, calm someone's anger, and deal with a student's sadness.

"Are you ready, Ricky? I thought today we'd take one of the practice tests to give you a feel for what it'll be like in a few weeks."

She held his gaze, seeing mixed emotions swimming in his eyes. Anger. Guilt. Frustration. She prayed he wasn't going to react to his uncle calling them pussies and decide to walk away. Time seemed to stand still as she waited, noticing even Trey kept his mouth shut as he looked up between them.

Finally, Ricky dipped his chin. "Yeah, Ms. Landers. That'd be good."

She sat on the chair, glad her knees hadn't given out earlier. Pulling out pencils and copies of the old state tests that had been released for students to practice with, she handed them to both. She sat quietly as they worked, and with each moment Ricky's uncle stayed in the apartment and did not reappear, she felt calmer. Since the boys were working on their practice tests and not talking, it gave her mind a chance to wander.

She imagined Jose's house and another smile curved her lips. She could see placing a few of her pieces of furniture there. She imagined the smaller bedroom being turned into a nursery for Suzette. The idea of a larger kitchen with a full-size stove where she could bake cookies filled her mind. She could see them there as a family. Suzette learning to crawl on Jose's floors and playing in the backyard.

And she thought of the king-size bed in the owner's bedroom and felt her cheeks heat. Jerking her gaze back down, she saw Ricky was almost finished with the test.

She was ready to get out of this apartment even though she'd only been here a short time. She wanted something better for Suzette. But looking at the two boys, she wanted something better for them, too.

Trey didn't worry her as much even though he had a follower's personality. He had a loving mom and seemed to have found a good friend to follow in Ricky.

Ricky was strong, not only physically but also mentally, and had a protector's instincts. But knowing about his father and having met his uncle, she could imagine that he'd been told he was no better than them for so long and wondered if it had settled deeply into each crevice of his soul. She now suspected he struggled to find a way to improve.

Ricky finished, and not too long after, Trey did also. She graded the tests, then smiled at both, clapping. "You both passed!"

Trey immediately leaped to his feet, dancing around and waving his arms, not caring that he didn't look like a cool teenage boy. On the other hand, Ricky remained still, but his eyes lit with a spark she hadn't seen since she'd met him.

While Trey continued his impromptu celebration, she leaned forward to hold Ricky's attention. "You can be whatever you want to be. I say that knowing that sometimes life is about not only taking chances but having opportunities presented to you. But I will say this... if you graduate from high school and want to join the Navy, you can do it."

He remained silent for a moment, swallowing deeply. Then he said, "That man who's been coming around to see you. He looks like the military."

She nodded slowly and said, "He's been in the Navy."

She saw the spark flare larger in his eyes and continued. "He works... well, he still works on the water. If you want, I'll have him talk to you sometime about what it would be like in the Navy."

She wasn't sure why she didn't mention that he was in law enforcement other than she had a feeling that would shut Ricky down. But if she could get Jose to meet Ricky, she felt sure it would make a difference in the young man's life.

"You know, Ricky, you don't have to work with your uncle," Trey said, a hopeful expression on his face. "I mean, you don't gotta do what he says when you turn eighteen. You don't gotta—"

"Shut up, Trey," Ricky growled.

Trey quieted, but his brows lowered as he pouted.

Melanie hadn't seen his uncle going and coming as though he had a job. Certainly not one during the day. Curious, she asked, "What kind of work does your uncle do?"

"Boats." Trey snorted. "He works with boats—"

"Shut up, Trey," Ricky repeated. This time, the harshness of his voice increased. "You don't gotta talk so much."

"Well, maybe if he works with boats, that's where your interest in the Navy comes from," she said, trying to understand why Ricky didn't want Trey to talk about his uncle's job.

Ricky snorted. "Yeah, sure." His hands fisted at his sides as a tic appeared in his jaw. Instead of looking at her or Trey, he stared out over the parking lot.

"Sorry," Trey mumbled, then turned his puppy-dog eyes toward her. Unable to stay upset for more than a moment, he finally grinned and said, "I'm gonna tell my mom that I passed your practice test."

"Well, hang on. I made something for you two." She hurried inside and grabbed the plastic container filled with cookies from the counter before returning to the doorway. "Here you go. Make sure to share them."

"Cookies!" Tray exclaimed, his hands reaching forward as he bounced on his toes. He popped open the top and looked down. "Homemade cookies! You made these for us?"

Glad that the earlier tension had been cut, she nodded.

Ricky peered down into the container, and then his gaze shot back up to her. "How did you know we would pass the practice test?"

She held his gaze for a long moment, feeling the strong young man in front of her wavering in his attempts to stay unaffected. "I knew how hard you had worked. I knew how much you'd learned. And while you won't succeed the first time in everything you do, I knew you wouldn't give up. So I made the cookies to celebrate because I knew you would pass."

Trey already had one half eaten and was trying to shove in another one. But Ricky just stared at her.

"Come on, man. You've got to have one! They're even better than my mom's!" Trey exclaimed.

Without taking his eyes off her, Ricky reached into the container, pulled out a cookie, then took a bite and chewed slowly, as if savoring each morsel. Swallowing, he said, "Ain't nobody ever baked cookies for me before."

"Just because something hasn't happened in the past doesn't mean it can't happen in the future. Remember that, Ricky. You have a chance to rewrite your story's ending. Do you want the Navy? Then you write your story so that you can make that happen."

Ricky's gaze still did not waver.

"Huh?" Trey said, his mouth half full. "Are we going to have to start writing for you now?"

She smiled and shook her head. "No, Trey. We're just doing biology. I thought maybe Ricky needed to hear a little extra."

Ricky nodded, then finished his cookie.

She gathered their papers. "Well, that's it for today."

As she stood, Trey, still celebrating his success, wrapped his thin arms around her and hugged her. "I know you're a teacher, but you're the first teacher in a long time that cared this much about me. And my mom says sometimes a hug is just what you need."

As his arms let go, his smile was wide, and her heart squeezed. She glanced up at Ricky to see him smiling with affection at his exuberant friend and, for once, not rolling his eyes. He stepped forward and thrust out his hand.

"Thank you, Ms. Landers."

She blinked back tears from the handshake that was as warm as a hug from Trey.

"Just because you two passed today doesn't mean we're finished. We still have some work to do to ensure you can pass the state exam, so I'll see you two in a few days."

Trey waved goodbye and headed back down the

steps, carrying the folding chair. She stepped back, but instead of leaving, she turned to look at Ricky, who was still standing in place. She grabbed a piece of paper and scribbled a phone number on it. Walking over, she thrust it forward. He took it, glancing down before lifting his gaze, waiting.

"There's something I didn't mention earlier," she said. Pressing her lips together, she rubbed them back and forth while second-guessing herself. Finally, pushing forward, she said, "The man I'm seeing was in the Navy, and he still works on the water. But I didn't tell you that he works for the Virginia Marine Police."

She saw Ricky startle and rushed, "I didn't say that earlier because... because... I didn't want it to make a difference if you decided to talk to him." Ricky stayed stone-still, and she was terrified her words might push him away. "If it doesn't matter to you what his job is, then you'll contact him so that you can talk about the Navy. If it does matter, for whatever reason, then just remember that talking to him might be the first step in rewriting your story."

He held her gaze unflinching for a long time, his fingers clenching and unclenching. Finally, he lifted his chin before following Trey down the stairs.

With a huge sigh, she had no idea whether she had made a difference. Rubbing her forehead, she decided that getting them to pass the state exam in biology would have to be enough. She stepped inside just in time for Suzette to wake up from her nap.

24

Jose sat at his table, smiling down at Suzette in his arms. Melanie had insisted on cooking, and with someone else taking care of Suzette, she had gifted him with a dinner of roast beef, homemade au gratin potatoes, and green beans with almond slivers.

At first, they hadn't been able to talk much while she fixed dinner and he entertained Suzette. But once she latched onto her bottle, Melanie had been able to tell him about her day.

"So you can see why I'm concerned about the boys," she said.

He had taken the opportunity to check with Hunter to find out more about the situation, another reason he wanted Melanie to move into his house as soon as she could. "I know the principal told you that his dad was in prison and that his uncle wasn't much better, but I have more information about them now."

Eyes wide, she looked over. "You do?"

"I know you accepted the only apartment you could get right away, but some of the people I've seen there have records. I wanted to make sure I knew what we were dealing with."

She leaned back in her chair, her brow scrunched. "I'm not sure how I feel about that, but I'd be stupid to turn down your interest and your professional ability to find things out. What can you tell me? I feel like anything I know can only help me with Ricky and Trey."

"What Trey's mom told you is right. Trey's dad was killed in a car accident when Trey was only six years old. Since then, his mom has worked full-time, sometimes two jobs, to give Trey what he needs."

"My only fear for Trey is that he's more of a follower than a leader. Yet I have to say, his choice of friends with Ricky is smart. Because Ricky is a really good guy."

"Yes... for now."

"What do you mean, *for now?*" She winced, and they glanced at Suzette's wide eyes peering at her over the bottle. "Sorry, I didn't mean to bite your head off and scare her."

He chuckled. "That's okay. You're passionate about these kids. Ricky's dad, Curtis, has been in prison for about four years. He was involved in a local gang, arrested, and convicted of armed robbery. His brother, Cory, Ricky's uncle, was also at the scene, but it was never proven that he had a weapon or was actively involved in the holdup. Ricky's mom died of an overdose when he was five. So saying he wasn't raised in a very nurturing home wouldn't be a stretch."

"And that's why he lives with his uncle."

Jose nodded.

"I don't trust his uncle."

Jose snorted. "And you shouldn't. Honestly, Cory may even be worse than Curtis. But so far, he's been able to stay out of jail for whatever he's been involved in."

"I just don't want to see Ricky fall into the trap of perpetuating the same mistakes over and over," she groaned. After a moment, she sighed and crinkled her nose. "I did something I probably shouldn't have, and I need to tell you about it."

He looked at her but didn't say anything as he waited with a lifted brow.

"Because Ricky had been asking about the Navy, and I told him you'd served in the Navy, I said that you would talk to him sometime if he wanted."

"Sure, that's no problem."

"Well, there's more. At first, I didn't reveal your current job, but that didn't seem fair. So I told him that you worked for the Virginia Marine Police, and he could call you if he ever had anything he needed to talk to you about."

Jose held her gaze, then his lips twitched. "You gave him my phone number, didn't you?"

"Oh, that wasn't good of me, was it?" Her nose scrunched again, and he thought it was adorable.

Chuckling, he shrugged. "Don't worry about it. Chances are, he's already tossed my phone number in the trash. But if he ever decides to call, I'll be glad to talk to him about the Navy."

She leaned forward, her hands clasped together on top of the table. "And if he wants to talk to you about anything else?"

"Sweetheart, if he calls and wants to tell me what his uncle is up to, I'll be glad to pass that on to the sheriff's department."

She leaned back, seeming to struggle. He waited, knowing she would speak when she was ready.

"You know," she finally said. "I love being able to influence young people. But sometimes, I just can't always tell if I'm getting through to them."

"Teachers get to see a lot of instant gratification," Jose said, bouncing Suzette slightly. "You teach them something, and they pass a test, so you feel like they've learned something. But many times, the words you say to them need to settle deep inside before they're ready to take them in and then make a change. You might not ever see it, but don't doubt how much your words would mean to someone."

She smiled, then stood and grabbed the now empty plates. "If you keep holding her, I'll clean up."

He looked down at his daughter in his arms as she clapped her hands and then batted them on the table. "Holding her is easy." He glanced over to watch as Melanie hummed while puttering in the kitchen. *And taking care of you is easy, too.*

When she made her way back to the table, he stood, and they walked into the living room together. She spread a blanket on the floor, and they both sat, letting Suzette lay on her back and look up at the toy bar that hung over her. She batted and kicked with the multicol-ored objects dangling down.

"I wanted to talk to you about something," he said. "And I'm not going to lie and pretend it doesn't have something to do with what we've just discussed."

She was sitting cross-legged and looked up to hold his gaze. "Okay, I'm intrigued."

"We said that we'd wait until I got more work done on my place before you two move in. In the past week, I've had some friends over, and Jimmy and my dad helped, too."

She smiled and nodded. "I can tell. I took a sneak peek upstairs and saw that you had the bedrooms and the bathrooms painted, and your floor stained. I was stunned at how much work you'd accomplished."

"I just don't want to wait any longer." He held his breath, wondering what she would say, fearing that she thought it might be too soon or that she wasn't comfortable until the house was absolutely finished.

Instead, he saw her eyes light as her smile widened and beam toward him. "I have to confess that I've been thinking the same thing."

They were sitting on opposite sides of Suzette on the floor, but both leaned forward, kissing each other lightly before settling back.

"I know you wanted us to wait, and I certainly wouldn't consider moving in before the painting and floor finishing was complete. But Suzette won't be crawling for a little while, and even when she does, we can easily keep her out of certain areas with baby gates."

"I don't have this Friday off, but Dad said he'd come

over and be here while the granite contractors bring in the counter and sink for the upstairs bathrooms. Once that's in, then I can make sure all the electric plates are screwed on, and Rosemarie was bringing a bunch of electric socket plugs for keeping little fingers out."

She nodded and said, "We can certainly go around and make sure the place is baby-proof."

"Jesus, that makes me nervous. But I can't wait until you two are here with me." Her expression grew pensive as she glanced to the side, the crease between her brow deepening. Usually waiting until she was ready to talk to him, he couldn't wait. "What's wrong?"

Her head jerked upward, and she sighed. "Nothing. I mean nothing about me and Suzette moving here. I'm ready to get out of the tiny apartment even though I've only lived there a month. I'm ready to take our relationship to the next level. It'll be nice to be home when you get in at the end of the day."

"But…?"

Her shoulders rounded as she admitted, "I just feel weird leaving Trey and Ricky." Giving her head a little shake, she amended, "Not so much Trey, even though I love being around him. But he has his mom, and his grandparents are nearby."

"It's Ricky, isn't it?"

As she nodded slowly, he felt her anxiety.

"It's been so slow and subtle, but I feel like I've made a difference with Ricky, and staying there, seeing him often, I think I might have a chance to make that difference more permanent. There's another month before school starts, and I'm afraid that whatever is going on with him and his uncle, in the month before I can see him again in school, I'll lose whatever gains I have attained."

"Will you still want to tutor them?"

"Yes. They will re-take the state assessment at the end of the summer."

"Then at least, you'll be able to keep seeing them a couple of times a week. But I don't want you back over at the apartment building. I just don't think it's safe." He waited for her to argue, but surprisingly, she didn't. Instead, a visible shiver ran through her.

"I never felt unsafe there until recently. I mean, all kinds of people live there. And most seem really friendly. But I must admit that Ricky's uncle was very unpleasant."

"Unpleasant? How?" he growled.

"He stopped me when I went outside for tutoring before the boys came up—"

"Are you serious? He approached you?"

She nodded, and her nose scrunched as though remembering something unpleasant.

"Babe, tell me what happened."

"Nothing bad. It's just he was rude and insinuated that it was ridiculous that I was helping Ricky. I could tell he's the type who would rather his nephew drop out of school than actually put in the work to graduate."

"Let's go back to him being rude to you," Jose said, feeling the heat of anger rising. It was hard for his brain to move past anything other than Ricky's uncle had been threatening.

"Jose, I don't need you fighting my battles for me."

"So you're saying there is a battle?"

"Will you stop putting words in my mouth!"

"Melanie, tell me what he said."

She huffed and rolled her eyes. "Well, he called me an uppity... " She looked down at Suzette babbling as she continued to play with the toys, then looked back up and whispered, "The b-word. And he told me he didn't want me filling Ricky's head with...um... stuff."

"I don't want you around him. We need to get you out of there ASAP. You and Suzette can stay here tonight and—"

"Jose, stop. You're scaring me."

He sucked in a deep breath and let it out slowly, then closed his eyes for a moment, working to find a sliver of peace. Opening his eyes, he stared at the beautiful woman staring back. Reaching over, he linked hands with her. "I don't want to scare you, but I do want you to be cautious, aware, and even suspicious. The robbery that Curtis is now incarcerated for wasn't their first brush with the law. And undoubtedly, it won't be the last from what it sounds like. I suppose it's a miracle they haven't influenced Ricky."

"It sounded to me that Ricky doesn't want to be around his uncle. Or at least doesn't want to work for him."

"Cory Montgomery doesn't have a job."

"Well, I haven't seen him go in and out as he does, but I figured he might work at night. I think he might work in fishing around here somewhere."

"What makes you say that?"

"Well," she said, chewing on her bottom lip. "Maybe he works on boats."

"Boats?" He scrubbed his free hand over his face. "Where did this come from?"

"It was something Trey said. Trey told Ricky that he didn't have to work with his uncle. He commented that Ricky wouldn't have to do what his uncle says as soon as he turns eighteen. Ricky got upset and told Trey to stop talking. I was curious because I didn't realize Ricky had a job. So I asked him what his uncle did. Trey was the one who answered and just said he works with boats. Once again, Ricky shushed him. Trey gets so exuberant that sometimes he talks without thinking. Anyway, nothing else was said, and we went on with our lesson."

They were silent for a moment, as the only sound was Suzette kicking her legs to hit the squeaky toys. Melanie scooped up her daughter, placing her in her lap and bouncing her lightly.

He watched the two of them, his heart aching at the sight of his daughter and the woman he'd fallen for. "I no longer feel that your apartment is safe. For whatever reason, you've gotten on Cory's radar. I don't like that, babe. And I'd rather act precipitously and get you with me than live with regret later."

She pressed her lips together, rubbing them slightly, and he knew she was pondering what he said. Finally, she nodded. "Okay. I agree. But we can't do it tonight. I need to have her crib, and formula, and bottles, and—"

"Okay, then I'm going back with you and will stay there tonight."

She laughed. "Honey, you've seen my twin-sized bed. We won't fit."

"I can sleep on the sofa."

"It's not long enough." When it looked like she might argue, he cut her off. "Melanie, it's happening. I swear there won't be a lot of times that I'll put my foot down, but when it comes to your safety, then I will."

She held his gaze, and her lips slowly curved upward. "Okay."

A whoosh of air left his lungs, and he chuckled. "You're easy."

She burst out laughing. "I'm not sure a woman wants to be called easy."

He shifted closer and kissed her lightly, feeling Suzette's hands pat his neck. Leaning back, he nuzzled his daughter, kissing her cheek. Shifting his gaze back to Melanie, he said, "You're easy to please, and you're easy to talk to, and you're easy to agree when you know something is the right thing to do. Not a lot of people are that way. But you are, and I'm thankful."

"You have the best way of saying things," she said with a smile.

He kissed her again. "As much as I'd like to keep this going, we need to get packed up so we can get over to your house tonight. Tomorrow, tell the landlord you aren't re-upping for another month."

"I need to talk to the boys tomorrow, too."

I'll arrange to get some friends to help us move things over here. What furniture we're not sure what to do with can go in my garage for now."

"I've got a small storage unit at the apartment that must also be cleaned out."

"Not a problem."

She grinned and glanced around the room. "It sounds like you've got it all planned out."

His smile widened. "When it comes to you and Suzette... yeah, I've got lots of great plans."

25

Melanie carried another box down to her SUV. She'd left Suzette with Mary so she could grab what they would need from the apartment until Jose and some of his friends could get the rest.

"Ms. Landers?"

She turned and spied Trey and Ricky approaching. "Hey, guys!"

They looked at the box in her arms, and Ricky immediately took it from her and carried it the rest of the way, placing it in the back of her vehicle.

"Thanks," she said, smiling at him.

"Where are you going?" Trey asked, peeking into the back of her SUV. He whirled around and stared at her with wide eyes. "Are you moving out?"

She sighed, seeing Ricky's intense stare. "Yes, I am, but I'm not abandoning you. I'll be back three mornings a week, just like always, for our tutoring. We've got to make sure you're completely prepared for the testing next month before school starts."

"Where are you going?" Trey asked, bouncing on his toes.

"Well, I'm moving in with a friend. They have more room for the baby and me."

"Huh," Trey grunted as he ran around her SUV, bouncing his basketball.

Ricky stayed in place, his stare remaining intense. "You'd come back just for us?"

She always had the feeling that Ricky was searching for something when he stared. Searching for a lie or searching for hope… right now, it seemed as though he was searching for both. Unwaveringly holding his gaze, she vowed, "Yes, I'll come back just for you two."

"Why?" he bit out. His face contorted, breaking his normal stoicism.

She stepped closer, peering up. "Ricky, I care a great deal for you and Trey. I care about all my students, but you two have been the first to welcome me to the area, and you've worked so hard." Shrugging, she added, "So I promise that I'll see you in school and will positively be here to continue the summer tutoring."

"I still don't get why you spent all this time not gettin' paid just so two fuckups you didn't even know could pass a test." He swallowed hard several times, blinking.

And she could have sworn his chin quivered ever so slightly. "Sometimes it's not about getting paid. Sometimes it's just about doing the right thing." She hefted her shoulders. "I had the time and the knowledge. You needed both. So it worked." Taking a chance, she stepped closer and lightly touched his arm. She felt the muscles tense underneath her fingertips. "Ricky," she softly called out, continuing to hold his attention. "Sometime, you'll have the chance to pay it forward. You'll have the chance to help someone, make a conscious choice, go against what might be popular or expected, and do the right thing." She smiled up at him. "And when you do, I'll be paid."

His chin quivered, but he remained steady. She stepped back to give him space, knowing he wouldn't want her to see him fall apart. Whatever was going on in his mind, he was wrestling with something. And she had a feeling it was all tied up in his asshole uncle.

Jose sat around the table in the VMP workroom with Ryan, the other officers, and Hunter and Sam.

All their eyes were on him. "So it might not be much to go on, but that's what she told me. I spent the night there last night after she said that Cory had approached her in a threatening manner and gave her a few warnings." He looked over at some of the other officers and said, "She's gathering enough things today to bring over to my house. I was hoping that I could get a few volunteers to help bring anything else over."

Jared waved his hand dismissively. "You don't even have to ask, bro. You know we can have her moved in no time between us and anyone from the American Legion."

"Appreciate it." Turning his attention back to the

others, he noticed a look between Hunter and Sam. "What have you got?"

"We're familiar with Cory Montgomery. But until you asked about him last week, we didn't have a tie-in or a reason to look at him. His brother, Curtis, served with a man named Ronald Jones for a while in prison. Ronald is out and back in the area. He's got a job, reporting regularly to his probation officer, and we've had no reason to suspect him of anything."

"I think I remember the name Curtis Montgomery. He was in high school about the same time I was. Armed robbery, right?" Ryan asked.

"Yeah," Sam said, looking down at his files. "Ronald Jones wasn't from here. But he met Curtis in prison and soon after he got out, came here to live. His crime is interesting, considering what we're dealing with. He'd stolen a car and was breaking it down in his garage to resell the parts. His next-door neighbor heard a lot of noise, peeked through the window, and saw what was happening. He recognized it as being stolen from a newspaper article."

Hunter said, "As we said, he hasn't been on our radar because his probation officer hasn't had a reason to think he's not toeing the line. He's got a job as a cook over at Max's deli. But when we looked closer, he recently got a new truck. So he's getting money from somewhere besides the deli."

Jose shook his head. "Okay, I'm not connecting the dots here."

Hunter continued, "Because the dots aren't easy to connect, and quite frankly, they're pretty far apart.

What you've told us about Cory—he may be the connection. Cory was tight with his brother and still is. He doesn't visit Curtis in person, but they communicate. The monitored phone calls report that Curtis has asked Cory for money and mentioned that Cory needs to *use the connection to make more*. Nothing illegal about that. But we now know that Cory and Ronald Jones have spent time together at a local bar, and that's probably the connection Curtis referenced."

Sam interjected, "Cory has sent money to Curtis's prison account. He had to get it from somewhere and he's got no employment that we can tell unless he's working for someone under the table. Cash only and not paying taxes or social security."

"Do you think Curtis is running a gang from inside the prison? That he sent Ronald to his brother when he got out?" Andy asked.

"We've got nothing to make that inference," Hunter said. "My guess is that someone else runs the show. Someone who knows boats… how to dismantle them and how to sell the parts."

"And the boating angle?" Jose asked.

"That connection only came in this morning, which is why we wanted to go over this with you," Sam said. "A man reported he took his outboard motor in to be repaired. He went to a business run by Devin Jackson, who advertises using new and used parts for repairs. Devin runs a shop here in North Heron, and he has another location in northern Accawmacke County, near the Maryland border. The customer talked to an employee and was told that it would cost more for new parts, so he should go with used parts. He did but was unhappy with the results. When he went back, Devin and the first employee weren't around. Another man was in the shop and told him that if he wanted to try another part, he could get it for him cheaper. The customer left but called the sheriff's department to report that he was suspicious of Devin's business dealings."

Callan shook his head. "How did that trigger the connection?"

"The man was concerned about the used parts and whether they were safe. Considering the recent boat thefts, the officer taking the complaint called me," Sam said. "Devin Jackson only has one employee on the books, which turns out to be Tucker Jones." For dramatic flair, he raised his eyebrows and added, "Tucker is Ronald's cousin."

"So the connection gets bigger," Jose said, nodding. A sliver of excitement surged through him that the case might finally show signs of being solved.

"And there's more," Sam said.

Hunter chuckled as he continued, "We showed the customer a picture of Tucker. He said that was the man who helped him first but not the next time he went in. Then we showed mug shots of Ronald, but it wasn't him either. Just on a whim, we showed him mug shots of Cory, and bingo, we got a hit. So while Ronald and Cory aren't official employees of Devin's, they are all connected."

Hunter added, "And very curious that Cory was in

the repair shop but made the offer to get something cheaper."

Leaning forward, with his forearms resting on the table and his hands clasped together tightly, Jose said, "So we've got Curtis Montgomery with armed robbery, having served time with Ronald Jones, who'd been caught trying to chop up a car. Curtis gets Ronald in touch with his brother, Cory, on the outside, probably knowing that Cory is a worthless fuck and would need money. Ronald's cousin, Tucker, works for Devin, who possibly runs his business off stolen boats and parts. So now we have a tie between Devin, Tucker and Ronald Jones, and Cory and Curtis Montgomery." Scrubbing his hands over his face, he battled a threatening headache.

"You got it," Sam said. Tossing his hands up, he added, "It's tenuous, I'll grant you that. But right now, it's all we've got. And when you called this morning to say that you wanted to talk about Cory Montgomery, the possibility that these men could be the ones involved in the local boat thefts was too much to ignore. Especially with the 'he works at night' and 'works with boats' comments."

"My thought is that Devin Jackson and Tucker Jones are using stolen parts to keep the boat repair business running at a larger profit. Ronald works for them by helping to steal boats. Cory gets in on the money by helping, as well. Everybody gets a cut, and Curtis gets money added to his prison account. It's profitable for everyone."

"And maybe, Cory is trying a hustle on the side.

Trying to undercut Devin by learning how to steal and chop up a boat motor, then sell them himself. And coerced his nephew to help," Jose said, leaning back in his chair, his gut now clenched at the thought of Melanie and Suzette so close to them.

"We're still waiting on the print match from the Bakersfield barn, but we're focusing on this group first," Sam said.

"And with the new information, I won't be surprised if it's Cory's, especially if he's working his own chop shop outside of Devin and the other's," Hunter agreed.

"As you all know, this is Colt's jurisdiction," Ryan reiterated. "But we still haven't located a place where they could've taken the larger fishing boat. Colt has his deputies looking at property for all known associates of any of these men. Other than Devin's business, none of the others own property. But there must be a place near the water they're using. Unless you are on an active callout, patrol each inlet north and south of here for about twenty miles."

Two hours later, Jose was frustrated, along with every other officer. They'd combed numerous inlets, looking for any sign along the banks where someone could bring a boat by water and then begin dismantling it without being in the eyes of anyone nearby.

By the time they had investigated another inlet that they knew wasn't a possibility but wanted to tick all the boxes, his normally staid demeanor was almost gone. Feeling his phone vibrate in his pocket, he looked down to see an unknown number. His finger hovered over the button before tapping accept at the last second.

"Officer Jose Martinez," he answered. When no one responded, he walked into the wheelhouse and stepped behind Bryce, who was steering. "This is Officer Martinez. Can I help you?"

Seeing Bryce cast a questioning gaze over his shoulder, Jose just shrugged. Just as he was about to disconnect, he heard someone clear their throat.

"Um… Is this… are you the water policeman?" a young male voice asked.

"I'm an officer for the Virginia Marine Police. Can I help you?"

"Um… yeah. Ms. Landers gave me this number to call."

Instantly on alert, he asked, "Is this Ricky Montgomery or Trey Blevins?"

"She told you about us?"

Hearing the suspicion in the voice that also wavered slightly, he said, "Yes. She shared how much she enjoys tutoring. So which one are you?" After a slight pause, he prodded, "Ricky?"

"Yeah…"

"Glad you called." He motioned for Bryce to cut the engine, and as soon as he did, he put Ricky on speaker. "What can I do for you?"

"I need… help."

By now, Callan had come into the wheelhouse as well. Jose's heart rate picked up. "Help? What's going on?"

"I'm in trouble… or rather, I know stuff. Stuff about my… shit," his voice trailed off.

Callan stepped away and radioed to the station, reporting what was happening.

"Just talk to me, Ricky. I can't help if I don't know what's going on."

"My uncle's gotten into some shit and made me get involved, but I don't want to. I never did."

"Okay. This is good for you to call me. Are you safe right now?"

"Yeah, man, he's not here."

"What kind of stuff is he up to, Ricky?" Jose asked.

Another hesitation followed, and Jose worried Ricky might shut down when the teen finally spoke.

"Boats. He steals boats. Breaks 'em down and then sells the parts," Ricky confessed. "I'm scared, though, 'cause he's had me go with him sometimes. He works with others mostly, but sometimes he gets the boats by himself."

"Don't worry about that," he assured, seeing two more VMP vessels approaching, the officers listening as he held his phone close to the radio. "Can you tell me where he takes the boats?"

"There was an old barn he used to use when he had some smaller boat engines. Those were ones he stole himself."

"Okay, good to know." Jose nodded as he realized that Cory was the copycat thief even though he worked with Devin, Tucker, and Ronald. And he felt sure with the different location, they had no idea what he was doing.

Callan stepped closer and mouthed, *"Sam and Hunter are on standby."*

Nodding, he said, "And any other places? Maybe somewhere bigger?"

"Yeah. Tucker got a place for the last boat they took. A big boat."

"Tucker?" A long silence met his ears, and he feared he'd spooked the young man. "Ricky, you're making a difference and doing really good. All this will help us and help you."

"Tucker Jones and his cousin, Ronald. My uncle works with them. He said something about my dad knowing them. Then my uncle said if I wanted to keep a roof over my head and not end up dead in a ditch somewhere, I had to help, too."

"Don't worry about that now, Ricky. Just give us what you've got."

"Fuck, I ain't seen it from the water."

"Doesn't matter. Tell me what you've got," he encouraged, staring at Joseph, Andy, and Jared on their vessel as they listened while he had his radio on so the other VMPs could hear.

"It was dark, but we went past that big chicken farm... um... factory."

Jose knew the location was at the northern tip of North Heron County. "Give me whatever you can. You're doing great."

"We turned just past it and drove down a few roads. It was dark, and there were no houses that I could see. Lots of trees all around... I couldn't see much." There were a few seconds of hesitation. "Oh, wait. My uncle Cory said something like Devin's old man's land."

"Devin?"

"Yeah... I don't know his last name. He seemed to know Ronald and Tucker."

Callan stepped to the side and began talking on his phone. Suddenly, Bryce nodded and started the engine again, heading north along with the other two vessels.

"Okay, Ricky, we're going to check it out. What else can you tell me?"

"Um... there was a kind of garage... a metal shed. Looked like a bunch of boat parts already there, but Cory said the big boat we'd just taken was gonna end up in there, too."

"Ricky, listen carefully. What you've done today is good. Really good. You've just proven what kind of man you are. But I want to make sure you're safe. So get where you know your uncle won't be around. Can you do that?"

"Trey's grandma was going to take us up to the Superstore to get some clothes for school."

"Good. Now, keep this phone with you, and I'll be in touch. And if you need me, then call back."

"Got it, Officer Martinez. Um... am I gonna get in trouble?"

"You've got my word that I'll be with you when any deputies talk to you to get details. If you keep making these good choices, you'll be fine."

"Thanks. She... uh... she told me."

"I'm sorry?"

"Ms. Landers. She told me that I could make a choice and do the right thing."

"She's right. And she'll be proud of you." Disconnecting, his chest filled with the fresh, briny air of the bay, eager to get to the location Ricky had given them.

Hearing his name radioed from Ryan, he answered. "Yes, sir?"

"Colt is sending Sam and Hunter, along with deputies, to the location. It's still in North Heron County. Devin also could have met up with Curtis and Cory Montgomery... they were at Baytown High School together back in the day."

"Tell Colt I promised Ricky I'd be there when deputies go to talk to him."

"He knows. Says it's no problem. Right now, I'm heading out to the site as well. Catch you there."

26

Jose's fingers twitched as he stood on the boat's bow as they neared the back of the property. It was farther north along the coast than they'd previously investigated. Once they turned into the small inlet, he still struggled to see where a twenty-eight-foot gillnetter boat could have been hidden before being dismantled.

"Holy shit," he muttered, staring just ahead. "Found it," he radioed, and Bryce immediately throttled the engine back even more. The inlet wasn't deep, but someone would have to be right up on it to see an old dock near the edge of the embankment, perfectly camouflaged with leaves and limbs coming down over a massive camouflage netting.

Underneath the covering, he could already see the hull of a large boat. Bryce maneuvered him close enough that he, Callan, and Andy were able to make it to the dock. Being careful not to tamper with evidence, they crossed over to the land, where they could see the also camouflaged large metal shed Ricky had told them about.

Colt had his deputies combing the area. As the VMP officers met him at the door along with Hunter and Sam, they looked inside, seeing the evidence of the boat chop shop.

"A lot of the parts are already gone," Andy said, surveying the scene. "Probably already made it to Devin's repair shop."

Stepping back out to allow the deputies to do their job, the VMP officers walked back to the docked boat with Colt, Sam, Hunter, and Ryan, who had just arrived as well.

"Up the lane are five other boats in various states of dismantling," Hunter reported. "We passed them coming in from the road."

"Devin Jackson was from this area originally, but he's been living up in Acawmake near the Maryland border. As soon as we got his name from Ricky's phone call, I contacted Sheriff Liam Sullivan. It seems Devin is also under investigation for fraud allegations in that county. One of his customers discovered that his repaired boat, which he paid for new engines and parts, was patched together, like a Frankenstein, using bits and pieces from old boats. But they never could find out where he was getting his parts. Their investigation had just started, so we hadn't heard about it."

"So Devin's running his theft ring down here. He's got a gang stealing boats, then they chop them up here to make it an easy transfer up there."

"That's what it looks like. He'll be indicted in both counties."

"I want to make sure that Ricky is okay," Jose said. "You heard the call– he was strong-armed, coerced, and threatened into helping. He didn't have to call me but thank God he did."

"How did he get your number?" Colt asked.

"Melanie. While tutoring. It came out that he wanted to join the Navy, and she gave him my number and said I'd be a good person to talk to. She also told him that I was in law enforcement and that if he ever needed help, to call me."

Hunter shook his head. "We can investigate every lead, but sometimes cracking a case comes down to a Good Samaritan giving us just what we needed."

"I just want to make sure his uncle doesn't find out that Ricky told us."

"Sheriff Sullivan said that they would pick up Devin right now. My people are getting fingerprints as we speak. But since we already have evidence that others were involved, my deputies will go pick up Ronald and Tucker Jones, as well as Cory Montgomery."

"Can we keep Ricky's name out of this, at least for now?"

"Absolutely. As far as we're concerned, the VMPs were searching areas for a boat, discovered this, and the rest is turning it over to us. That will give us a chance to pick them up, question them, and see what we can squeeze out of them first."

"Thanks," Jose said, with a chin lift. "I appreciate it. I know Melanie will, too."

While some of the deputies collected evidence in the garage and in the boats on the property, the VMP officers snapped on rubber gloves and slid shoe protectors over their boots to do the same on the old gillnetter. They worked most of the afternoon before heading back to the harbor.

Filled with the elation that comes from a case moving toward the end, he could hardly wait to get home and tell Melanie what Ricky had done.

"Mary? Is everything going okay with Suzette?"

"She's fast asleep for her afternoon nap," Mary assured. "Carlos is out with Jimmy, so I've got her sleeping in the playpen while I sit and read for a little bit. She's been an absolute dream. How's the move going? I don't want you to do too much because the men will be able to help tomorrow."

"Oh, it's not bad. I'm leaving all the heavy stuff for them anyway," Melanie laughed. "But the kitchen items and linens, toiletries, and all the baby stuff, I'm packing up. I've made one trip back to Jose's house and am back at my apartment getting the last couple of things. Since it's not much, I'm going to stop by your house and pick Suzette up on my way. So I should see you in about thirty minutes."

"That'll be fine. I'll see you then."

Disconnecting the call, she looked around the apartment and walked through the rooms, snapping pictures. She wanted to remind Jose what he and his helpers would need to move tomorrow. As she closed and locked the door, she decided to do the same thing with the storage unit.

She hadn't been in the storage unit since she moved in and thought a few pictures to see how the movers had left everything would be wise. Walking around to the back of the apartment building, she followed the short road leading to the long building housing the six-by-ten-foot storage units for each of the sixteen apartments. Taking off the padlock, she lifted the door and glanced around, glad that she didn't have much in there. *I can sell some things, give some other things away, and a few things will fit nicely in Jose's place.*

Banging could be heard from the back of the building just behind her unit, and she was curious as to what was there. Walking around, she discovered a second, smaller unit. Old rusty metal signs saying to **Keep out, Property of apartment management** hung on the outside.

One of the doors was open, and she walked over, curious to see if the property manager was inside. She'd only met him once when she first rented and wanted to let him know what day she would be moved out.

Stopping outside the open storage unit, she looked inside. It appeared to be filled with the kind of outboard motors she'd seen on boats.

"He works with boats," Trey had said about Ricky's uncle. Her conversations with Jose came back as well. *"Someone is stealing boats and then taking them somewhere to be dismantled."*

She jerked her head around, the air rushing out in

relief when she didn't see anyone around. Turning, she darted around the corner to head back to the apartment building, when she slammed into something large and hard.

Hands grabbed her arms, and she yelped as she jerked and looked up. Ricky's uncle Cory was glaring down at her. His gaze moved from her face to behind her where the open storage unit was, then back down to her face.

"I knew an uppity bitch like you would be a pain."

She tried to scream, but he quickly overpowered her. With one arm, he whirled her around and managed to pin her arms to her sides and clamp a hand around her mouth. He picked her up easily, and with her feet dangling above the ground, walked until they got into the storage unit. Giving her a shove, he tossed her to the ground. She sprawled on her hands and knees on the concrete floor, crying out in pain as her hip hit a jagged piece of a motor. He grabbed her before she could push herself to a stand, and she was helpless to get away. Her arms were jerked behind her, and she heard the rip of tape before he wound it around her wrists. Shoving her to her knees, he put his hand on her back and forced her on her face again. With her legs grabbed, he repeated the motion with her ankles. She felt her phone sliding from her back pocket.

"You won't need this," he said, crushing it underneath his booted foot. Bending, he sneered as he grabbed an old, dirty cloth and gagged her as he tied it tightly over her mouth.

She wasn't sure what he planned, but he began to pace, mumbling to himself. "What the fuck? Shit!"

Her heart pounded in her chest as her body ached. Terrified, she watched as his eyes bugged out.

"No, no. I'm not tellin' any-fuckin'-body about any-fuckin'-thing!"

He walked around the small shed, his wide-eyed gaze darting around as he dragged his hand through his hair. "None of this is my fuckin' fault!"

Finally, he stopped pacing and looked around as though forgetting he had a taped woman at his feet. "Ain't got fuckin' time to get rid of this shit. Goddamn fucking mess!" he walked to the door and then turned, his gaze now on her. "I'm out of here, bitch. I figure ain't nobody gonna find you here." He stepped out and lowered the door, plunging her into darkness. She heard a lock snap on the door before his footsteps retreated.

Thankful he hadn't killed her or harmed her worse, she also had no idea how she would get out. Unable to move easily with her wrists and ankles bound, staying in place and waiting to be found wasn't an option. *Maybe I can kick on the door if I can wiggle over to it.* Dismissing that idea, she doubted any of the residents could hear her.

Still lying on the concrete floor, her eyes slowly became used to the dark interior of the shed, as a sliver of light came from where the door did not seal against the concrete floor. As she attempted to move, pain shot through her hip.

Remembering the image of the boat propeller she'd

landed on, she wondered if she had cut herself on the sharp edges. A little gasp escaped. *If it's that sharp, then it should cut through the tape.*

She didn't know if Cory was coming back but didn't want to be taped up and at his mercy if he did. Whatever the person on the phone said to him freaked him out and may have saved her life because he was obviously thinking about getting out of there. But if he came back, she might find that he'd be willing to do anything to shut her up permanently.

Looking around, she could barely make out the boat motor lying on its side on the floor. She could see the propeller, and for a few seconds, she debated whether to try to cut through the tape on her ankles or her hands first. With adrenaline coursing through her body, she struggled to decide. Finally, groaning, she shifted around until she could feel the propeller blades pressing against the tape between her wrists. She moved slowly, not wanting to slip and slice her wrist instead of the tape. Bleeding out on the nasty floor of an old storage unit was not how she wanted to be found.

With that gruesome thought going through her head, she continued to saw for several minutes until she could finally feel the tape giving. Working her arms up and down in a limited motion since they were behind her, she finally felt the tape separate on one side of her wrists. Now gently pressing it all the way between her wrists, she continued to saw until they were free.

Elation shot through her. She tried to work the knot out of the gag but was unable to loosen it. Not wanting to waste more time, she shifted around, and using her hands, she worked the propeller blades against the tape on her ankles. Now that she could see what she was doing, she was able to go much more quickly. What she couldn't figure out was how to escape the prison once she was free of the tape.

27

"Jose?"

"Yeah, Mom? How was Suzette today?"

"That's why I'm calling, son. She's been an absolute angel, but Melanie was supposed to be here an hour ago. In fact, she called me to say she was thirty minutes out, and that was an hour and a half ago. I've tried calling, but I can't get anyone to answer. It just rings and rings and then goes to voicemail. I wondered if you knew where she was?"

A cold snake of fear slithered through his body. "I was almost home, but I'm heading to her place."

"Don't worry about Suzette. I've got her," his mom assured.

It only took him a few minutes to get to Melanie's apartment building, where he saw her vehicle still in the parking lot. He jogged up to her apartment and banged on the door. No one answered, but the unease shot straight to fear.

"Are you looking for Ms. Landers?"

295

He turned and saw a thin, young man, nervous energy exuding as he bounded up the steps.

"Yes, have you seen her?"

"She's moving out. In fact, I thought she was moving in with you."

"She is, but she was here today. Getting a few boxes."

"Yeah, me and Ricky saw her earlier. I'm Trey by the way. We had a chance to say goodbye to her. She said she was gonna keep tutoring, and so we could—"

"Have you seen her since then? Her vehicle is still here, and she hasn't shown up anywhere."

Trey turned and looked over the railing to the parking lot, his brow furrowing. He twisted around and looked back at Jose. "Yeah, it is there. But I haven't seen her."

"Where's Ricky?"

He shrugged his thin shoulders. "I don't know. We were gone earlier cause my grandma took us to the Superstore so we could get some new school clothes. She had some money saved up from her job, and Ricky also had some, so we were looking for some of the new—"

"Trey, I'm sorry, but we gotta stay on task here. Have you seen Ricky since you came back from shopping?"

He shook his head. "No, we usually hang out, but he was really nervous and said he was gonna try to stay away from his uncle this evening." Trey leaned closer, whispering conspiratorially, "Between you and me, his uncle is an ass. He tried to get me to work with him, but my mama said no. She said she didn't trust him and didn't wanna have anything to do with him—"

296

"Trey, call Ricky."

"Sure," he agreed readily, pulling out his phone. It rang several times, and then finally, Trey said, "Hey, man. Where are you? I got someone here. He wants to talk to you. No, no, it's not your uncle."

Jose held his hand out, unwilling to wait on Trey's phone. "Ricky? This is Jose Martinez. I'm at the apartment building, and Melanie is missing but her car is here. Do you know where she might be? Do you know where your uncle is?"

"I'm hiding out, Officer Martinez," Ricky said. "When I got home, my uncle was acting real twitchy. I heard him on the phone with Ronald, but I don't know what they were talking about. He was in a pissy mood, and when he got off the phone, he told me that he needed to move it, and I needed to help him."

"Move what, Ricky?"

"I don't know, Officer Martinez. I really don't. I told him I wasn't gonna work for him anymore, and he hit me. I fell back and hit my head against the door. I managed to push him back, then I ran out of the apartment. I didn't want to go to Trey because I didn't want Cory to come after Trey or his mom. So I headed down the road. I made it to the 7-Eleven about a mile down the road and then have been hanging out here."

"Okay, I'm glad you're safe, and I'm going to have a deputy come pick you up. You're not in trouble. I just want you to be safe."

Ten minutes later, with his heart in his throat and Trey dogging his heels, he raced around the apartment building, knocking on doors to check to see if anyone had seen Melanie, when several sheriff's vehicles pulled up. Seeing Sam, he called out, "Cory's not answering his door, but his truck is gone. I can't find Melanie. If you don't get me in there, I'm kicking the fuckin' door down!"

Ricky jumped out of the back seat of one of the sheriff's vehicles and ran upstairs, stopping just in front of Jose. The two men took measure of each other for a few seconds, then both must've liked and trusted what they saw. Pulling out his key, Ricky said, "Come on."

With the deputies right behind, Ricky unlocked his apartment, and as the deputies called out to identify themselves, they moved forward with weapons in front of them. Sam held Ricky and Trey back until they got the all clear as Jose rushed forward behind the deputies. He raced through the small apartment, checking each closet, his heart in his chest, searching for any sign of Melanie.

"Ricky, check to see if it looks like anything is missing," Sam said.

Ricky raced around the apartment, then came back and shook his head. "My uncle's clothes are still in the closet, and I don't see that it looks like he's packed up. I...I don't know where he goes." His face fell as his chest deflated. He turned to Jose as his hands lifted to the sides. "He never tells me where he goes, and I never cared. I just was glad he wasn't here with me."

"What if he'd seen Melanie? If I already know he threatened her—"

Trey gasped as Ricky growled, "My uncle threatened her?"

A HERO'S SURPRISE

Jose recognized the same anger flooding both young men. "That's why I was moving her into my place as soon as possible." He turned toward Sam, his face ravaged.

"If her car is still here, then she's got to be close unless he took her with him," Sam said.

Ricky planted his hands on his hips. "Maybe he went to see Ronald or Tucker? I don't know!"

"Deputies have picked up Ronald and Tucker. They're being taken to the sheriff's department for questioning."

Jose turned to Sam. "If Cory was hustling stolen boat parts on the side, he might go to the barn to try to get rid of them, especially if he didn't realize the barn had been discovered and searched." Turning to Ricky, he said, "Go down to Trey's apartment and stay. Deputies will be searching this place. If you think of anything else, call me."

Ricky let out a long breath and nodded. Jose raced out the door to Sam's SUV. Calling Ryan, he reported what had happened and where he was going. Ryan immediately called for some of the officers to meet him at the dock of the Bakersfield farm.

He remained quiet on the drive as he tried to calm his tangled thoughts. Finally pulling out his phone, he dialed his dad. "I don't want to worry Mom, but get home and stay with her and Suzette. We're looking for Melanie—" His voice cracked.

"Son, hang in there," Carlos said. "I'm almost home and won't leave until you bring Melanie here."

"Thanks," he managed to say before disconnecting.

He knew his dad would call the rest of the family, pulling in everyone the way his family always came together in times of crisis as well as celebration. Blowing out a ragged breath, he listened as Sam was on the phone.

"Hunter? Lean on Ronald and Tucker individually. Tell them that Cory was skimming and running a side hustle. Tell them that he had his own place. Doesn't matter that we don't know for... what? Seriously? Fuckin' hallelujah! Then definitely lean on those two. Get them to turn on him and find out where the fuck he might be! Call me when he's been arrested. I've got Jose, and we're heading to the Bakersfield barn."

As soon as Sam disconnected, Jose turned to him. "What?"

"The fingerprints from the barn are a match for Cory. And none were found there of Devin, Ronald, or Tucker."

"So that was his place on the side," Jose said. Swallowing deeply, he closed his eyes as fear continued to slither through his body. He wanted to find Melanie, but was terrified that if she was there...

"Don't go there," Sam said. "Just wait. No need to make it worse than it is."

He dragged in another breath and stared out the windshield, kicking himself that he hadn't insisted she move earlier. "I waited," he said, the words like shards of glass in his throat. "Why the fuck did I wait to move her in?"

"Don't go there, Jose," Sam repeated as he flipped on his blinker, making the turn to the old farm.

Jose looked over to see several deputy vehicles right behind them. They came to a hard stop, and he leaped from the SUV, his boots racing toward the barn. Seeing Andy, Bryce, and Joseph running from the dock, they reached the door at the same time, and with his heart in his throat, he threw the door open. It was obvious the small barn was empty, and his stomach clenched. He started in, but Sam rushed up and grabbed him, halting his progress.

"Hang on, man. Sorry, but the deputies cleared this out, and after the scene was processed, it was swept. Look." He pointed down at the dirt floor. Fresh boot prints were seen entering, then chaotically on the inside, and then leaving.

"He's been here. It's got to be Cory. He came and saw it was now empty and has left. But where the fuck did he go? And does he have Melanie with him?" Jose asked, his voice growing harder with each word.

"What if we missed him? Passed him?" Sam asked.

"Going back?" Jose turned to stare at the detective, barely following Sam's line of thinking.

Bryce nodded. "Maybe he came here to get rid of the evidence. Discovered someone compromised it... he wouldn't have to know it was by the deputies. But figured he needed to get out of the area."

Whirling, Jose gasped. "He'd go back to his apartment to grab what he could before leaving!"

While Andy and Joseph headed back to the docked VMP vessel, Bryce ran to Sam's SUV with Jose. Taking off down the road, Sam radioed for deputies to continue being alerted for Cory Montgomery's truck.

Then, calling into Hunter, he put him on speaker. "What have you got from Ronald and Tucker?"

"As you can imagine, neither knew he was side-hustling them, and they're pissed. Both are tripping over each other to give him up in hopes of lessening their charges. So far, Ronald is giving up more about Cory and is also turning on Devin. Tucker tried to be loyal to his employer, but as soon as he heard Ronald was confessing, he jumped in, too."

"Looks like Cory went back to the barn, but we missed him. We're on our way to his apartment again. Still searching for Melanie."

"Shit," Hunter cursed. "Jose, hang in there."

As the call disconnected, Jose remained silent, staring out the side window as the miles passed. His mind filled with Melanie's smiling face as she held Suzette. His baby had lost one mother... He couldn't fathom her losing two. But then, he couldn't fathom losing Melanie just when he'd found her.

28

Ricky paced in the back bedroom of Trey's apartment while Trey stayed right with him, nervously chattering with each step.

"Maybe they found him. Maybe they found her. Do you think they'll call? Did you check your phone? Maybe—"

"Jesus, Trey, you gotta be quiet, bro," Ricky cried, his nerves frayed. "I can't think."

"Whatcha thinking? About where your uncle went off to? And do you think that he's got Ms. Landers?"

"Trey!"

Trey's nose wrinkled as he quieted, nodding slowly. "I'm sorry. You know I think out loud. But I'll be—shit!"

Ricky jerked around, ready to send Trey into the other room when he realized Trey stood still, mouth open, staring out the window facing the back. Swinging his head around, he spied Cory driving his truck down the dirt lane that ran behind the building. Bolting into the living room, he called over his shoulder to Trey,

"Call Jose." Stopping only long enough to see Trey's mom hurrying from the kitchen, her brow lowered in surprise, he added, "Mrs. Blevins, call 911!"

As he threw open the door, he felt Trey right on his heels. "Stay back, Trey! I've got to see what he's doing, and I can't have you rushing in and alerting him! Stay here and lead Jose and the deputies back when they come."

With that, he darted near the tree line that ran by the lane, hoping to stay out of sight until he could determine what his uncle was doing. Around the bend, he spied the long, low storage building for the apartments. He and Trey had been back here exploring a long time ago but quickly discovered nothing was interesting about them. Each resident had a small unit with a padlocked door. On the back, the apartment manager also had a couple of units. He couldn't remember the last time he and Trey had been back here. But as he approached, he spied his uncle's truck in front of his unit. The door was open, and Cory was loading up the back of his pickup with some boxes and an old suitcase.

Determined not to let Cory get away, he raced forward.

As soon as they pulled up outside the apartment building again, Jose looked out to see a couple of deputies and Ryan and Callan arriving. Adrenaline coursed through his body as he, once again, leaped out of the vehicle.

"Anything?" he called out, just as Trey came racing out of his apartment.

"I saw Cory driving behind the apartments! I saw him! I told Ricky, and he went after him!" Trey called out, bouncing on his toes as he pointed.

Jose started running to the end of the apartment building to go behind it when Trey came up alongside him.

"There are sheds out there. Me and Ricky explored them before, but there's nothing to see. Maybe Cory's got stuff hidden in his!"

"What shed? Show me?"

Jose, Sam, and a few deputies ran around to the back of the building, with Trey jumping up and down, racing behind them.

Pointing at the lane, Trey called out, "They're here."

Shouting met his ears, and Jose ran toward the low building, seeing the storage building. A pickup truck was outside one of them, and he could see two men on the ground, fighting. Getting closer, he recognized Ricky and Cory outside an open unit. While he grabbed Ricky, one of the deputies apprehended Cory.

Pulling Ricky back, he calmed the angry young man who was sporting a split lip. "Chill out, we've got him. It's okay. We've got him."

Ricky's chest heaved as he gasped, "I tried to find out where Ms. Landers is, but he won't say!"

Jose looked inside Cory's unit but found no sign of Melanie. Then running to the one that corresponded with her apartment, he noticed the padlock was on the ground. Jerking the door up quickly, he spied a few pieces of furniture and boxes, but no Melanie.

Whirling around with his hands on his hips, he stalked over to where Cory was now handcuffed. "What the fuck did you do with her?"

"Not saying shit till I get to talk to a lawyer," Cory groused, refusing to make eye contact.

"You piece of shit—" Jose began, his adrenaline turning into rage as Ricky started yelling at his uncle as well.

"We'll start looking," Ryan said, pulling out his phone.

Sam added, "Got deputies all over the county searching."

"Do you guys hear that?" Trey said, his head moving from left to right quickly.

No one responded as Sam radioed to the station.

"Hey, guys, don't you hear that?" Trey said louder, jumping up and down.

"Trey, you gotta be quiet, man," Ricky said, wiping his bloody lip. "They're trying to find Ms. Landers."

"I know, but don't you hear that banging?" Finally, he yelled, "Listen!"

Suddenly, everybody stopped, and the faint sound of something hitting metal could be heard. Jose sucked in a quick breath and darted past the others around the back of the building, spying a couple of doors labeled for the management. All had padlocks on them, but the distinct sound of someone banging could be heard.

"Melanie!" he yelled.

He quickly found the one with the sound and called for one of the deputies to get a lock cutter.

"Melanie, is that you?" His shouts were drowned out by Trey banging on the door and jumping up and down while Ricky tried to pull his excitable friend back.

A muffled voice was heard from the inside, and Jose was climbing out of his skin by the time one of the deputies jogged over with lock cutters in his hands. With a few snips, the padlock fell away, and Jose bent to grab the handle, lifting the door with a bang. Melanie stood inside, her face bruised, and a dirty gag filled her mouth. Remnants of duct tape hung from her wrists and feet. Blood ran down her leg, and she was covered in dirt and dust. His heart threatened to leap out of his chest at the sight.

He scooped her up in his arms and carried her outside. Her tears made dirty trails down her face. Setting her down, Callan stepped behind her to slice off the gag while Jose gently pulled it from her mouth.

"It was Cory Montgomery," she gasped, lifting a hand to try to remove the rest of the duct tape from her wrists, wincing as it pulled her skin.

"Don't touch anything. We'll get something to get that off you," he promised, his heart still pounding a staccato beat.

"Suzette!" she cried out, her face filled with terror. "I haven't called your mom—"

"I've already talked to Mom and Dad. She's fine. And as soon as I get you to the hospital, I'll call Mom to let her know what's going on."

Melanie grabbed his arms. "Jose, listen. Cory got

really nervous and upset before taking off. He's got all kinds of boat stuff in there."

Sam looked over and said, "Looks like he was using this place as well as the barn. Another place Devin, Ronald, and Tucker probably don't know about." Turning to the deputies, he said, "Rope it off and start processing." Walking over, he moved his gaze over Melanie's face. "Ms. Landers, I'm Detective Shackley. Glad to see you. We'll need your statement as soon as you're up to it."

"I want to get her to the doctor," Jose said.

"Trey? Ricky?" she said, looking at the two standing nearby. "Are you okay?"

Ricky's face contorted as he said, "I'm so sorry, Ms. Landers. Jesus Christ, I'm so sorry."

Trey had a big grin on his face and said, "I heard you! I knew I heard something, and it was you!"

Hunter pulled up in his vehicle just when they made it back in front of the apartment building. "Ricky? I'm Detective Hunter Simmons. I want to ask you some questions, but I know Officer Martinez wanted to be with you."

"He's got to take care of Ms. Landers, sir," Ricky said. "But I'm fine to go with you and talk to you. Whatever I know, I'll tell you."

"Jose, honey, I'm fine," Melanie said.

"You're fucking hell not fine," he bit back. "I don't want to be separated from you."

"Then take me to Judith. I don't want to drive all the way up to the hospital just to wait in an ER. Take me to Judith and let her check me out." She looked over at

Hunter and Sam. "Detective Simmons. Would it be possible for me to come to the station as soon as I'm checked out?"

They glanced between her and Jose, then both nodded before heading to their vehicles.

Turning her gaze back to Jose as she clutched his cheeks, she said, "You need to do this. You promised, and that boy has had so many broken promises."

"Baby, you and Suzette will always be my top priority," he countered.

"Yes, I agree. But we're fine. Suzette is with your mom. But you need to be at the station sitting with Ricky. Please, do this for me and do it for him."

"I'll go as soon as Judith checks you out."

"Deal," she said, jerking her head in agreement.

As Hunter and Ricky walked away, they left Sam with the other deputies to investigate the storage unit. Jose carried Melanie to his vehicle and carefully placed her inside.

She leaned back and sighed, then looked over at him as he slid behind the wheel.

"You need to stop worrying about everybody else," he admonished gently.

She smiled softly and touched his cheek. "I'm a mom. It's what we do. We worry."

He couldn't help but smile as he drove into town.

29

Melanie sat behind the two-way mirror in the North Heron Sheriff's Department. She had been questioned, giving them all the details of what Cory had done to her when she surprised him at the storage shed.

Now, she sat and watched as Ricky described everything he knew about the boat thefts in detail to the investigators. Just as he'd promised, Jose sat next to Ricky, a silent but steadying presence.

The painkillers were wearing off, and she knew she'd barely be able to walk when it was all over, but for now, she was right where she wanted to be.

The nurse had cleaned the cut on her hip, and Judith sutured it with just three stitches. Jose had been hanging on to his rage during the process but managed to hold her hand gently at the same time. By the time they'd made it to the sheriff's department, Ricky was just starting his interview.

She could tell Ricky was nervous, but his voice remained strong other than when he described the times Cory would hit him to "keep me in line." Tears pricked her eyes as she watched him struggle with the fear of what the future might have in store for him. He admitted he wanted to hit his uncle in return but, as he got bigger, was afraid to give in to the urge. "I never wanted to end up like my dad or him."

He gave details about what he knew about the operation, which, it turned out, wasn't much. Cory hadn't involved Ricky until the night of the fishing boat theft because they needed the extra eyes to keep watch.

At the end of the interview, Sam told Ricky that his uncle, Ronald, Tucker, and Devin, were all under arrest and would not be getting out on bail anytime soon. "You're not quite eighteen, but we've talked to a social worker. It seems Mrs. Blevins has volunteered for you to live with her while you finish high school as long as you stay out of trouble and graduate on time."

A gasp slipped from Melanie's lips at the gesture from Trey's mom. Blowing out a long sigh of relief, she stood with a little difficulty, then slipped out of the room. Standing at the end of the hall, she watched as Ricky and Jose walked out of the interview room together. They chatted for a few minutes, and she was sure Jose gave him whatever words and assurances he needed to hear. Jose was a man who stepped up and stepped in. He'd done that with Suzette, and he'd done that with her.

They turned and headed down the hall, Jose seeing her first. His smile, just like the first time he turned it her way, made her heart squeeze in her chest.

As they approached, Ricky finally turned and saw

her standing there. His large body stuttered to a halt, then he raced forward, pulling her in for an unexpected hug. She felt his body quiver, and as he pulled away, she saw him blinking furiously before he finally lifted a hand and wiped underneath his eyes.

"I'm so proud of you, Ricky," she said, her hands clinging to his arms. "What you did took such courage."

He shook his head, his face crumpling. "Ms. Landers, if I'd said something earlier, he would've never gotten to you."

"Don't take that on, Ricky. That's not your guilt to bear. He's the one who kidnapped me. Not you. Don't take on his sins."

"But if I had spoken up earlier—"

"You're young, you were afraid, and you were in an untenable situation. But if you need to ease some misguided guilt, then just learn from this. After all, you've already started rewriting your story."

He held her gaze for a long moment, and she was once again struck by how he seemed to be searching for either lies or hope. He must have finally found hope because he nodded slowly. Then, with a small smile, he said, "I'm going to live with Trey and his mom while I finish my senior year."

Her lips curved as well. "I heard about that. I think that's wonderful."

He shook his head. "That means I'll have to share a room with Trey. He'll probably drive me crazy the first night."

She laughed, then snorted and clapped her hand over her mouth. "You're right."

"Nah, it'll be cool."

"Well, remember, we still have a lot of tutoring to do in the next month before school starts."

"I'll be ready."

"I'm sure you will."

Sam walked over and clapped Ricky on the shoulder. "Mrs. Blevins is out front, ready to take you home. You've got my card? If you need anything, you give us a call. And I'll stay in contact to let you know when we'll need more from you."

Ricky thanked the detective, then turned to shake hands with Jose.

"The same goes for us, you know," Jose said. "And soon, you and I will talk about the Navy."

After more handshakes, Sam walked Ricky out front, followed by a much slower-walking Melanie. Jose's smile was now gone, and he scooped her up carefully in his arms.

"You can't carry me out of the sheriff's department!"

"With your injury, you're walking slow, and I've got to get you to Suzette," he said.

She wrapped her arms around his neck and tucked her head against his. "Then go faster." She laughed, urging him on.

Five Months Later

Melanie sat on the porch swing with Suzette in her arms, both bundled against the December chill. The day was filled with sunshine, and she relished the time they spent swinging back and forth. She was out for the holiday break and loved the time she and Suzette could spend together.

The evening would be busy when her parents arrived in town and Carlos and Mary came over. Christmas morning would be busy with gifts at their house and then off to be with the whole family and more gifts at his parents' house.

But for right now, it was just her and Suzette swinging as they waited for Jose to get home from his early shift.

Her daughter had already been crawling and had pulled up to a very wobbly stand just today before plopping back down on her well-padded diaper butt. Melanie sent a video but couldn't wait for Jose to see it himself.

Suzette's dark hair was thick, and while she mostly took after Jose, Melanie could also see bits of Karen in her. As Suzette giggled on the swing, Melanie breathed in deeply, her heart full. "You would be so proud of her, Karen."

Karen's voice had receded, but it didn't matter. Melanie knew Karen looked down on them, a smile on her beautiful face. She would tell Suzette all about her sweet birth mother one day when she was older, but for now, she reveled in the adorable sounds of clapping when Jose's SUV pulled into the driveway. He waved and parked just outside the garage. Hustling up the front steps, he gently sat on the swing, wrapping his arm around both of them.

"How are my girls?" he asked, kissing Suzette's cheek before leaning over and kissing Melanie.

"We have had a wonderful day. I baked cookies while she napped. We played, and I even managed to wrap a few more presents."

"And your parents come this evening."

"I haven't forgotten. I was thinking about the next couple of days and how busy they'll be. That's why I decided to come out here onto our magical swing to wait for you."

He chuckled and shook his head. "Magical swing."

"Hey, don't make fun. I want her to know a magical swing just like the one at my grandmother's house."

"Well, since the next few days are so busy, and we are all out here on the magical swing, how about we make some magic now?"

Lifting a brow, she laughed. "Um... I'm not sure that I know what kind of magic you're talking about making, considering it's chilly, and we have a baby here!"

He shifted around and stuck his hand into his jacket pocket. "This was going to be your Christmas present, but I don't want to wait. And I don't want a bunch of family around when it really should just be you, me, and Suzette."

He pulled out a ring box, and her breath caught in her throat. As he opened it, her gaze landed on a gorgeous engagement ring. Before she could speak, he shifted on the swing again, making sure to keep Suzette secure in their arms while he held Melanie's gaze.

"We met under unusual circumstances but quickly

realized how we met isn't important. What's important is what we felt when we were together. The connection. The spark."

Tears welled in her eyes as she tried to breathe past the lump in her throat.

"And I want to keep that spark with you and our beautiful daughter for the rest of my life. So will you, Melanie, do me the greatest honor and become my wife?"

"Yes!" she cried, barely giving him time to finish his question. She pressed close to him as he slipped the ring on her finger and kissed him, holding a squealing Suzette between them at the same time.

And as their lips touched, a warmth surrounded them on the magical swing.

Eighteen Months Later

Melanie sat in the audience next to Jose as he gently held and bounced a two-year-old Suzette in his lap. Melanie's hand rested on her stomach, with her secret known only to him. They had just confirmed the pregnancy but didn't want to tell anyone until she was further along. But the idea of their family growing kept the smile on her face.

They watched the Baytown High School graduation ceremony, cheering as Trey walked across the stage, and she laughed when it was obvious he was trying to stay calm instead of bouncing on his toes as he accepted his diploma. The year before, they had watched Ricky make the same trek across the stage. She was sorry he wasn't here to see Trey graduate but knew it couldn't be helped.

Soon, the graduates tossed the caps into the air, and they filed out of the football stadium. They had an arranged place to meet with Trey and his mother, so they made their way toward them at the side of the crowded parking lot.

Trey grabbed her in a hug, his exuberance finally spilling over. "I made it, Ms. Martinez. Graduated and heading off to auto mechanics' school!"

"I couldn't possibly be prouder of you," she exclaimed truthfully.

Suddenly, Trey stiffened in her arms, and she looked up to see what was the matter. His gaze focused behind her, and as she turned, her eyes widened in surprise.

"Ricky!" they all shouted.

Ricky grinned widely as he approached, wearing his Navy uniform, looking every inch the man she always knew he could be. Greetings, hugs, and handshakes followed.

Knowing the local restaurants would be crowded, Mrs. Blevins had invited them all over for a post-graduation meal. Her parents had passed in the past year, and she moved into their small house, claiming it was plenty of room for herself.

Later in the day, as Jose placed a snoozing Suzette into her car seat, Melanie hugged Trey and Ricky goodbye. Trey moved over to speak to Jose, and she reached up to place her hand on Ricky's arm.

"I'm so glad you got to come today," she said. "I know it meant the world to Trey. He's a bit of a follower, and you were the perfect person for him to follow."

Shaking his head, he said, "I'm not sure about that, Mrs. Martinez. But I know that you were the person who was placed in our lives for a reason. Without you, I don't think I could have re-written my story."

She hugged him again, not surprised when tears fell. "Then I can't wait to find out the rest of your story."

He blinked his eyes several times, then nodded. "Yes, ma'am. Who knows? I might come back and work for the police on the Eastern Shore."

Her breath caught in her lungs. "I can't think of a worthier man for them to have."

After final goodbyes, she and Jose headed home. That evening found her on the porch swing once again with Suzette and Jose sitting beside her. "I sometimes can't believe this is my life," she whispered, noting that Suzette had fallen asleep. She pressed her lips together, rubbing them slightly, as thoughts of Karen moved through her mind.

"It's *our* life." Jose said. He held her gaze and added, "I know what you're thinking."

She snorted. "You always seem to know what I'm thinking."

"We can't change the past. You taught Ricky that lesson. And you need to take it deep inside yourself as well. We can only write our story. So while thoughts of Karen not being here fill you with sadness, she's still part of our story."

Smiling, she leaned into him. This man, this child, and the one she was carrying. And Karen. It was their life. And it was a good one.

Don't miss the next Baytown - Bryce's story!
Hopeful Hero

If you enjoy Facebook groups, please join my reader group for fun, giveaways, and the latest on my books!
Maryann Jordan's Protector Fans

Sign up for my newsletter for the most up-to-date info on my books!
https://maryannjordanauthor.com/

Finding a Hero

A Hero for Her

Needing A Hero

Hopeful Hero

For all of Miss Ethel's boys:

Heroes at Heart (Military Romance)

Zander

Rafe

Cael

Jaxon

Jayden

Asher

Zeke

Cas

Lighthouse Security Investigations

Mace

Rank

Walker

Drew

Blake

Tate

Levi

Clay

Cobb

Bray

Josh

Knox

Lighthouse Security Investigations West Coast

Carson

Leo

Rick

Hop

Dolby

Bennett

Poole

Hope City (romantic suspense series co-developed

with Kris Michaels

Brock book 1

Sean book 2

Carter book 3

Brody book 4

Kyle book 5

Ryker book 6

Rory book 7

Killian book 8

Torin book 9

Blayze book 10

Griffin book 11

Saints Protection & Investigations

(an elite group, assigned to the cases no one else wants…or

can solve)

Serial Love

Healing Love

Revealing Love

Seeing Love

Honor Love

Sacrifice Love

Protecting Love

Remember Love

Discover Love

Surviving Love

Celebrating Love

Searching Love

Follow the exciting spin-off series:

Alvarez Security (military romantic suspense)

Gabe

Tony

Vinny

Jobe

SEALs

Thin Ice (Sleeper SEAL)

SEAL Together (Silver SEAL)

Undercover Groom (Hot SEAL)

Also for a Hope City Crossover Novel / Hot SEAL...

A Forever Dad

Long Road Home

Military Romantic Suspense

Home to Stay (a Lighthouse Security Investigation crossover novel)

Home Port (an LSI West Coast crossover novel)

Letters From Home (military romance)

Class of Love

Freedom of Love

Bond of Love

The Love's Series (detectives)

Love's Taming

Love's Tempting

Love's Trusting

The Fairfield Series (small town detectives)

Emma's Home

Laurie's Time

Carol's Image

Fireworks Over Fairfield

Please take the time to leave a review of this book. Feel free to contact me, especially if you enjoyed my book. I love to hear from readers!

Facebook

Email

Website

ABOUT THE AUTHOR

I am an avid reader of romance novels, often joking that I cut my teeth on the historical romances. I have been reading and reviewing for years. In 2013, I finally gave into the characters in my head, screaming for their story to be told. From these musings, my first novel, Emma's Home, The Fairfield Series was born.

I was a high school counselor having worked in education for thirty years. I live in Virginia, having also lived in four states and two foreign countries. I have been married to a wonderfully patient man for forty-one years. When writing, my dog or one of my four cats can generally be found in the same room if not on my lap.

Please take the time to leave a review of this book. Feel free to contact me, especially if you enjoyed my book. I love to hear from readers!

Facebook
Email
Website